AYA MCHUGH

Cursed World: Initial Sparks

For Caleb, who I love more than anything else I can imagine.

As well, I'd like to thank all my supporters and Beta Readers.
Without you, none of this would have been possible.

Beta Readers
Baylee Shlichtman
Caleb
Sylvia
Saria Sappho
Robin
Jack Guan
Sean
John Dufee
James Walter Raskopf

And for Seth.
Gone, but never forgotten.

Chapter 1

Sparkling lights, wavering fire. Swirling air and heat. It felt as though the world was burning. Fire snapped and crackled, white hot sparks breaking free from a cherry red flame. She wondered why she felt like this, so calm within the blaze. Then a ringing sound, hard against her ear. She tried to block it out, but it drowned out even the roar of the inferno.

Rei's eyes peeled open under the weight of sleep, the alarm on her cell phone blaring. She reached for it, slow and clumsily. Finally, she found the source of her hateful wake up call, right where she had left it. After some further fumbling she silenced it and sat up, vision blocked by the tangle of cherry red hair streaming down her face. Rei spent an idle, lazy moment pulling it back with her hands, then crawled out of bed. She quickly dressed herself; a simple pair of forest green sweatpants and a well-fitting white t-shirt, and made her way down stairs, the scent of pancakes wafting up from below.

"Good morning Mom," Rei said, sitting at the dinner table. The pancakes had been laid out for her in advance, golden brown and slathered in strawberry jam.

Her mother, Aria, had equally red hair, though tied in a long purity knot to keep it from the food and stove top. She spared her daughter a glance as she cooked her own breakfast.

"Same to you, Rei. Better hurry though, you're going to be late at this rate," Aria jabbed a thumb at the kitchen clock. It read half past seven, only thirty minutes to finish eating and walk to school.

Rei cringed in embarrassment. Sleeping in this late sucked, especially when her mother made her breakfast every morning. She wanted to savor every second of it, and now she had to rush. Still, as she stuffed them into her face, she could tell the soft and tender pancakes were full of love.

"I'll be... fine, honest," Rei said, not without some degree of hesitation. With a joking wave she swung her backpack over her shoulders.

"Thanks Mom! Breakfast was great!"

"Ok Rei, just be safe. And *don't* be late!"

Rei's mind wandered as she made her way to school. The simple suburban neighborhood she lived in was row upon row of near identical white houses with gentle sloping rooves, and sturdy well-kept sidewalks. Not a stone was out of place. The occasional sign advertised such-and-such person vying for the position of mayor of Laketown, the signs dotting the crisp green lawns. More ambitious folk were gearing up for parliamentary elections, seeking to leave the sleepy town for the big city. Rei mostly ignored them, preferring to have an unobstructed view of the grass before the coming winter hid them away beneath a chill blanket.

Homes soon gave way to what her tiny town considered a commercial district, bustling shops advertising soon to come holiday deals and painted up in reds and blues like gaudy showpieces. But not even fresh paint could hide the imperfections to those familiar with them. Chipped walls and small cracks along the bricks, the occasional piece of litter or fallen leaf or petal from the town's ever-present desire to hang flower pots from lamp posts and to plant trees in small gouges in the sidewalk. Of the tallest buildings, few reached ten stories, impressive only to someone who'd lived here her entire life.

Which she had, of course. Truth be told, Rei loved it all, a vibrant feast for the eyes.

A view spoiled by the occasional cars roaring by, some of the fancier electric models ONY Manufacturing had released a few years ago mixed among the regular gasoline driven vehicles. They'd soon be replaced once the former became more affordable.

Though the air held the distinct sharpness of coming winter, the lack of wind and high sun left Rei feeling warm all the same. The sky was a brilliant light blue, faint clouds hanging high. The street was crowded with pedestrians, insofar as Laketown's slow to wake populace could crowd anything. Mostly adults, who paid the seventeen-year-old girl little mind as they went about their morning business and daily lives.

Rei ignored them in return, imagining what it must be like to soar through the air. A small robin flitted across her vision and she stopped to watch it briefly, the tiny bird coming to rest on a digital sign showing the temperature for today.

It also showed the time. She had ten minutes left and was still only half way. A chill ran down her neck and she bolted, equally thanking the bird as cursing it.

Rei struggled for breath as she made it to the entrance of her school, a great wide lobby covered in windows from top to bottom like an atrium at a zoo she'd seen in a travel guide once. The building itself was large and wide, two floors separated by ramps instead of stairs. The walls were cement, painted blue and fading with age.

The grassy fields that served as its schoolyard nearly matched the building's size inch for inch, only broken up by the parking lot. Rei was late by a scant few minutes, but her teacher's weather-beaten sedan was just as absent as she was. That was a relief, at least.

The only problem was that something was nagging her as she made her way up the ramp towards the top floor of her school. She couldn't quite put her finger on it but something was slipping her mind. She lost herself in wondering.

Let's see, what was it... something today is special right? Rei thought. That she was sure of. At least, she was sure she was sure. *It's probably not prom. God, I hope it's not! Is it a test? No... no, no tests coming up. I think. Pretty sure anyway. Oh no, is it about "the incident"- no, it can't be that. They cleaned up the burn marks days ago! What is it...?*

The slowly building panic in her mind was interrupted by a familiar, though dry, voice.

"Ah hey, Rei! You finally made it!" The sudden sound jolted her in surprise, ripping Rei from her thoughts.

Ahead of her in the hall was a rather short girl with tangled, dirty blonde hair. As always around this time of year she wore a large woolen green sweater, which consumed her petite frame. Large round glasses like an owl's face made her seem even smaller.

"Verde! Heeey, how you doing?" Rei asked with a bright smile and quick wave, leading her to put aside her forgetfulness for now.

Verde sighed with an exaggerated shrug, "Eh, things are fine. Was wondering when you'd show up. I've been waiting for*ever*. I was *going* to remind you about today; you're always forgetting stuff like this."

"Aw, thanks Verde! I... totally remembered," Rei said, the obvious lie going without comment. "But I wouldn't mind a reminder. You know... just in case?"

"God, you need to pay more attention, girl. The new transfer students are coming in today. How could you forget?" Verde said, mock anger making her words sting like tiny pinches against Rei's arm.

"I-it slipped my mind, that's all!" she tried to explain.

Verde rolled her eyes and grabbed Rei by the wrist, dragging her off to class.

"Yeah yeah, sure. Knowing you, you spent all night playing 'Knights of The Stars' again. You better of finished your studying, I still need to crib off your notes."

That complaint was genuine, and Rei let out a nervous sigh. Verde was right of course. No wonder she was always losing track of things...

###

The two girls had barely gotten to their seats when the teacher pushed his way through the door, pulling at the too tight neckline of his shirt. Behind him trailed two students and-

Rei blinked once, then twice.

The first was a girl wearing an elegant frilled blouse, a wavy skirt patterned

with butterflies trailing her legs. Rei could almost envision the little tag marking them from some fashion designer from the south. Curly, chocolate brown hair flowed behind her as she walked, and she carried a small umbrella (or was it a parasol, Rei always confused the two) underneath her arm. Her skin was smooth and pale, soft features accented with a sharp nose and sharper green eyes.

The second was a guy, and his appearance set a fire in Rei's brain. Rugged features despite his age and with dark brown eyes that matched his skin tone. His hair was inky black, clean cut but with enough frizz to look just a bit controllable. He wore faded blue jeans and a graying hoodie that clung to his body enough to tell he was clearly athletic, a toned chest hiding underneath. From a distance he looked so confident in his movements, but there was something about him that felt different. His expression was shy, and he seemed lost in thought, likely overwhelmed by the experience.

Rei's mind exploded with sparks, heat in her cheeks rising, mind burning with attraction. A sharp jab between the shoulder blades broke her out of it, friendly and familiar pain replacing unbidden feelings.

"Rei. Wake up Rei. Teach's talking to you," Verde said, jabbing her with her ruler again for good measure.

Rei cursed inwardly as she did, but it woke her out of her stupor, so she appreciated it as much as one could.

"Miss Scios," the teacher said, the typical frustration of a grumpy teacher plain in his voice, mixed with the mild irritation that came with the boredom of teaching young adults. "Do pay attention. I *said*, would you like to be our class representative for Kestrel?"

"Uh, sure thing sir!" Rai said, voice cracking.

She sounded far more excited than she intended, and felt heat flush to her cheeks for an entirely different reason. She suddenly realized she didn't even know which was which. Much to her relief, the boy moved toward her with a small wave and a stiff smile.

Oh good, the boy. That's much better, Rei thought to herself, immediately followed by *wait shit!* and a chorus of inward screaming.

"Hey," he said simply. "I'm Kestrel."

His voice was cool and collected, and reminded Rei of what she imagined ice would sound like if it had a mouth.

He took the desk next to hers. "I guess we're going to be stuck together today, huh?" he asked.

Rei could tell he was nervous. He was tapping a finger against the desk, and she recognized that look in his eyes. Deep in thought, low-key preparing to panic. She had to play it cool.

"Yeah. Not that I mind of course, it'll be uh, nice, to have a new face around. I'm Rei. Rei Scios," she held out a hand to him.

He took her hand gently. "It's nice to meet you Rei. So, what's first?"

Rei was almost certain she would die. She'd never crushed on someone this hard before, at least as far as she could remember. She shook his hand, and tried to calm herself.

"Well first up is math. First period's always math. It's not *that* tricky though, and I can try and show you a few tricks I picked up to figure stuff out."

He smiled, the stiffness starting to fade from his face. "Thank you, Rei. It's appreciated."

"After that we've got sci. I'll show you around the school a bit on the way to the science room. I think you'll really enjoy it. You'll probably be partnered up with me, and when I get going, things uh, get reactive."

Rei was rambling and she knew it. All she could do was hope it sounded coherent. Telling Kestrel that she tended to explode things wasn't the smartest move she could have made, but he seemed into it.

"Hm. Sounds like you really know your stuff then. I'm not that interested in science, but... it'll be interesting to watch you work."

Rei's heart skipped a beat, and she was about to say more when the teacher cleared his throat, demanding attention. Rei sighed; she had wanted to talk more with him. But there would be time, she told herself. She tried to focus, but could still feel the lingering heat from his hand. Her fingers tingled.

Today was going to be a long day.

###

The first half of the day came and went like a fever rush, Rei's head spun as she tried and failed to focus on school. Her math assignment was a mess and she knew it. When she'd tried her little trick to solve math to Kestrel... it had failed, entirely. But he had assured her that talking it out with her had helped him better understand it, so she couldn't feel all that bad about it.

Then there was the meandering tour towards their science room. That at least went far better. She showed Kestrel the few sights worth seeing on the way, informing him of all the schoolyard myths they had about classes and telling jokes that landed flat on the floor. Their eyes met more than once, sky-blue staring into piercing brown that made her nerves spark with excitement.

Finally, lunch came and Rei collapsed at her favorite table next to Verde. Kestrel sat across from them, a small bowl of meaty soup cooling before him.

Why do I even care anyway? the thought came to the young girl suddenly as she drank some water, the icy taste cooling her head. *I mean yeah, he's cute, and new, but you JUST met him? Isn't that weird? And he's been so quiet. But then you've just been rambling on and on. Of course he's been quiet. He's probably just shy like you are. Shy, and new, and neat, and attractive, and-god, I've gotta think of something else. Anything.*

Thankfully, Verde provided a suitable distraction.

"So, how's the tour with Sir Stoic over here going? Ella's been a total cakewalk for me," Verde said, an eye on Kestrel gauging how he'd react. He was stirring his soup, looking off to the distance. If he had a response to Verde's teasing nickname, they couldn't tell.

"... that's the umbrella girl, right?" Rei asked.

Rei had completely missed the girl's name, focusing on Kestrel as she had been. It felt like as good a guess as any.

"Yes, obviously. You doing okay, Rei?" Verde asked in return.

Rei tapped her foot against Verde's under the table. A simple signal they'd developed. "Yeah, just got some stuff on my mind. We can talk about it later, in computer class."

"Ah," Verde nodded, and turned back to her own lunch, some salad and a sandwich.

At that moment, the so-called umbrella girl appeared with a school tray filled to the brim with every manner of lunch room meal. She sat next to Kestrel, and the contrast between the two could not have become any sharper.

"Someone's hungry, eh Verde?" Rei asked, elbowing her tiny friend in the shoulder.

Ella nodded with a slight smile, "Oh yes, I couldn't quite choose which to eat, so I picked all of them. My old school down in Exova was far less generous with portions. You're free to share of course." Ella said, voice dainty and with a practiced elegance to it.

"And what about you, Kestrel? You sure that's... gonna be enough?"

Kestrel just shrugged, "It's fine. Reminds me of home. I don't eat much anyway."

He continued to stir it gently, heat slowly bleeding off it in faint steam.

"Where you two from anyway?" Verde asked, "Teach's a bit hands off, if you catch my drift. Didn't tell us anything but your names, and I haven't really had time to ask."

Rei felt Verde's heel tap against the top of her shoe, encouraging her to agree. Verde loved geography, so she couldn't help but oblige and add with a nod, "Yeah, tell us."

"Well, as I said I'm from Exova, the Southern Provinces, just along the border of the Felisian Hub," Ella answered. "Judging from his appearance, our silent friend is most likely from the Trestaria, the Eastern Provinces, correct? I would guess somewhere closer to the coastline."

Kestrel simply nodded.

Ella gave them all a self-satisfied smile before continuing. "You, Miss Rei, must have been born up north here in Dulace. No one not built for the weather could walk around in a t-shirt otherwise. And though she lacks the accent, given her name Miss Verde must be from the Hub itself, yes?"

"Correct on all counts," Verde said, impressed. "Most people can't tell Rei's from up here. Usually think she's from the west, in Kaiga, cause her name's all foreign. How'd you manage that?"

Ella took a quick bite of a sandwich before stashing it back on the tiny buffet table that was her lunch tray before answering. "Ah, that'd be a hobby of mine," she wiggled her fingers before her face mysteriously. "Divination!

Nothing can hide from my spells, you see~."

Rei laughed at Ella's small joke, but Verde just rolled her eyes. Kestrel, however, glanced her way.

"I'm serious! O-or at least, mostly. Truth be told I'm really only good at love fortunes," she said.

As her laughter subsided, Ella's tone got through to Rei. "Ah... wait, you're being serious?"

"Oh, come on Rei, really? Don't tell me you believe that," Verde said, adding "no offense, Ella."

"It... I mean," Rei paused a moment. Her eyes shot over to Kestrel, then to Ella. "I just mean, a love fortune would be nice. You know?"

Verde scoffed at that, but Ella's face brightened.

"Oh, I know the feeling quite well Miss Rei. Just give me your hand, and we can begin."

Rei held out her hand, palm up, and Ella took it. Her finger tips felt like small matches, delicate and thin. As Ella traced a fingertip across Rei's palm, she could feel the faint tingle of heat again.

"Deep breaths, Miss Rei. This is a delicate process. I need to read the chaos in your blood," Ella said matter-of-factly. The words held a dream-like quality, and Rei felt herself being pulled in. If it was really magic, or just a tinge of infatuation from close contact, she couldn't say.

Then there was a loud popping sound, like a firecracker. Rei recoiled, palm stinging and fingers suddenly numb. Ella pulled her hand back with a shout. The sound wasn't loud enough to interrupt the goings-on of the other tables in the lunchroom, but it was more than enough to turn Verde's head. Even Kestrel, stoic as he was, jumped in his seat.

"Ah, E-Excuse me. That was... startling," Ella said. "The air is dryer than I thought. I wasn't... expecting static. My apologies."

She brushed it off like it was normal, like nothing serious had happened.

But something *had* happened. Rei was sure of it. For a split second, Rei could have sworn she saw a spark of fire come to life. She shook her head, trying to rid herself of the image.

"N-no, that... that was *not* static. Don't tell me you didn't see it," Rei said.

Ella and Verde gave her a confused look.

"Do... don't tell me you didn't *see* it. There was a-a... a fire. A small one."

Verde rolled her eyes again. "Rei, you're seeing things. Ella, what did your little 'spell' tell you?"

"Oh, not much sadly," Ella said. "I lost my concentration. Best I can manage is... I suppose Miss Rei here has a shocking personality."

Rei laughed despite herself. "Haha... alright, alright. Enough making fun of me. God, it's not like I believe in that stuff anyway. Any other hobbies, umbrella girl?"

"Yes actually. Reading, though I don't imagine that counts... I also do ballet, or did back in Exova."

"Ooh, cool," Rei said, trying not to imagine her in a frilly tutu. With everything else on her mind her head was already on fire, the last thing she needed was more kindling. "There's no way I could do something like that."

Verde laughed. "Yeah, you're way to clumsy for that. You'd end up tripping over your own feet. So, how about you Kestrel? Or are you gonna stay quiet all lunch?"

Rei and Ella echoed her question. Kestrel looked away for a moment, as if in thought.

"I... train. Work out," Kestrel answered. "I like to stay fit. You know... just in case."

"In case of what?" Rei asked.

He smiled, as though remembering something. "Moving, mostly. My parents work for ONY Manufacturing. Marketing, so they move around a lot to get a feel for the country."

"What kinda marketing would ONY need? Don't they make everything?" Verde asked.

He shrugged, clearly unsure of the answer as much as they were. When it was clear that was all they'd get from him, Verde turned to Ella with her next question.

"So, Ella, what's with the umbrella?"

Ella popped it open, causing some shouts of concern from nearby students, and lifted it so they could see the inside. Though the outside was sturdy black plastic, the inside was inset with embroidered lace depicting a fanciful scene of two foxes dancing along rocky steppes while followed by a mass of red, silver, and black snakes.

"Whoa, that looks so cool," Rei said.

Verde adjusted her glasses. "Uh... what is it?"

"It's a folk story from back home. Nothing all that interesting, just a cautionary tale about how looks can be deceiving. The south is very rocky you know, so you've got to be careful when wandering around."

She closed her umbrella and set it down next to her. "It resonated with me, so I had it sewn into my favorite umbrella so I could always keep it with me. It's an Exovan tradition, of sorts."

"That doesn't really explain why it's an umbrella, but sure, I get it," Verde said with a nod.

"Oh, that," her cheeks flushed pink. "My mother is Kaigan, Miss Verde. So, my skin's a little... fair. It gets all splotchy in the sun."

Verde shrugged and took a bite of her sandwich. "Makes sense to me."

"Well I think it's super cool. You've gotta tell us that story later," Rei said.

To their surprise, Kestrel chuckled. "It *does* sound interesting. Who is chasing who, the foxes or the snakes?"

Ella took a further bite from her food pile. "Well, they're not really chasing or being chased. They just need to watch for danger among the cliffs and cracks of the land."

"Makes sense. We've got a similar story in the east. Though for us, we're the snakes watching for desert foxes on the hunt." Then he finally took a sip of his soup, now cool enough to eat.

The talk continued, slowly giving way to school based chatter and Ella trying to get Kestrel to have his fortune taken. Rei smiled and laughed along, but in the back of her mind she couldn't shake the feeling something had happened.

And every so often, Rei would look at her palm and see the faint black burn where Ella's fingertip had touched her.

######

Chapter 2

Rei sat down at the computer desk next to Verde and cracked her knuckles. Her diminutive friend gave her a sidelong glance that Rei did her best to ignore. It was time for computer studies, and Rei did what came natural in such a class; goof off. But after today's lunch, she had a mission.

A mission the world seemed determined to interrupt.

"Spill it, Rei," Verde said.

"Spill what?"

"You *know*. You've clearly got a crush on one of the new kids. Is it tall dark and brooding? Or was the whole fortune thing a sign?"

Verde shoved her hand out towards her for emphasis. Rei shushed her as best she could.

"N-not so loud. Someone-*they* might hear you," Rei said.

Rei gestured over to a group of three blondes chatting and laughing it up in one of the corners of the computer room. They were cruel, twisted girls who played at being haughty rich kids. As though having more money than most in a town as small as theirs mattered. They'd tormented her relentlessly for years, from insulting her clothing to pulling her hair.

They were busy today, clearly fawning over Kestrel, his assigned computer tragically right next to them. No doubt they had been waiting for him to stop being so attached to Rei's hip.

After making sure they were absolutely focused on the new boy, she whispered an answer to Verde.

"Kestrel, actually. Ella's cute and all, but... something about Kestrel's just dragging me in. What do you think?"

"I'd say Ella, myself. The hand thing was pretty smooth. Sparks *literally* flew, and she seems into you."

"I mean I guess, but... I don't think she's my type. And I'm uh... not sure I want to be open about being bi at school. Just yet, anyway."

It wasn't that she wasn't proud of who she was. Far from it, in fact. But giving that gang of losers more ammo to fire at her felt like a poor idea.

Verde sighed. "I know. You're gonna have to tell someone other than me eventually, Rei. I think the school could use some more colour. Center City's way more open about that stuff, and people are a lot happier as a result. One of the few things I miss about the Hub."

"Well, I think we can drop it for now. I've got some stuff I need to look up."

"Yeah, I get it. Sorry for bugging, I just hate seeing my friend get all twisted up about this stuff. And what're you looking at?"

Verde peered over at Rei's screen. It was open to a news website, 'The Hidden Layer'. The particular article opened was about a fortune teller predicting chaotic storms in the near future. The page was laden with ads, and the title was a catchy tagline about how the sky would rip asunder and the moon would fall from the heavens.

"Really, Rei? You get zapped one time and you start believing in this stuff?"

Rei felt her cheeks flush from embarrassment. "N-no, I just... I got a weird feeling, you know? I had to check it out. And like, look at this one."

Rei navigated to an article showing a businessman talking with some scientists. "It says here President Yamata's given funding to people for an underground think tank. They're studying ESPers and stuff."

Verde gave Rei a dead-eyed stare.

"Rei you don't *actually* think I'm going to believe the president of ONY is secretly paying people to study psychic powers, right? Some whack job probably misread a report on the... the little auto-complete features on phones and went overboard."

"Predictive texting. And it's not just that, weird stories like this pop up all the time, you just gotta know where to look for them," Rei clicked through a handful of stories as she spoke. One spoke of a little girl who'd been raised by wolves and how she was having trouble in modern society. Another talked about people vanishing, only to reappear with strange symbols etched into their skin. And yet another was of a Dulacen farmer finding a red bone fragment that dissolved overnight into a fine, cold ash.

"You really believe this, huh," Verde said. "You realize that site looks sketchy as hell, right?"

Rei hesitantly nodded. "I mean, yeah. But think about it this way. How would people know if it's true or not? This other one I read talked about how like, demons run most big businesses nowadays. Creepy stuff like human sacrifice, shadow cabals to control the prime minister. I don't believe stuff like *that*, but like, there's a *lot* of these if you go looking for them. You're really going to say *every* supernatural story is fake? That not even *one* is real?"

Verde thought on it a moment, and Rei was certain she'd caught her interest.

"Hm. Alright. How does that relate to you, exactly?"

A smile came to Rei's face. "You remember *the incident*, right?"

Verde shuddered, and had to control her voice for fear of shouting. "Yeah of course I do Rei. You set a table *on fire*. With *a Bunsen burner*."

"Yeah, exactly! And I swear, I *swear* it wasn't turned on. But it went up. And now with Ella, she made my hand kinda spark, with like fire or something. That's a connection."

Verde's expression was blank. "Rei, the teacher *said* the thing had a fault in it. It's not some magic explosion or whatever."

"Look, I know it sounds ridiculous, but come on. Like... at least, look at my hand?"

Verde sighed, and took a hold of it. "Okay, what do you want me to see?"

"Can't you see it, there's like... like, a burn mark on my palm."

Verde squinted, adjusted her glasses, and looked a little closer.

"I mean... I guess? That could be anything. You sure you're not high? On like endorphins or something? Last time you had a crush on someone you had trouble walking and-"

"That's just it, Verde. I've been feeling flustered all day, and read this," Rei navigated to another site-'The Laketown Times'. It had been a local newspaper, but had gone to digital years ago. The head image of the article she'd dug up was of a burnt-out building, intact but otherwise ruined by flames.

"It says here this place used to be a club. A lady was dancing, she felt everything get hot, and then... fwoof. Flames, everywhere. She later described how she felt, and... I mean, it's not *dissimilar* from me, right? I was getting frustrated setting it up and I got flustered and, well... fwoof, again."

"It also says a woman in a purple coat with a cat tail saved everyone's life by throwing them out of the building. Rei, buddy, you've gotta calm down. Not everything you read is true, you know?"

"In that case," Rei said, "let's go check it out after school. The article was updated recently, says there's been noise complaints and they think it might be haunted. I wanna... go see if I can feel anything."

"Feel anything...? What, you mean like *you* might be magic now?" Verde rolled her eyes, and turned back to her own screen.

"What? N-no, not at all. I just... I know it was probably just static or whatever, but it felt weird. Felt it might be neat to check out, right?"

Verde shrugged. "Sure, sounds like a plan. Gonna invite Kestrel? Seems like a good excuse as any."

"I-well, I mean, maybe. I *was* thinking of asking Kestrel-"

A voice rang out, not loud enough for the rest of the class, but enough to attract the attention of the clique of girls who always bothered Rei. They leaned in to watch, their attempts to talk to Kestrel forgotten in favor of what was about to befall Rei.

"Did I hear that right? *You* are going to ask our new classmate out on a date?" the voice said.

It was a haughty tone, thick with venom and bile. If not for that, Chloe would have almost sounded musical. She wore a sky-blue coat with matching pleated skirt, a white dress shirt underneath. An ocean blue tie served as a solid exclamation point to her ensemble. Her gold-blonde hair bounced as she walked up to the computer desk. Even in the monitor's dull reflection, she looked like she shined.

"Hello, *Chloe*," Rei said, typically sunny voice going as monotone as possible.

"Hello *MISS* Chloe, Rei," she said.

Rei cringed. With Ella it was clearly a verbal tic of hers, but with Chloe it was

15

just a way of showing how superior she was to the rest of them.

"Hello *Miss Chloe*. What do you want?"

"That much should be obvious," Chloe leered over Rei's shoulder, chest pressing against the back of Rei's computer chair. "I want to know what you intend to do with Kestrel."

"Really? Why do you care?" Verde asked as Rei slumped face forward into her keyboard.

Chloe scoffed at that. "I mean, it's my *business* to care. Rei *is* my friend after all. Besides, his family is fairly worldly. He needs someone more his speed. She would just have her heart broken when he left her."

Verde looked about ready to pop her in the face, but Rei managed to grumble a response. "It's fine Ch-*Miss* Chloe. Just do whatever, I'm not interested in him anyway."

A lie, of course. But enough to satisfy Chloe and shut her up. Her friends in the corner were starting to laugh, the tallest of them high fiving the others.

"Wonderful," Chloe said, eyes darting over to her pack of friends. "I'm sorry, Rei, but I have to. You've got to understand I've only your best interest in mind yes?"

"Yes, Miss Chloe," was Rei's deadened response.

She patted Rei on the head, ruffling her hair dismissively. "Good to know. I can't stand to see you waste your time like that. It's not that you can't be friends, Rei, it's just... you're *you*. You'll have other options, options that *aren't* my future boy-toy."

Without waiting for a response, she flounced off to her awaiting gang of sycophants, who were laughing up a storm.

As normalcy returned to the computer room, Verde let out a frustrated groan. "Man, what's her damn problem?"

Rei sighed, finally lifting her face off the keyboard. "I don't... I don't know Verde. It's... blegh. It sucks."

"You *used* to be her friend, right? What happened? And when're you gonna stand up to that asshole?"

"No clue," Rei shook her head, "One day she was fine and the next, a total jerk. I've tried asking her before, but she'd always brush it off with some snide comment. I gave up trying to 'get' her. And uh, actually, keep it quiet but I've got a secret weapon for that."

Verde leaned in close, eyebrows rising. "Oh? Do tell."

Rei poked herself in the chest. "Right here. Chloe's got like, a breast pocket. You can see a little bulge in it whenever she leans over. She's got a lighter in there, and a pack of cigarettes in her jacket. If she goes too far, I'll tell her dad."

Verde blinked, face a blank slate.

"Right, you don't know! Yeah, Chloe's dad wants her to be a pop idol or something. Small, community run singers are super popular in Kaiga, and since Chloe's dad runs a tourism board..."

Verde nodded. "Yeah, yeah, that sounds pretty good. Two questions though. One, how'd you know that? Two, you look at her chest *how often* to end up noticing that?"

Rei started sputtering, face turning crimson. She pulled at the collar of her shirt. Verde just started laughing.

"N-no... no, no not at all. What? That's disgusting. You're disgusting, Verde. Even... ugh, even thinking about it makes me feel gross. That'd be worse than dating *you*."

"Oh please, if I was into girls, you'd be all over me. I'm fun-sized."

"You wish. You're the one who came onto me."

"It was one time, and if you *recall* that was just so I could, you know, figure out where *I* stood. So, don't get a big head about it."

Rei laughed and gave her friend a sharp jab in the shoulder, a smile bright on her face. They spent the rest of third period like that, frustration at Chloe and concern about love forgotten for the moment.

###

Gold Row, the oldest part of Laketown's history. Rows of buildings made from aged wood and cracking concrete, their painted walls chipped and flaking, peeling from wear and tear. The sidewalks were cracked and had been worn down by years of winter snow, and were constantly littered with trash, mostly old cigarette butts and discarded fast food wrappers. For ages smokers lined up against the buildings, and the stench had marked the place like a scar.

People had lived here once, when it was new. In townhouses that stood alongside local businesses. There was a sense of community back then. But slowly Laketown had grown, and it was deemed too expensive to improve the old buildings, that it was too 'historic' to restore them. So ONY had built up a proper, cleaner suburban neighborhood instead.

Now just a handful of people remained in that forgotten third of Laketown, and only the occasional vagrant- or someone looking for a cheap, stiff drink from one of the scarce few bars still open walked the streets here.

Those, and three teenage girls.

"According to the GPS we should almost be there," Rei said, face half buried in her phone. Verde followed behind her at a leisurely pace, Ella close enough to put a hand on the smaller girl's shoulder. Her other hand held the umbrella close, like a club.

"Are uh... you sure we should be down here?" Ella asked. The concern was clear in her voice.

Verde grabbed her hand. "Oh yeah, don't worry about it. It looks all run down and grungy, but it's actually quite nice once you get to know it."

The sarcasm wasn't lost on her, who squeezed Verde's hand a little harder.

"Besides, you *did* volunteer to come along," Verde said.

"O-only because you couldn't find Kestrel, Miss Verde," Ella said. "It felt important to come along, for protection, but..." her words trailed off.

"Ah, finally!" Rei shouted. "We're here."

It was almost exactly like the picture on the website. A former dance club and late-night bar. Not all that popular given its location, but with just enough clientele to stay open. 'The Laketown Times' claimed it was a small piece of local flavor by day. The rusty iron door at its entrance suggested its late-night activities were less than family friendly.

But now it was just a burnt-out shell.

The town was lucky the building was brick instead of wood, or it may have spread to the adjoining businesses. Instead, it was just blackened by flames, any colour the building once had on the outside roasted away, leaving wavy patterns on the walls. Afterimages of what felt like an ancient fire.

No one had been injured, thankfully, but the owner never recovered his losses.

Any signage the building once had was long gone as well, and the windows and door were boarded up. About twenty feet around the entrance was a steel-barred barricade, the sort you'd see at music concerts. Waist high, enough to dissuade anyone from jumping over.

"You feel anything, goofball?" Verde asked.

Rei grumbled an answer. "No... no, not yet. I'm gonna get closer."

"The hell you are! I think the cops condemned this place for a reason."

"I'm *gonna* get closer," Rei said. She took a deep breath and jumped the fence.

Or tried to, anyway. Her knee hit against the top of the barricade and she fell flat on the road. Shouts of surprise and concern came from her friends, but Rei scrabbled to her feet as quickly as she'd fallen.

"I'm okay, I'm okay!"

Verde rested her arms on the barricade's edge, her chin on her arms. "So, feel anything *now*? Other than embarrassment?"

"Oh Miss Verde, don't be so mean. Are you sure you're okay, Miss Rei?"

"Yeah, I'm fine. Don't worry about it, Ella, just... give me a second," Rei said.

The stinging in her face said otherwise, but it was more of a distraction than anything else. Rei closed her eyes, and tried to concentrate. Tried to feel... something, *anything*.

Nothing. She couldn't feel a thing. Or... she could? No, she was sure she could. It felt warmer as she approached the dance club.

"I feel something. It's like... warmer, over here."

"Girl, it's called *drafting*. Buildings block wind," Verde said. "Read a book or something!"

Rei grumbled again, walking around the building's perimeter. She took the occasional picture with her phone, hoping to catch something. "How about you, Ella? You're the one with magic."

"I-It's not magic, it's... it's more of a skill. And besides it's also just a *hobby*,"

Ella answered, stammering. "I can't feel anything!" She took a step back, holding her umbrella in both hands now. Tightly.

Verde sighed and leaned over the fence for emphasis. "Come on Rei, you heard her. What do you expect to find here anyway?"

Rei tried to ignore her, but the question lingered. What *did* she expect to find here? Ghosts, if that newspaper was to be believed. Fire, probably? Maybe even some heat, a faint sign that what she'd seen when Ella touched her hand wasn't her seeing things.

"Give me... give me just a second," Rei said. She reached out to touch the door.

Nothing. She didn't feel anything.

Just the dull buzz of disappointment.

I'll have to get inside then.

The instant the thought crossed her mind, Rei recoiled. Pain pulsed through her fingers, like a firecracker had gone off in her hand. A dark mark had appeared on the rusted old door in the shape of her palm. Sparks fell from it and sizzled against the wooden planks keeping the door closed.

A pang of fear lit across her nerves like wildfire, and she didn't understand *why.* A hazy, sick feeling bubbled up at the back of her head, and a chill ran up her neck like an icy finger. Rei's eyes went wide and she bolted, vaulting over the barricade. Her friends scattered to avoid her.

"Jeez, you okay Rei?" Verde asked.

Rei only now realized she was sweating. She felt burning hot, and it was from more than just fear. Her heart was racing. She looked at her hand, and saw nothing but dirt and rust flakes, clearly singed from the fire. Likely rubbed off on her hand when she'd touched it.

Nothing had happened, she'd freaked out over nothing.

What's worse, the burn mark on her palm was gone. If it had ever been there at all.

Rei sighed, shaking her hand clean. Her cheeks flushed red. "Yeah, I'm... I'm fine. Just uh... got spooked. Don't tell anybody, okay?"

"No promises Rei. Now let's get going," Verde patted her friend on the back, and the three turned to leave.

But as they did, Rei took one look back.

It was faint. She'd almost missed it, was *certain* it wasn't really there, but littered across the distance between the club's entrance and the fence were dying embers.

Before she could say anything, Rei felt a tug on her arm, Verde's hand had slipped into hers.

"Come on, girl. Let's get out of here."

Rei hesitated, took another look back. But there was nothing. She sighed, and turned away.

"Yeah, let's get going."

Crystal blue eyes trailed them as they left, focused intently on the red-haired girl. The other two with her were so caught up in her sudden dash from the door, they hadn't stopped to take notice of what she left in her wake.

He had, watching through gaps in the boarded-up window. He saw her walk up to the door, watched her touch it. Saw her run. Saw her footsteps leave a flickering path of quickly dying flames.

Once they were gone, he descended back into the darkness. As long as she didn't try to get in to his new home, everything would be fine.

######

Chapter 3

As they walked home, Ella started to shiver, as much from nerves as the cold. "How do you two manage this anyway? It's so chilly up here."

Verde shrugged, and given her woolen sweater the others could barely see her shoulders move. "I mean, I imagine my answer's pretty obvious."

"To be honest Ella I don't know," Rei answered. "I guess I'm just used to it. It's usually not until the snow falls that I even think about wearing something warmer. Speaking of, how's that space heater of yours looking Verde?"

Verde sighed, kicking at a broken off chunk of what passed for Gold Row's sidewalk. "It's looking pretty shit honestly. I've been fiddling with it, but I think it's done for."

"You're trying to fix it yourself?" Ella asked. "That's quite impressive Miss Verde."

"Oh yeah it's great. Verde's always doing stuff like that," Rei added.

Verde blushed slightly. "It's not *that* impressive. Besides, I couldn't actually fix it remember. At least not entirely."

The light changed, and they began walking again.

"Well if you can't fix it, why not bring it to an electronics store?" Ella asked.

She shook her head. "Yeah, that's not happening. No one in town can fix it, and trust me I've checked. The only way I'm fixing it is if I send it off to ONY for repairs and that's way too expensive. May as well just buy another and hope it doesn't break again."

A question formed in Rei's mind. "Hey, why *can't* anyone fix it? You were able to get it going again, at least a little. There's gotta be someone who could do it, right?"

"I agree with Miss Rei. In fact, I believe there were a few repair shops down south..."

Verde shrugged again. "I bet it's just some proprietary thing that ONY's keeping hidden or something. Can't afford to risk their monopoly and all that. That's what my mom says anyway."

"Huh. Weird," Rei said. That had never really occurred to her before.

"I'm sure you'll fix it if you keep at it, Miss Verde."

"Thanks," Verde said, suddenly stopping in place.

She looked back at Ella, an eyebrow raised. "Hey, so, what's with the 'miss' stuff anyway? That's like, super formal. I'm Verde. You can just call me Verde."

Ella's cheeks flushed pink. "Oh, sorry. It's a uh, habit of mine. I believe I mentioned earlier my mother is from Kaiga, yes?"

"Yeah, you did," Rei said. She was curious as well, though she'd probably never think to bring it up herself.

"Well, the Kaigan language is *very* formal," Ella continued, "and my mother was a *geisha*, a sort of dancer. She had to be very polite on top of typical Kaigan formality. She raised me with the same values. I've got a hard time *not* using honorifics, to be honest. I could call you Verde-*senpai*, if you'd like."

Ella smirked, and Verde's lips curled in mock disgust. "Eugh, no. Rei's already *way* too into Kaigan stuff. There was like a week, a couple years ago, when she *insisted* on talking like that. No thanks. I'm fine with the 'miss' thing."

This time it was Rei's turn to blush. "V-Verde! You can't just tell people that. That's super embarrassing!"

The other two laughed, and Rei did as well despite herself. Embarrassing or not, it was a happy memory, and sharing it with her new friend felt... right.

The laughter suddenly cut off, as Verde stopped to elbow Rei in the side.

"Oh hey, Rei, isn't that Kestrel?" Verde said, pointing over to the other side of the road.

And there he was, alternating between looking at his phone and looking around his immediate area. As odd as it was for the three of them to come down to Gold Row, it was odder still to see someone there alone, even if they didn't know its shadier reputation. They ran over, only Ella delaying enough to look for cars.

"Kestrel! Hey! How you doing?" Rei called to him.

He turned to look at them, the briefest hint of surprise on his face.

"Oh, hello Rei. It's good to see you," he said, nodding her way as the other two caught up.

"Yeah, it's uh, good to see you too. What're you doing down here?" Rei asked.

He looked at them, clearly still in thought. "I'm just trying to find my way around town. We live near here, and I need to get a proper mental map."

Verde cocked her head to the side. "Wait, people can live down here?"

He nodded. "Yes. It was more affordable than in the regular neighborhood, and my family wanted to be closer to this part of town for their work."

"Oh, that's cool. I guess ONY's cooking up something to help out areas like this?" Rei asked.

He nodded again, and put his phone away. "So, what are you doing down here Rei?"

"Well, we were checking out a condemned dance club," Rei said. "I read a news article about it and it seemed cool. I think it might be haunted, honestly."

She immediately realized how creepy that sounded and started stammering. "I, I mean not that we *believe* that or anything. I mean, I uh-"

Rei was dead. Absolutely dead. Whether she believed in something so outlandish or not was irrelevant, she just admitted to doing something weird *to her crush.* Her face was starting to burn with so much embarrassment she started to hope it *was* real and would melt her into a puddle.

To her surprise, he smiled. It looked gentle now, like he'd worked out some of his initial shyness. "Interesting. Did you find anything?"

"I didn't," Ella said. "Even though they insisted I could, given my fortune telling."

Verde rolled her eyes. "We didn't insist. Rei did. I think it's all nonsense really. But still, it was a burned building. That's kinda neat. *Definitely* worth the cigarette stench."

"I see..." Kestrel said. He looked off in thought for a moment, towards where the dance club was.

"I'd be careful if I were you. My parents mentioned they heard there had been some break-ins in the area. That might be your 'ghost'."

At his comment Ella brought her umbrella up for defense. "O-oh, a break in? That... hmm, we should leave."

The other two nodded. It wasn't that Rei was scared, but something about Kestrel's tone had sent an anxious spark up her arms that was hot and itchy. It made her think back to the weird, hazy feeling she'd felt back at the dance club. Reminded her of what she was *sure* she saw.

Of course, bringing it up with him would be further social suicide.

"Yeah, agreed. I'll uh, see you at school, Kestrel?"

He nodded. "Of course, Rei. I'll see you at school. Stay safe." and with that he departed, pulling out his phone to look at it once more.

Once he was out of ear shot, Verde whistled. "Wow, and I thought I was dry. He seems like one of those professional types."

"W-what?" Rei asked.

Verde shrugged, then she nudged Rei in the side. "I mean he seems so serious. It's not like there's anything *actually* dangerous down here, not really. And hell, he didn't even offer to walk you home. Lost out on his opportunity to play the white knight and everything."

Rei blushed, and the both of them laughed. They started walking after Ella, who had stopped to wait for them after getting a few feet away.

"Oh, I'm sure he's just shy," Rei said between laughs. "And maybe a little intimidated. Who wouldn't be, walking home with the three of us?"

"I suppose that's true. Ella is a pretty scary fortune teller."

Ella's face scrunched up in frustration, but it was clear from how quick she joined their laughter she was having fun. "Oh, Miss Verde! I'm not scary at all. It's my mother who is terrifying."

"Pffth, not as scary as mine. Pretty sure I've seen her put a patient in a head-lock once."

As the others laughed and chatted on their walk home, Rei felt her pace slow. She still couldn't shake the images from her head. As though something had burrowed its way into her brain and refused to leave.

Rei fished her phone from her pants pocket and checked the time. It was six o' clock, half an hour from when her mom typically had supper ready. Did she have enough time...?

She decided she did.

"Hey uh, guys?" Rei started.

Verde and Ella stopped, turning to her.

"Yeah Rei? You okay?"

"I'm fine, I just... go on ahead. I'll meet you at that corner store. You know the one Verde, on fifty fourth street?"

Verde tilted her head to the side. "Yeah, I do. What're you up to Rei?"

"Oh, I'm just uh-I'm going to go back to see Kestrel," Rei said, words leaving her mouth before her brain could catch up with what she was even saying.

"I'm gonna get his number," she shook her phone for emphasis.

It wasn't *necessarily* a lie. If Rei ran into him on the way there, she'd at least give it a try.

Verde laughed and turned to walk away.

"Alright Rei. Go get'em. Come on Ella, let's go get some snacks while we wait for lovestruck over there."

"Good luck Miss Rei," Ella said with a wide smile, waving as she followed after.

Rei smirked, grip tightening on her phone. Then she turned, and ran.

Rei made her way down the sidewalk with more than a little trepidation. A part of her mind was screaming, telling her what a stupid, reckless, idiotic idea this was. But another part of her was sure, as sure as she could ever be, that she *had* to do this. That she *had* seen something, and that her head wouldn't stop buzzing till she found out what.

So, she found herself back at the burnt-out dance club. The cigarette stench that permeated Gold Row seemed more like fresh kindling in the presence of the old, flame-touched building.

The first thing Rei noticed was that the barricade fence she'd vaulted over was warped. The top part of it- a smooth round tube of iron- looked like someone had pressed their fingers into it, leaving faint divots in the otherwise unscarred metal.

Her fingers fit into them near perfectly.

What the hell happened? Rei thought, running a finger along the now bumpy fence. She looked at the building, as though it could give her an answer.

One of the boarded-up windows had been busted open. The boards had been ripped from the frame, wood splintered and cracked. Looking in through the window was like staring at a starless sky.

Well... that's ominous. Let's check the door.

Rei hopped the barricade fence and went up to the door.

Through the rust and grime, she could see a clear scorch mark along where she had touched the door.

And that's three. Something definitely happened here... though at least the window's not my fault.

Rei cracked her knuckles. Now that she was certain something was going on here, she had to get inside. Curiosity and the burning, hazy feeling in her brain demanded it.

Rei grabbed at the planks of wood bar boarding up the door and pulled.

All she got for her trouble was splinters. The boards were drilled into the dance club's wall, and no amount of force was pulling them free any time soon. For the first time in her life she felt glad her mom had insisted she pack a med-kit with her whenever she went to school.

A cautionary measure she'd said, one that Rei found funny and a little overbearing. Less so now, as she used a pair of tweezers to pull out the painful wood chips.

Okay, looks like the door's a no go. I guess there's the... window.

Rei looked over to the window, gaping back at her like she was an idiot for even trying the door. Rei cursed herself out under her breath, and checked out the scattered boards around the window.

They had been drilled into the building too. She tried not to think of how strong one would have to be to rip them off, and carefully climbed through the window.

Rei's nose twitched at the musty, ashen scent. It felt strangely calming, like incense. She fumbled for her cellphone and switched on the flashlight app, illuminating the club before her.

The dance floor was warped and burnt; old scuff marks from excited dancers partially overwritten by the scarring touch of fire. There had been a checkerboard pattern once, but Rei could scarcely make it out with how twisted it was now. It felt like walking on uneven gravel, each footstep crunching under her feet.

Against two of the walls were a line of seating booths, cushioned seats rent down to nothing but black smears and ruined frames. The firefighters had done as good a job as they could to save the place, the few pieces of flame-touched furniture still standing a testament to their effort.

Rei walked along the dance club's perimeter, tracing a hand across the dusty, burnt-out table tops. They creaked, and she was certain that it could crumble at any moment if she just put in a little more pressure. She tried to imagine what it'd be like to be here, before the fire, and came up blank. The entire place felt dead in a way she'd never experienced before, and had no real words for.

Rei could definitely feel something now. A tingling sensation up the back of her neck, sparking against her skin. The neckline of her shirt felt like it was closing in on her.

Finally, she found it. The source of the fire. It wasn't on the dance floor, like the report online had said. It was at one of the booths and had completely obliterated the seating there, leaving a permanent scar along the floor like a black starburst. Rei couldn't imagine why, but it felt like she was drawn to it the way moths fluttered towards flame.

Hesitantly, Rei knelt down and put her hand down in the center of it. It felt like her hand was sizzling, but when she looked at her palm there was nothing but more grime and dust, the blackened ash rubbing off on her palm.

"Why was I drawn here..." Rei asked herself, the words escaping before she could realize they'd been spoken. The tingling was growing worse, and she could feel her nerves sparking like fireworks. She got up and turned, to explore the rest of the dance club.

The club's bar had suffered much like the seating, scarred by the inferno but saved quickly enough to still be standing. Shattered glass and melted bottles littered the countertop and the shelves behind it, old decorations and knickknacks that would have once given the place flavor now lost to fire and time.

And climbing over the counter top was a glistening red figure.

Its body caught the light of Rei's phone, shimmering like a multifaceted crystal, its form lithe and sharp and bright red. Its arms ended in three pointed talons, and it had backward jointed legs. The joints themselves didn't seem to properly connect, like a skeleton bereft of all flesh floating in front of her. And yet it moved, with an unnatural heft to its jittering gait.

Its head, shiny smooth like a featureless skull, seemed to stare blankly towards Rei. Its head tilted to the side, as though regarding her with some level of curiosity.

Rei felt a scream live and die at the back of her throat, taking a step back. Her entire body was quivering, sweat beading at her forehead. Her right eyelid twitched.

Her brain erupted in thought as the thing approached her. *I-I'm just... just seeing things, right? This isn't real. This isn't REAL! It can't, can't be real, it can't...*

Slowly, it reached out one of its tri-fingered hands, the crystalline talons spreading out to touch her cheek. Rei felt them brush her face, smooth and chill like icicles. Then, the crimson figure pulled its hand back, bringing its hand up to its face as though regarding its own fingers curiously.

Rei saw the blood on its claws, dark against its red form, before she felt the thin line of life roll wet down her cheek. It'd sliced her across the cheek, more a nick than anything else. But seeing her blood broke whatever hold fear had on Rei's nerves.

She screamed and tried to run. The crystal skeleton jolted forward, elbowing Rei in the stomach hard. She reeled back, smashing into the table behind her. Rei and table both collapsed in a heap of rubble, a sharp breath escaping Rei's lungs. The red thing loomed over her like a predator. It held up its right hand again, still fresh with her blood.

Red mist started to rise from the blood, flowing towards its head. The mist swirled around the thing's face, forming into dull, pale flesh. A single blood-red eye peered at her; a small chunk of face now attached to the smooth skull like an errant tumor.

It started to rear back its arm, claws moving to form a singular, sharp point. Its aim was obvious.

I'm going to die, aren't I? she thought. There it was, concrete and solid in her mind. She was going to die. This strange crystal monster was going to impale her, rip her to pieces and use her blood to grow flesh upon its skeletal form, or whatever the hell it wanted with her. She wanted to avert her eyes.

But she didn't. Or more, she found she *couldn't*. She locked eyes with the thing's blood red gaze. If she was going to die, she'd at least stare it in the face. Let it know she wouldn't go easy. There was nothing she could do, she knew that... but she refused to die so easily.

A shout echoed out across the burnt-out dance club.

"Get DOWN!"

The crystal being shuddered for a moment, head turning, distracted from its prey. Before it could react something- some*one*, leapt onto its back. He grabbed the thing's arm, still poised to strike, and twisted.

There was a loud crunching, cracking sound, like bone grinding and snapping against rock. The monster's arm splintered and bent at an angle that would look unnatural if not for its twisted form. Its head recoiled in a silent scream, the blood red eye bulging in panic. It collapsed under its assailant's weight. He grabbed it by the head, fingernails scratching against the smooth surface.

Once, twice, he lifted its skull up as much as its warped neck would allow it, then slammed it down into the dance floor. It shattered, first the floor, then its head, crumbling like broken glass. The flesh latched to its face dissolved into mist.

The man stood up from the thing's corpse, and for the first time Rei got a good look at him.

He was young, barely twenty by her guess. He wore nothing beyond ragged, ratty blue jeans. His feet and chest were bare, and he was lean and muscular, though purple bruises and healing cuts marred his skin. His hair was a tangled, jet black mess, covering half his face.

Crystal blue eyes, dark like the dusk sky, stared down at her. His face was surprisingly serene, but held a hard edge to it. He took a step backward.

Or, rather, tried. His knees buckled, and he collapsed onto the remains of the skeletal creature with a resounding crash.

"A-oh shit! Are you okay?!" Rei shouted. She palmed around for her cellphone, so she could better see what was actually going on, unsure where she'd dropped it, or when. She couldn't find it, but her eyes had adjusted to the dark enough that she could at least see what the problem was.

Her face went pale when she did.

Among the other myriad wounds along his body, a massive gash was cut across his side just above the waist. It looked a little larger than a grown man's hand, and was deep enough to be oozing blood out from the inky black scab that was trying, and failing, to form. Faint black threads were hanging loosely from the edges, as though he'd tried to stitch himself up, poorly.

For an instant Rei forgot her pain, and threw off her backpack. Rei retrieved the med-kit once more, and quickly popped open the container, bandages and cotton falling loose in her rush. She dug out the disinfectant spray and a cloth.

"Ok, ju... just hold on. I'm gonna patch you up, okay?" it wasn't a request, though her voice shook as she spoke it all the same. Adrenaline burnt through her veins, as though her blood was on fire.

"N-... no, stay ba-aagh!"

She ignored his protests, and pulled him off the crumbling corpse of the red creature he'd fallen on top of. It was starting to dissolve into the air like smoke. She knelt beside him.

"Hey so, uh... this is going to sting, a little. But don't like-like freak out, or anything. I'm not gonna hurt you," Rei said. This close, she could smell the foul stench coming from the gash in his side. It was almost certainly infected, and she wondered just how well the spray would work. With little other options available, it'd have to make do.

His wound sizzled as the foamy white bubbles came to life, tinted red by blood. She cleaned it gently, the occasional twitch or groan from the young man telling her when she pressed too hard. Once the gash had finally stopped bleeding, she carefully packed the wound with gauze and wrapped it with bandage. With some amount of effort, he was able to lift himself enough that she could wrap it fully round his torso, nice and tight.

Despite the panic, despite the blood pounding through her head, she felt almost impressed with herself. She'd remembered way more of the week-long first-aid course her mother had taken with her than she'd expected. Rei made a note to thank her, then fished out a bottle of painkillers.

"Here, this um, should help," she held out her hand, two of the little white pills in her palm.

Rei's hands were filthy with dried blood, a sight that only added to how woozy she was feeling. Nothing in the course could prepare her for this. The real thing was far, far worse.

He took them with a groan, and they waited for the medicine to work through him. Rei watched over him as she cleaned her hands with what remained of the kit's wet wipes, waiting for a reaction

After what felt like an eternity, he spoke.

"You... shouldn't have come here, mancer," he said.

He tried to sit up, only able to thanks to Rei grabbing his shoulder and gently pulling him forward. Rei shook her head as she did.

"Man, you're telling me. Note to self; don't jump through boarded off windows," Rei said with an awkward laugh. He simply stared at her, with an expression Rei couldn't quite read.

"What I want to know is, why did you save my life?" he asked.

Rei scoffed, with another unsettled laugh. "Save you? Dude, you saved *my* life," she picked up one of the slowly dissolving chunks of the red creature. "I don't have a *clue* what the hell this thing was, and you... well, you killed it. You saved me."

The man looked at her, then at the remains of the crystalline figure.

"I suppose I did. We're even, now, so get out of here."

His voice had lost that softness it'd had earlier, gaining a sharper edge.

"Oh, believe me, I'd love to," Rei tossed aside the chunk she had been holding in her hand. It shattered like glass. "But after *this*, I'm uh, gonna want some answers. Who *are* you, and what the hell was that thing?"

"That *was* a puppet, though not one I'd ever seen before. As for who I am," he looked away from her. "That's none of your concern."

"Like hell it's not! You really think those bandages are gonna keep?"

Rei gestured at his side. The bandages were already tinting pink from where the gash was.

"You're lucky you're so busted up or I'd drag you to the hospital myself."

"No. No hospitals," he said. "I've had enough of those for one life."

It was pretty clear by his tone this wasn't something he was going to budge on. Rei sighed. If he got any worse, she really *would* drag him to the hospital, but she was in no mood to argue right now.

"Then you better get used to me. You saved my *life* dude, I'm not letting you die of like, sepsis or whatever," she poked him in the shoulder for emphasis, and he flinched.

"So, answer the question. Who *are* you? How did you get this beat up? Did that... puppet, do this?"

He grumbled, but relented. Seemed like he wasn't in the mood for arguing either. "No, the puppet didn't do this to me. Not that one anyway."

"Okay, so a puppet *did* hurt you, great. Got it. What're you doing here? Not that I don't uh... 'love' the ambience here."

"Where else would I live? It's warm, there are a lot of places to hide if I need to, people rarely come here, and those that do can't get in."

He looked at the crystalline corpse not five feet from him.

"Mostly, anyway."

"So... you really just live here? Where're you from? How'd you get here?"

He shook his head. "*How* I got here isn't your concern. I walked through a forest, managed to find shelter here three days ago, and I've stayed ever since. As for where I'm from... I don't really know. Really, I don't even know where I *am*."

Rei sighed. A forest could mean pretty much anywhere. Laketown had only one real road out of it, the rest surrounded by wild forests and a massive lake. It made for great camping in the summer, but did little to help her narrow down where he'd come from.

But something about how he'd said he didn't know where he was from struck a chord with her. She patted him on the shoulder and he flinched again, though less so.

"Well, I mean... I could help with that? I've got like, geography textbooks at school and shit, I could help you out. It's the least I could do."

"No, the least you could do is get out of here. Forget about this, all of it. It's too dangerous. You're not involved, not really."

That she completely understood. She could, and *should*, just leave. Put it aside. Ignore that the supernatural exists. Ignore the thing, the fire, that she saw with her own eyes.

"Yeah that's not happening, dude. I'm involved," Rei stood up, and stuck out her hand, expectantly. "I'm Rei Scios. Who're you?"

He glared at her. But, reluctantly, he reached out and shook her hand.

"My name... is Gamma."

######

Chapter 4

After ensuring Gamma really would still be there when she next showed up, Rei hopped through the window and made her way out of Gold Row. It took her five minutes to get into the proper commercial district. It only took one minute for the adrenaline to die down, after which the full impact of what had just transpired hit her like a train.

Rei fell to her knees and screamed. In the distance, birds flew off.

"Holy shit. Holy SHIT! That... that didn't just *HAPPEN*! Th-that... that didn't... really happen, did it?"

She looked at her hands. There were faint flecks of red under her nails, and her sweatpants were filthy with dust and grime. She didn't need to touch her face to remember the faint pain of a healing cut on her cheek.

Huh. That all really did happen, huh? What the actual fu–

Before she could finish her thought, a voice ripped her from her mind. It was Verde.

"H-hey! Rei! Are you okay!?" she said. The diminutive girl was running towards her, the doors to the store she had just been in swinging behind her from the force of her shoving through them.

"Oh, hey Verde. I uh... I-I'm fine," Rei said. She rubbed her face with the back of her hand, brushing against the star-patterned bandage on her cheek.

"Rei, you're on your knees in the middle of the street and I'm *pretty* sure I just heard you scream! Are. You. Okay?"

It wasn't often Verde sounded that serious. Her hazel eyes were locked on Rei's. It reminded her of when they first met.

"Yeah, Verde. I'm fine. I just... tripped."

It hurt to lie to her, but after all that had happened it felt like the only thing she could do.

From the way Verde was looking at her, Rei knew she wasn't buying it. The shorter girl sighed.

"Okay. Sure. You 'tripped'. I'll... believe it, if it was something serious you would actually tell me. So, uh... did you get it?"

"Get what?"

Verde's expression went blank.

"Kestrel's number. You went back to get it, and then said you'd meet us here."

Rei mentally cursed. She'd forgotten about that entirely. Now she needed a cover story for her cover story.

"O-oh, that. Uh, no, I forgot. Cause we talked a bit. About stuff!"

"Uh-huh," Verde said. It sounded deadpan even for her. "You didn't find him, did you?"

"Ye-... no, I didn't find him. Guess I'm a little distracted, so I uh... fell. Flat on my face. Again."

Verde rolled her eyes.

"Okay, now *that* I can believe. Let's get you up, you big lug," she held out her hand to her.

Rei took it, and made a joke of having trouble getting up without Verde's help.

"Oh, Verde! You're so strong!"

Verde laughed, hard. "Hell yeah I am, girl. You're the brains, I'm the brawn."

She struck a pose, flexing her arms. The effect was lost by her arms being concealed by her sweater. Rei laughed, voice cracking just a little.

The shop door opened up again, Ella exiting with a graceful step. In one arm was a small plastic shopping bag, and in the other her umbrella, casting shade down on her. "Oh, Miss Verde, why did you run o- oh! Miss Rei, Are you alright?"

"I'm uh... I'm doing good, Ella. Just need to dust myself off. Thanks for waiting for me."

Rei tried to wipe the dirt off her pants and pointed at Ella's shopping bag.

"Find anything nice?"

Ella held up the small plastic shopping bag, veritably bursting with king size candy bars. "Oh, *absolutely*! I had heard they still had these up here, and I *had* to buy some. Feel free to help yourself!"

Both Verde and Rei gladly took a bar each. Rei in particular suddenly realized she was starving. The nougat-y chocolate mixed with peanut butter was deliciously sweet, and exactly the thing Rei needed right now. Almost dying did that to a person, she figured.

"So, Miss Rei, are you excited for Saturday?" Ella asked between bites of her chocolate bar.

"About what?" she asked.

Verde bopped Rei in the stomach, causing her to double over and start laughing, partly from pain and partly from how sudden the strike was.

"Come on Rei, the fighting game tournament's in like, two days. Are you sure you're doing okay?"

Rei suddenly felt like her feet had taken root in the sidewalk. *I KNEW I forgot something today!*

"Oh god I almost forgot I signed up for that! Today's been..." a myriad flash of romance and horror flashed past her eyes. "It's been one of those days."

Then realization hit.

"Wait, how do you know about that anyway, Ella?"

Ella chuckled softly. "That would be because of Miss Verde. She's been talking about it all evening, after you left. In fact, she told me how excited sh-"

This time Ella was punched in the gut, though far lighter than Rei was. Ella barely reacted beyond looking down at her stomach.

"Oh no, I've been felled," she said, and with an over-elaborate gesture collapsed on the sidewalk. The three girls started laughing, hard enough that Ella almost had a hard time standing back up.

Rei prodded Verde in the shoulder. A smirk had come to her face. "So, you were... talking about me?"

Verde pushed her face into the collar of her sweater, blushing furiously. "I-it... I just mean, it's cool, you know? I couldn't do something like this. I was just hyping it up for her."

"Oh, *suuure* you were Verde. I believe you, don't worry. Anyway, I uh, probably need to get going now. That took longer than I expected. I'll see you tomorrow?"

They nodded, and Rei went to leave. But something stopped her.

Verde was still holding onto her hand. She'd been holding on the entire time.

"Yeah, I'll see you tomorrow, Rei. But... please. No jokes. Are you okay?"

Her face was stone serious, and behind her glasses Rei was sure she could see the beginning quiver of tears. Concern for her made crystal clear.

Rei felt a pang of guilt pulse through her, and took a deep breath.

"I'm fine. Really, Verde. I'm good. And thanks. Really."

Verde blinked, and for a moment even Rei doubted her words.

"Okay. I believe you Rei. Have a good night. And better luck next time," she gave Rei a faux dismissive wave and walked off, Ella following after her.

Rei waved back as well and proceeded to walk home, the setting sun casting an orange glow over her.

Rei slinked through the front door of her home, dropping her backpack on the well-trodden welcome mat along with her shoes, and headed towards the kitchen. The typically inviting atmosphere of her home's white walls, laden with photos of happy times, was diminished by two burning thoughts in Rei's mind. One, the ever present feeling of fear from what she had experienced at the dance club.

Two, the realization that it was seven thirty. Her mom almost always made sure dinner was on the table at six thirty.

It was with great relief then that, when Rei turned the corner into the kitchen, her mother was stirring away at a large pot, humming a little tune to herself. As Rei sat down, she could feel the heat emanating from the burner. The clock on the nearby wall ticked methodically, and sounded to Rei like a foreboding omen rather than the passage of time.

"Welcome home. Dinner will be ready in just a second," Aria said, turning to her. She wore a pleasant, motherly smile. "How was your day?"

"Hey Mom. It was uh... it was pretty good. The transfer students came in today," Rei answered.

Hesitantly, she added "I uh, got picked to show one of them around. Sorry about being late, I, um, lost track of time." A small lie, and one that dug at her conscience. The real reason she was late would probably terrify her poor mother. Her mom was always averse to danger.

Aria sighed. "That's alright Rei. I can cut you a little slack, this time. I just worry about you, you know?"

"I know, Mom. I know," Rei said. It was a little harsh, being 'worried about', as though she'd end up hurt. But now more than ever, she understood where her mom was coming from.

"So, tell me about them. Who's the new friends?"

That was a harder question. "Well, there's Ella. She was paired up with Verde," Rei answered. "And I was partnered up with a guy called Kestrel. He's uh, pretty cool. He works out."

Aria raised an eyebrow, eyes glinting like only a mother thinking something devious could. "Oh, a boy is it? Well that explains things."

"Er, explains what?" Rei said, acting dumb.

"Why you were late. Ah, I understand, my little bell. I was in love once myself." Aria clasped her hands together, sighing happily.

Rei rolled her eyes, red rising to her cheeks. As embarrassing as it was, her mom teasing her was better than any punishment. And though she'd never admit it, she still loved the cute nickname she had given her when she was five.

"Y-yeah. He is pretty cute," Rei said. She looked over to the pot, partly out of hunger and partly out of trying to avoid her mother's teasing gaze. "I uh, won't be late again. Promise."

"Good to hear," her mother stepped closer, and ruffled her daughter's hair. "But you don't need to apologize. I just get concerned. I don't want you to get hurt. *And* I want to make sure you actually eat on time, you know?"

"I know," Rei said. Her mother had always been a stickler for schedules, and Rei had never really broken one before. She was glad it didn't seem to faze her.

Rei was about to say more, but something caught her eye. She smirked. "Hey, Mom, you better go check the pasta. I think it's ready."

The pot of pasta let out a guttural roar as it suddenly boiled off, accompanied by the sizzle of water touching the burner. Aria let out a small yelp and rushed over to the stove.

"Ah! Da... dang thing. Must have lost track of time..."

Rei laughed, hard, as her mother scrambled to get the pot off the burner. Dinner was saved, though the faint burning smell lingered over the meal.

Rei lounged on the living room couch, feet dangling over the edge. She was stuffed with pasta, and the walk upstairs to her room seemed far too daunting at the moment. From the kitchen came the sound of running water, as her mother cleaned up the dishes. Rei lazily flipped through the channels, as she let her mind wander.

Okay Rei let's recap. You were almost killed by a crystal skeleton, a weird murder hobo saved your life, you saved his life, and you've got a crush on the new mysterious transfer student. Cool, my life's gone to hell. How do I deal with this?

As she worked her mind over such an impossible question, the television lingered on the beginnings of a commercial. A thin-lipped man in a pristine white suit and slicked back grey hair was advertising the latest in home-computer technology. He was smiling, as the commercial proudly announced who he was. President Yamata, head of ONY Manufacturing.

Man, I wish I could get one of those. My laptop's so slow. Whatever, one thing at a time Rei. Easiest thing first; Kestrel. Rei thought. Her face flushed, a mix of remembered embarrassment and still flickering immediate attraction. *Okay, yeah. He's cute. Gotta... see if he's interested. Maybe ask him out? Oh, I know, ask him to the game tournament... that's not weird, right? It... no, no it's- no, I should give it a shot. And maybe Verde and Ella can come too, or um... maybe only if he doesn't come.*

The commercial continued unabated, listing off the specifications of their new desktop computer. It was some top of the line stuff, which came as no surprise. ONY had designed and built almost everything the country used. According to history class they'd even made weapons once. The government had used them to end the civil war one hundred years ago.

The commercial teased something about a trade show happening in a week's time. Rei flipped the channel. She was too broke to afford a new computer, and couldn't really care less about the other technology they might be showing. She wasn't the techie that Verde was.

Rei sighed looked at the palm of her hand.

Okay. That's... not settled, but definitely sorted. Now this. This... sparky fire thing. And Gamma. Is that two things or one? Anyway, what was it he called me? Manser? Is that like, Felisian or something? And what was that skeleton thing? I- okay, losing track. One thing at a time. Just... ugh, it's too much to think about! Does this mean ghosts ARE real??

Rei's forehead started to buzz, the beginnings of a headache if she wasn't careful. Unpacking everything that happened today in just an afternoon would be impossible, let alone actually sorting through and *understanding* it all. She resolved to put it out of her head for the time being; for now, all that mattered is that the supernatural was real and that she was way more invested in this stuff than she let on in computer class.

Rei bolted up from the couch. *Actually, that's an idea! I should search up the uh, the thing he said online. The word, what was it... mancer, right!*

Half a second after nearly leaping off the couch, her mother's voice froze her in place.

"Where do you think *you're* going, little bell?"

She didn't sound mad, but the words felt like lightning up her spine all the same.

"Wh... up. Upstairs, to my room?" Rei said.

Aria made her way towards her daughter, eyes sparkling with that devious glint only parents could have. She held a DVD case in her hand, and the faux painted cover showing a massive bloody hook made it clear what type of film it was.

"Don't you remember, Rei? Your birthday's coming up... tonight's the start of the festivities!"

Rei felt all the heat drain from her. *Oh my- oh my GOD I forgot it's my birthday soon! That's what I forgot!*

"O-of course I remember, Mom! I just uh, just... didn't realize it was tonight. I had um, plans and I-"

Aria waved off her comment. "Oh hush. You know how busy work can be, little bell. This is the only time I can really get to spend any *real* time with you, you know?" she reached out and ruffled Rei's hair again. "You used to love movie night, right?"

There wasn't anything Rei could say in response. Her mom was a lawyer of some sort, and they'd let her work from home despite all the trouble it might have caused. And though she didn't know the specifics, Rei knew one thing.

Aria did it so she could take care of *her.*

Rei smiled, unsure how forced it was. She *did* love movie night after all.

"Okay Mom. But you've gotta let me pick the film one of these days. If that's alright."

Aria's smile brightened immensely in return. "Oh, wonderful. And okay...but only if you don't get scared, little bell~."

Rei lowered the blanket down to her chin, body shivering. Aria was across from her, face unchanged from the warm smile that seemed to be chiseled into her kind face. The grim satisfaction was clear, even if Rei couldn't see it.

"Was the movie too... spooky, Rei?" her mom asked. Not a hint of fear was in her voice, it was as though the last two hours of suspense had rolled off her like nothing.

"That was cruel. That was rude. That was *horrifying*, how could you let me watch that?" Rei answered, voice shivering as she fell sideways on the couch, pulling the blankets around her like a protective cocoon. "That was awesome. That movie ruled."

"Good to hear," Aria's smile twisted into a smirk. "It's my favorite series, you know. *Hopefully* you'll be okay with watching the rest, little bell?"

Rei nodded, though not for lack of considering otherwise. She never took to horror films the way her mother did, though to say she didn't enjoy them would be a lie. But it had always been Aria's preference, ever since Rei was a kid. Truthfully it was wearing thin but spending time with her was more than worth it.

That, and it made her feel closer to her dad. He and Aria would have horror movie nights almost every week, back when he was-

Rei shook the stray though from her mind, and briefly wondered if her mom remembered telling her about it. Wondered how she'd feel about it. Another worry screwing its way into Rei's head.

"Thanks, Mom. For...everything," Rei said.

"Any time, my little bell. Don't stay up too late now, you hear?"

Unlike her concerns about getting to school or home late, that one felt more like a joke.

Rei smiled. "Oh, don't worry Mom, I won't. I'll be up in my room if you need me!"

"Alright, Rei. I'll be in my office. Try to keep it down, just a little."

That one felt more real. Rei rolled her eyes.

"Don't worry Mom, I will."

Without waiting for a response, Rei ran up the stairs. After everything that happened today, she needed a way to de-stress, and she had just the thing in mind...

The axe hit the ground with a resounding crash, chunks of detritus flying from the impact, but she had avoided it unscathed. It was an obvious blow, of an amateur. With gale-force speed she dashed forward, her blade crunching into his armour with a sickening impact. He was knocked into the air by its force, limbs flailing helpless. Her eyes shone with a brilliant white light, and in an instant, she leapt after her disabled foe. With flashing silver steel, she struck at multiple angles, his body shattering as easily as the ground had previously. She landed with grace and struck a triumphant pose, a series of stars tracing out a lion's face sparkling behind her.

"Celestial Finish. Perfect!" the digitized voice called out, declaring Rei's victory. The action was far more impressive in her head than on screen, but the results were the same.

A flawless victory. Rei felt a surge of satisfaction, her opponent flinging violent obscenities her way over voice-chat.

He was quickly kicked, though the cheering of the others in the online lobby had drowned most of it out anyway. Rei stood up on her bed, cleared her throat, and unmuted her headset microphone.

"Once again, another challenger falls to my blade!" Rei said, in the most comedically exaggerated voice she could, full of pride and bluster.

"I am the great Spectral, Queen of 'Knights of the Stars'! None can stand before me!" she pointed triumphantly into the air with her controller, grandstanding for no one but herself. The game screen switched to the scoreboard for today's fights, her screen name sparkling at the top.

The three players beneath her couldn't reach her record even if they'd combined their wins.

Hm. I did pretty alright tonight, I think, she thought to herself. The others within the lobby began talking over each other, discussing strategy. Much of which was centered around how to dethrone her.

Rei ignored it for the most part. She muted her mic, and with a triumphant shout leapt from her bed, swinging her controller imitation of the knight she'd just played as.

She didn't stick the landing near as well, heels slipping out from under her and sending her butt first into the ground and back first into her hard, wooden bed frame.

Rei groaned, mostly in pain. But it couldn't dull her victory.

Aaah... that... mm, felt nice. The victory, not... the other thing. She took a deep breath and let the feelings, both pain and joy, wash over her. The white noise of faceless voices shouting over each other dulled everything around her but her sense of self.

Man, I really needed that. And probably needed the practice. I'll... aah, I'll worry about this supernatural shit tomorrow. I'll get my answers from Gamma or something. Now then... let's focus on good shit, alright Rei? Happy thoughts. Clear your head...

Rei sighed wistfully, watching the next round play out. Two others, challenging for the opportunity to take her on. She let the sound wash over her and focused her mind on something more immediate. It was no surprise what Rei's mind turned to.

Why did Mom have to say love, anyway? It's not that serious, not really. It's just a crush. I mean a big crush, but still! Why does she have to be that serious about everything all the time. I'm eighteen- or, I mean I will be, soon. Let me breathe a little.

Rei could feel her face starting to heat up, fingers tingling as though sparks danced between them.

Why is she so overprotective anyway? Okay, dumb question, I did almost get killed today. But that's- that's not a common occurrence! Right? God, I hope not! Besides, this... this is fine. Everything's fine. Hell, if I told her she'd probably be proud of me. But... I mean, she'd also freak out. At least, I think so... she is pretty calm...

Her train of thought eventually slowed to a crawl. Rei was unsure what to make of it. Aria had, truthfully, always been rather strict. Always concerned about her getting hurt, concerned she wouldn't make it on time. Concerned she wouldn't eat enough. Given the quality of her meals, that last one wasn't going to happen any time soon.

But after what happened today, a part of her understood it. Stifling at times, but still kind. Rei had felt worried about being late, but it ended up being all for noting. Her mom understood.

Before she could dwell any longer on it, her controller buzzed. The fight was over, and she was up next. Rei unmuted her microphone, grinning like a predator who'd just caught the scent of prey.

Aria yawned; piles of paperwork spread out across her desk. The digital clock read two in the morning. She was thankful she could work at home like this, but when it backed her up this much it was like living a nightmare.

It was worth it, though. Carefully, she tiptoed upstairs to check on Rei.

She found her daughter sleeping on the floor of her room, controller still in hand. At least she'd taken off the headset, so the game's vibrant, Kaigan pop-music wouldn't keep her awake.

Aria cracked her knuckles, and carefully lifted Rei back up onto her bed. She gently laid a blanket across her sleeping form. Rei's chest rose and fell, breathing lightly, sleeping softly. A tired smile came to Aria's face.

"I can't believe how old you've gotten, little bell," she said. It reminded her of all the times she'd do this, when the both of them were younger. It felt like soon that wouldn't be possible. Aria cleaned the room as best she could, returning the headset and controller to their place. There was a small burn mark on the rug that she filed away for fixing later, when Rei was out of the house.

With everything done she tiptoed out, letting go a content, if sad, sigh.

And as she left her daughter's room, she saw it. A wedding photo hung upon the wall, of her and Samson. Her husband.

She bit her lip, but smiled warmly through it.

"I wish you could see her," Aria said, stroking the picture frame. She lightly made her way back to her own bedroom and turned in for the night.

######

Chapter 5

"So, you gonna ask him today?"

The question shook Rei from her stupor. She'd woken up early today, and had even managed to catch up to Verde on her walk to school. A rare occurrence for the two now, but one they'd relished in the past.

"Uh, ask him what?" Rei asked back.

"Him *out*, or if he wants to date you or whatever. Between lover boy and this supernatural kick, you can barely focus," Verde said.

"Wh-wait, really? It's only been a day! Has it actually been that bad?"

Verde bopped Rei in the cheek with a rolled-up notebook.

"Absolutely. These math notes are terrible. How am I gonna copy off them?" Verde swung the notebook again, though this time Rei managed to grab it and put it back in her backpack.

"More importantly, I don't want my friend to get hurt. You've obsessed about stuff before, but going up to a condemned building, acting like you're gonna *break in*, it... I mean you're gonna get yourself killed. Or worse."

Rei shivered but tried to play it off as coolly as she could.

"What could possibly be worse than dying?"

Verde shrugged. "Look my mom's a *doctor*, I've heard of some painful shit. And the last thing I want is for my best bud to end up like that."

"Awe. Well, thanks Verde, it's appreciated. Don't worry, I wasn't planning on going there today anyway," Rei sighed, shaking her head. A lie, of course. *I doubt she'd believe me even if I told her. And Gamma is uh... probably not someone she'd want to meet any time soon.*

"Good to hear. I'd be failing half my classes if it wasn't for you."

Rei punched Verde in the shoulder jokingly, and she returned it with an elbow to the side, the former doubling over in mock pain. They laughed, and continued on their way till they hit a cross walk.

"Why do you care so much about school, anyway?" Rei asked as they waited for the traffic signal to change.

"Why do- Rei, come on. School's super important. Besides, I've got big plans you know!"

She spread her arms out to emphasize her point. Given today's sweater reached all the way to her knuckles, the effect was less than impressive. She looked like a plush toy. Rei laughed harder, and Verde just scoffed.

"Look, one day I'm gonna be a doctor too. And when you come crawling in with a busted leg one daye cause you fell off a tree or something, you're going to be *thankful* you helped me out."

This time it was Rei's turn to scoff. "Oh please. I already am thankful. I'm just bugging you."

They laughed again, only interrupted by the sound of a sedan driving past. As the traffic signal changed to walk, and they sped off to school.

It was only first period, and Rei could feel the day starting to drag already. Glazed eyes looked over her work sheet, and nothing but a blank piece of paper stared back at her. Verde was right, she needed to focus. Otherwise, Verde wouldn't be the only one failing half her classes.

"Hey. Need some help?" a calm voice said. Rei looked up.

It was Kestrel.

"Uh, er... y-yeah, sure. I'm just a little confused, is all," Rei said. She felt less on fire than yesterday, the immediate draw of 'something new' fading overnight. But his sudden approach had startled her, and she could still feel the lingering embers of attraction crackle with a reminder of how she felt.

He pulled up a chair beside her. "So, what seems to be the problem, Rei?"

"Well, I kinda took crap notes yesterday. I was uh, distracted," she answered. "By you. I-if you don't, mind me saying."

To her shock he laughed. It sounded almost cute, with how soft and smooth his voice was.

"I don't mind at all. I imagine carting me around all day was quite distracting. Sorry for that, by the way. It just takes me a bit to get used to a place. Can I see your notebook?"

"You really do move around a lot huh?" Rei asked. "And uh, sure. I'm not sure how it'll help though."

He started looking over her notes as he answered. "Yeah, I do a lot of run–I mean, yes, my family does move a lot. Sorry, I thought you meant-"

"Your hobby. Yeah, I get it," Rei said, laughing to herself. She hadn't expected to catch him off guard like that. Somehow, he'd thought she meant exercising. It was adorable.

Kestrel laughed with her, a small bit of red coming to his cheeks. He looked so cute when he laughed, and Rei couldn't help but feel a blush rise to her cheeks as well.

He continued reading, writing his own notes over hers.

"So, what's it like back home? I heard the east is like... almost all desert, right?"

Kestrel nodded. "Yeah, basically. Get closer to the coast and it starts becoming a beach. A lot of resort towns and stuff. Getting out of there is why my parents took this job."

"Hey, at least you got to meet a ton of people."

"It's not all that special, really. People are people. More often than not, you see one and you've seen them all."

Rei nodded. Laketown had its fair share of tourists, the northern flair of Dulace a steady draw even in the coldest weather. Rei enjoyed watching them herself, but she could see how Kestrel might get sick of it, growing up in an actual resort town.

He handed Rei back her notebook. His writing looked machine precise compared to her wide scribbles. It was also incredibly easy to understand, simplified in a way even a child could read.

"Wow, thanks Kestrel. I uh... hm. You're pretty good at this stuff."

"Thanks. I try to be. When you move around so much, you miss a lot."

He sounded wistful, and for a moment she could see some sadness in his eyes. He was open, vulnerable even. This was her chance.

"Yeah, I can imagine... hey, Kestrel. I've got a question."

"Sure, shoot."

"Do, do you wanna go out with me? Like, on a date?" Rei's face flushed red. Being forward about it didn't make it any easier, at the end of the day. She wondered how he'd react.

Kestrel's face didn't budge an inch.

"Where would you want to go?" he asked. It wasn't a yes.

But it also wasn't a no.

"W-well, I mean, uh... this weekend, I've got an um, fighting tournament going on and-"

That caught his attention. His eyes, briefly, grew sharper.

Oh my god he thinks I mean for real, the thought exploded in her brain like an atom bomb. Rei flailed her arms wildly.

"N-no, I don't mean like, like actual fighting. It's just a video game!"

The teacher shushed her, but otherwise didn't look up from his book.

Kestrel's expression softened, and for a moment it looked like he was blushing too.

"Ah, sorry. I just thought-"

Rei laughed, voice cracking. "How did you even *think* that-"

He started to laugh as well. The teacher shushed them again, louder.

After they had calmed down, Kestrel spoke up again. "I mean...I do martial arts myself. As part of my train- working out, I mean."

"Oh? I... well, I've done some boxing. Just a little, though," Rei said. *Yeah, if by 'a little' I mean two years of it. I only stopped like, a year ago because it was starting to hurt, and Mom said it was okay if I did.*

"Oh, cool. Maybe later we could hang out, and you can show me your moves"

Rei started stammering. He seemed so into the idea of it he was even smiling.

She felt a smile cross her lips herself. "Y-yeah, I mean sure. If you want. Sounds cool. So... about my question...?"

"Unfortunately," Kestrel looked away. His expression had darkened again. "I won't be able to make it. I'm busy, this weekend."

Rei felt as though a hole had opened up beneath her. In retrospect, maybe her mom was right. Maybe it was love, not just a crush. But when he looked back over to her, he was smiling again.

"But after that, sure. I'm free. We can hang out, do...whatever."

Before she could respond the bell rang. He wished her well and got up, the rest of the class bustling over to second period. Rei blinked once, twice, thinking over her question.

He hadn't said no.

But he hadn't said yes, either.

Verde gagged.

"Really? What non-committal bullshit," she said between bites of her sandwich.

"I-Come on, Verde. He wasn't negative about it! That's basically a yes, right?" Rei said.

Ella thoughtfully drank her soda from a straw. "I don't know Miss Rei, that seems suspect to me. If it were me, I'd give them a simple yes or no."

The three of them were eating lunch together, Kestrel's answer turning the rest of Rei's morning into a blur. She was still mulling over it in her head.

Rei felt Verde kick the side of her foot, a signal to 'go for it'.

Really Verde? Hm... why not. Doesn't hurt to ask, Rei thought. "Well in that case, wanna go on a da-"

Ella answered before she could even finish. "Oh, no. Sorry, but I'm ace. No offense, Miss Rei, you are quite lovely. I just hope I didn't lead you on."

Verde started snickering. "Jeez Rei. I didn't think you'd *actually* ask her. Or that she'd shoot you down so hard."

It suddenly dawned on Rei what she'd asked, and to who. She planted her face in the table, partly to shake the Kestrel thoughts distracting her and partly out of embarrassment.

"You didn't, Ella. And uh, thanks for sharing that. Wish I could be that confident about myself."

"Well, you *did* just come out to me," Ella said, sipping on her soda again. "That matters."

"Yeah, true... so um, could you keep that on the down-low, actually? I don't want that to get around."

"Don't worry, Miss Rei. In Exova we keep the secrets of our friends like treasure. It'll be safe with me, and I'm honoured to have it. Even if it was by accident," she giggled.

Verde's snickering turned into a laugh, and she patted Rei on the back. "So, guess you're stuck with me then Rei?" Verde said. "If you want me to film your first big win, you uh, might need to invest in a step ladder."

The reminder drew a sigh from her. *Right, the tournament.*

Rei *had* wanted to do that. Her town could be so dull sometimes, she had all but literally jumped at the opportunity. This could be the only time she'd ever get to be in one, the only time she'd get to really show off and she wanted the memories. Of course, Verde being too short didn't matter in the first place; a video camera was way too expensive.

Ella cleared her throat. "Miss Rei, I never said I didn't want to come to your... game, thing. I'd love to. Just, as a friend."

"O-oh. Well, that's great to hear! I was going to ask, but, well, you know."

"It's the least I could do, Miss Rei. You and Miss Verde have been such good friends to me," Ella said, bowing her head slightly. When she raised it, a finger had come up to her chin in thought. "You're the only two who've expressed interest in my divination. At my old school, everyone loved it."

Rei sputtered, almost spitting out her drink. "The only *two*. Verde, did you-?"

Verde blushed red, barely perceptible behind her massive glasses and sweater collar. She buried deeper into it. "Y-... shut up! I needed a question answered. That's all."

"Ohoo, little Miss Skeptic needed a *love* fortune?" Rei prodded at her friend's shoulders. Whatever answer Verde got it clearly wasn't what she wanted.

"Oh, actually no, she had a more practical question," Ella said. "She wanted to know if she'd ever gr-"

Verde threw the rest of her sandwich at Ella, who deftly caught it. With her mouth.

The three girls erupted in cheers, Ella's more than a little muffled. Once she'd managed to eat enough of the sandwich to talk again, they turned to idle school chatter, the other two filling in the rest of the morning Rei had blanked through.

It was Ella who found the next topic of discussion.

"Oh, Miss Rei. I've an offer for you as well," she asked.

Rei looked up from the remainders of her fries. "Sure, go ahead Ella."

Ella extended a hand towards Rei's own. "Would you... like a fortune? Just a simple one, nothing love related. I feel I've the concentration now to properly assist you."

Rei looked to her tinier friend. This time, Verde didn't roll her eyes.

"Eh, what the hell. Tell me a fortune, Ella. How about... how's my fight going to go?"

"Of course. That's something I can *easily* do," Ella said confidently.

She took Rei's hand, and for the first time Rei realized just how soft and pale her skin was. Elegant and smooth, like Ella herself. She started tracing her finger down the lines of Rei's hand.

As she did, Rei could feel it. A hazy twinge at the back of her mind, like when she'd first broken into the dance club. Her heart started to beat, as if it was all happening again.

What... what is this? Is this real? Is Ella...?

As though Ella could hear her thoughts, she poked a finger into Rei's palm sharply.

"Sorry, Miss Rei. You've just... got to clear your mind, for a moment."

Rei did so, or as well as she could, and watched Ella draw intricate patterns into her hand. She could feel heat rising but couldn't see a spark. Her fingers were starting to burn, the way they did when you cut off the blood flow and let it all come rushing back suddenly.

Then, there was a small snapping sound in the back of Rei's head, and the heat dissipated. Ella let go of Rei's hand, and the hazy feeling went away.

Something about Ella's expression was off. The edges of her bottom lip quivered, just faint enough that Rei wasn't sure what it could mean. From the looks of it, Verde didn't even notice.

Finally, Rei spoke up. "So... you okay Ella? My fortune?"

Ella snapped to attention, coughing. She shook her head, hard.

"O-oh, sorry. I zoned out a little there. Fortune, yes... right," Ella coughed again, clearing her throat. "I... your fortune is, good. It is a good fortune. I suspect you'll win. Just, be careful. Don't do anything rash."

"Huh. Not what I expected," Rei said. "But uh... thanks, Ella."

Her answer was unsettling. Not in any bad way, just... a general feeling of *wrong* in Rei's gut. She had to find out. With all that had happened yesterday, she *had* to.

"So, Ella. Are you actually magic?"

For the slightest second Ella froze. Then she made an elaborate hand gesture that ended in her biting at her fingernail slightly. The one she'd used on Rei's palm.

"What? No, not at all. I can't do-I'm not *magic*. Like I said it's just... a skill. Truthfully it's more like guesswork really..."

Verde jabbed Rei in the side with her elbow, snatching some fries off her plate in the process. "You heard her Rei. Hey, did you check any of those photos you took yesterday? See any ghosts or whatever?"

Rei turned the physical jab with a verbal one. "You're just changing the subject because you don't want to think about *your* fortune being true."

"That being true doesn't mean I'm trying to change the subject. Show us the pictures girl!"

Rei relented. Badgering her friend about it was pointless; if magic was real, she'd get it from Gamma. She put it from her mind and reached for her phone.

Her phone wasn't in her pocket. It only took half a second to realize where it was.

"Shit. I lost it."

Verde groaned, clearly disappointed. "How do *you* lose your phone? You can hardly wake up without it!"

"Well, I don't know Verde! I woke up early today!" Rei grumbled, slouching in her seat. "There's really only one place I could have lost it, too..."

"W-wait, does that mean we... have to go back?" Ella shivered at the thought of it.

Rei sighed. "No, you guys don't *have* to come. I can like, find it myself. Don't worry."

Ella abruptly pounded the table with her fists. "Really? Isn't that dangerous? Mister Kestrel said there might be... ruffians."

Rei and Verde both started laughing, hard. Ella's face twisted into a pout, but eventually she broke and laughed with them.

Once the laughter died down, Verde took a breath and said "don't worry about it, Ella. Rei can handle herself. Besides, I've uh, got something I need to do after school anyway. You do too, *right* Ella?"

"Oh, yes! Right, yes," Ella said with a nod.

Rei blinked. "Wait, what're you guys talking about?"

The stony-faced silence from Verde and the less than stoic biting of Ella's tongue made it clear it was a secret. Rei sighed and shrugged exaggeratedly, rolling her eyes for emphasis.

"Well, guess I'll go to the spooky, maybe haunted, *ruffian* infested dance club myself then."

"Wait, you're going back downtown today? Do you want me to come with you?"

All three of them turned at his words. Kestrel had walked up without any of them noticing, bowl of soup in hand. Rei's heart just about stopped.

"We-well, I mean, yeah if, like, you want. Or whatever," Rei stammered, barely getting the words out of her mouth. "How much of that did you hear?"

Kestrel shrugged. "Just the end of it. Why're you going back to Gold Row?"

He sat down with them, right across from Rei, and smiled.

"My phone," Rei said. Her brain went into overdrive. "I um, lost it. After we saw you. No idea where I dropped it."

"Hm. Well, I'll help you look for it," Kestrel said with a smile. He seemed to be smiling more in general.

Then he blushed, ever so faintly. "And sorry, about yesterday. I'd have offered to take you home, but I didn't really know where *I* was, so if I'd walked you home, I'd... probably have gotten lost."

Rei blushed as well, the thought of Kestrel wandering around confused too funny not to imagine. "Oh, don't worry about it. It's probably for the best anyway."

Verde kicked Rei in the side of her foot and gave her a quick side-glance. 'Go for it', though this time she didn't need the encouragement.

A plan was already forming. They'd go down, look around a bit, give up... and then Rei could walk *him* home, and maybe get his phone number. Write it down on a piece of paper, or her arm if she had to. Then she could double back, get her phone, check on Gamma, then get home. It was perfect. It was *foolproof.*

"But yeah, that sounds great! I'll uh, meet you downtown, near the dance club?"

Kestrel smiled. "Sure thing. I'll meet you there."

Rei couldn't stop a smile from spreading across her fate. She'd gotten her date after all.

######

Chapter 6

Rei kicked at her heels, back pressed against the cleanest wall she could find. The tobacco-stench of Gold Row was starting to feel normal, and that was a little concerning.

More concerning was that Kestrel was a no show.

Ugh... where is he? It's like, nearly five. Or something, I can't tell the time because my damn phone is missing. Maybe I could just... no, if Kestrel DOES show up and sees me sneaking into the dance club he'll absolutely follow and something awful will happen.

The thought brought to mind the image of Kestrel leaping heroically in front of her, arm outstretched to protect her. From what she wasn't sure, Gamma was *probably* still too injured to move. He probably wouldn't attack them anyway; he was her friend. Sort of.

Still, the thought of him protecting her, with a quippy line of 'sorry, I got lost' made her heart flutter. Then they'd beat up whatever nasty monster it was menacing her together. Rei punched the air in time with her thoughts, imagining a solid uppercut knocking their opponent flat. Kestrel would then get closer, lean in, and-

Rei's cheeks flushed and she pulled at her collar, awkwardly fanning herself off with her other hand. *Okay Rei,* that *was going too far. You're just gonna hang out a bit. Don't get ahead of yourself.*

She took a deep breath and looked around. Still no sign of Kestrel. No sign of anyone, save three teens her age on the other side of the road. Rei sighed and kicked at her heels again. *Damnit... I should have told him I'd wait outside the school. That would have been-*

"Are you sure about this man? Wasn't that place like, on fire or something?"

"Yeah! There's definitely gotta be a hidden safe or somethin' right?"

Rei froze in place. The relative silence near the dance club had been broken by the boisterous voices of the young men across the street. She normally didn't eavesdrop if she could help it, but at the mention of fire it was clear what they were talking about.

The first of the teens, in a dingy sweatshirt and jeans, spoke up again. "A safe? Wouldn't the owner like, take that with him?"

"Well yeah, but what if he didn't? It's worth a shot man." The second one said. He wore a tank-top, showing off what a teenager would likely consider an ample amount of muscle.

The third one, the smallest of them in a woolen tuque, spoke up next. "I mean the last place had some cash under the floorboards. Even if we don't find anything, we can store our shit there."

"Hah, yeah. That's a good idea man. Let's get goin'" said Tank-top, clearly their leader. He thrust a finger backward, towards the dance club, and the three went towards it.

Rei's mind exploded like a rocket. *Kestrel had mentioned break ins, Ella warned me about ruffians, they're going to the dance club. Gamma is there-* the image of Gamma crushing the puppet monster's head against the ground played back through her mind, and Rei just *reacted*.

"Hey, losers!" she shouted. The three of them stopped dead, Tank-top turning to her first.

"What do *you* want?" he growled. Literally growled, as though trying to scare her off.

Rei pointed a finger at him. "Don't think I didn't hear you. You've been breaking into people's homes and shit."

Tank-top scowled, and Rei felt the venom coming from it even across the road. She was starting to sweat bullets, a number of colourful expletives coming to mind.

"What're you going to do about it?" It was Sweatshirt, joining Tank-top in glaring at her.

Rei forced a smirk. "I'm going to call the cops, dumbass!"

It was as if time had stopped. Rei standing there, fingers tingling, slowly reaching for the phone she knew wasn't there. The three would-be criminals across from her, fists clenching and brows furrowing. For a moment, Rei really thought they might turn tail and run.

With a shout of "get her!" from Tuque, the three ran across the empty road towards her. Rei turned on her heel and booked it down the nearby alley, out of convenience more than anything else. If she could lose them that would be great. If not... well, she hadn't reached that part yet. But she'd make it work. As long as she stopped them it was okay.

Laketown's alleys were far wider than most big cities, often opening further into parking lots or back-alley entrances. It was one such lot, full of the discarded remnants of construction materials and trash piles, that Rei's mad dash led her to.

Three paths; one blocked by trash cans and garbage bags used by what Gold Row counted as businesses, one clear but a fair distance away, and the one she came from. There was a door, but it was likely locked, and bringing three ruffians- the word sprung to mind in Ella's worried tone again- into someone's home or business would be about as bad as what she was trying to prevent. She went for the open path.

Too late. The delay was enough for Tank-top at least to catch up. He ran past her, blocking off the exit. The other two made their way closer, all three of them looking more than pissed off. Rei found herself with nothing but trash behind her, and in front of her.

"What was that about callin' the cops, again?" Tank-top said, taking a step towards her.

Sweatshirt cocked his head to the side, cracking his knuckles. "How about you give us that phone of yours; and any cash you've got. Maybe we don't rough you up so bad?"

The other two laughed, and Tank-top took another step forward.

Rei let her backpack fall to the ground behind her and took up a boxer's stance, left foot and fist forward, right hand and foot closer to the body. It wasn't perfect, after a year of no practice that was to be expected. Arms a little stiff, legs not quite far enough apart. But, she hoped, it would be enough to scare them off.

Tuque laughed harder. "Hey, look at that. She wants a fight."

"A shame. Hate to bloody that face of hers," Tank-top said.

Then he charged forward with a right hook.

Rei had fought before, sparring off and on with her teacher and a few other kids way back when. So, she could see how untrained her opponent was. But in a fight, the first to act tended to be the first to hit. The tank-top wearing goon socked Rei across the face, causing her to stumble backwards, nearly tripping over her bag. Her face stung.

But he was in range. Rei countered with a right jab to the chest, pushing him back and at least surprising him. Surprising him enough for a left-handed hook to slam into his cheek. He hollered and reeled backward, having to turn full around before he could right himself.

Tank-top spat a mix of blood and spittle to the ground and growled again.

"Kill her."

The other two ran towards her. Rei braced herself.

She didn't have to.

Tuque, the slower of the two, was suddenly struck in the back of the head. He fell, and Sweatshirt stopped at the noise, only to get one across the face in return.

"Rei! Get back! I'll handle them."

It was Kestrel. Rei hadn't seen him come rushing through the further entrance to her rescue, focused on her assailants as she was. But he was here, now, standing before her, iron pipe in hand. He looked back at her with a small smile.

Tank-top was helping Tuque up from the ground, while Sweatshirt was bellowing in pain, holding his face. The latter's face was bloody.

Rei's mind buzzed, but before she could say anything in response Sweatshirt charged, pained shouts turning to rage. Kestrel was still looking at her.

Rei stepped forward, almost pushing Kestrel out of the way, and threw a strong right hook at the bloodied teen. It slammed into his face hard, knocking him to the ground with a resounding thud. Rei flicked a thumbs up Kestrel's way, only just being able to return his smile.

Tank-top and Tuque stepped over their fallen friend, the later taking a few swings at Kestrel- who had turned back to the fight as Rei pushed past him- while the former attacked Rei with a wild series of punches, separating the two and pushing Rei back. She raised her fists to her face, her forearms and shoulders taking the blows.

Each one stung. Tank-top was strong, that much was clear, but each blow knocked the rust off of her. All she had to do was find an opening. It came from an unexpected place; the ruffian stumbling over her backpack. Rei lunged, a quick left jab to the gut followed by a devastating right straight to the middle of his face. She cringed, feeling the cartilage of his nose break. She pulled her hand back.

He didn't fall. Tank-top rounded on her with a rabid left hook that rattled her brain and struck her in the right eye. Rei dropped to one knee. Her head burned, a hazy fog building in her head. Everything felt too real. Tank-top put his hands together, lifted them into the air.

Another opening. It was small, but if she didn't take it, he'd bring both fists down on her head. Instinct more than what she'd learned kicked in, and in that briefest of moments she rose up. Her torso twisted to the right; her right arm shot upward. Pain shot through her as her uppercut landed square on her assailant's jaw.

And sent him flying backwards nearly six feet with a resounding thud.

Rei nearly fell herself, her rising uppercut throwing what balance she had left off completely. For a moment, the tank-top wearing teen just laid there.

Holy shit! I jus-he went flying! I... you can't do that, right? What's going-aah, oh wow everything hurts! Rei thought, heart thrumming in her chest so hard she could barely hear herself.

A second thud rang out, Tuque- now hat-less- falling to the ground. He managed to pick himself up again... only to start running, the other two peeling themselves off the street to follow after.

"Hey, Kestrel, are you al... right?" Rei asked, the adrenaline slowly burning off. She only noticed mid-way through her sentence that he was unscathed. Save for flecks of blood on his sleeve. The iron pipe in his hand was painted red with it.

Somehow, despite all that just happened, the heat in the air and the back of her head, she felt a shiver up her spine.

Kestrel smiled, tossing the pipe aside. "Rei! I told you to get back, are you alright?"

Rei heard the concern in his voice and shiver went away.

"Don't worry! I'm fine!" She struck a pose, flexing her arm- and immediately regretted it, with how sore she realized she was feeling.

"Your nose is bleeding."

Only when he said it did she feel the hot, damp feeling of blood streaming down from her nostril.

"Oh, shit. Um, hold on a second," Rei held up a hand and quickly opened her backpack, fetching out some tissue. She cursed under her breath, both from forgetting to refill the damn kit and from the weird embarrassment she felt from Kestrel seeing her bleed.

Once her face was wiped clean- the cut she'd received on her cheek previously had also been split open- and her nose stopped with tissue, she got to her feet with an awkward stretch.

"Hey uh... sorry about that." Rei said.

"No problem," Kestrel said. He looked away for a moment. "I was late. Sorry. What even happened?"

"It's alright. And uh... I heard them talking about breaking into places. Figured they were the guys your parents mentioned." Rei flashed him a nervous smile. "One thing led to another. You know how it is."

To her surprised he chuckled at her lame joke. "That's very... community minded. Though dangerous. I'd try not to do that again."

"Well, I'll try," Rei said. Her cheeks flushed an off pink, faint bruises beginning to form. "Though um, if it means you'd show up to help out, I might pick another fight."

Kestrel smiled, softly. "I don't imagine you'd need my help most of the time. I caught a few glimpses of it while taking care of mine. You're pretty tough."

Rei's head was swimming now; Kestrel not only not minding she got in a fist fight but *complimenting* her was mixing with the adrenaline's aftereffects and the buzzing pain in her hands. She grabbed her backpack and slung it over her shoulders with just a little cringing.

"Well, thanks. You're uh, pretty tough yourself," Rei glanced over to where he had been fighting; the ground as stained as much as the pipe was. "Did you have to go that hard on them though?"

Kestrel looked away again, towards the bloody pipe. "I was just concerned. And I did think I'd be fighting all three of them."

"That's fair," Rei said, though the sight of it still made her uncomfortable. Wounds like Gamma's where one thing, but actively hurting someone so much... she could still feel Tank-top's nose crunching under her fist. She felt a shiver, and suddenly realized she was starving.

"Hey uh, Kestrel? I'm... going to be getting home," Rei said. "Sorry for dragging you all the way out here just to get you involved in something like this."

He shrugged but gave her a smile all the same. "Don't worry about it. Did you find your phone? I could... help, if you haven't."

"Ye-yeah, I did. I guess I'll see you... Monday, if you're busy all weekend."

He nodded, and waved her off. Once he was out of sight, Rei let out a heavy sigh.

Well, that was a disaster. Never been in a fist fight before! Kestrel seems okay with it though, that's cool. Probably just underplaying it so I don't panic. I did get kinda beat up.

Rei touched her cheek at the thought and flinched. She was going to be sore for a while.

Still though... he did jump in to save me. That's cool. It was a bit more... violent, then expected, but... it was nice. Shitty I had to lie about the phone. I'll get it tomorrow. For now, I've gotta get... home.

At the thought of home, Rei felt something 'click' in the back of her mind.

Being late was one thing.

Getting into a bare-knuckle brawl was another thing entirely.

Without her phone, Rei had no idea what time it was when home finally came into view. With hunger cloying at her stomach and her injuries slowing her down, the sun was beginning to set, and that was all she had to go on.

The door creaked as Rei made her way inside. A dozen lies ran through her mind, to explain what kept her and why she was battered and bruised and had a tissue wedged in her nose. Everyone was insufficient, too complex to believe or too vague to hold any water. She swallowed the lump in her throat and stepped into the living room, ready to face the music.

Aria was there, sitting in her chair, reading through a book. Without looking up from it, she spoke, voice as calm and warm as ever in every way but the words.

"You're late, Rei. Where've you been?"

Rei's brain frizzled, one last bit of grasping for straws. She came up with nothing.

"I got in a fight."

Aria just about tossed her book through the ceiling with how hard she stood up. "R-what?! Rei, are you hurt? Who did this?! Oh, look at you, you're so bruised, and, and-Rei, what *happened* today?"

She was on Rei in an instant, carefully looking at her face, checking her over. Rei almost felt embarrassed. A welcome emotion, given she was more concerned than anything else.

"It's... a long story."

"Then tell it, little bell."

Rei took a deep breath.

"It's not -*that* long. I just... I was waiting for a friend, and I heard some people talking about breaking into some houses downtown. I uh, guess I wanted to stop them and..."

With all the tension gone, Rei felt herself start to get teary eyed. Her right eye stung.

"The three of them chased after me when I told them I'd call the cops, and we ended up fighting. I uh... got a little roughed up. But I chased them off though. Actually beat one of them myself."

Aria stroked her hair gently, pulling her in for a warm hug "It's okay, little bell. It's okay now. Take a breath. The fighting is over now."

They stayed like that for a moment, Rei hugging her mother back hard. Finally, Aria spoke again.

"So, little bell... what were you doing... downtown, you said?"

Rei's scratched the back of her neck, looking away. "I'm... I'm an idiot. Yesterday me, Verde, and Ella went to check out something in Gold Row. Ella's new- you know that- so we just, wanted to show her around. I uh, dropped my phone somewhere. We were trying to find it."

A lie. Another one. When her mother was being so vulnerable herself. Rei couldn't remember the last time Aria had raised her voice like that. A little bit of guilt poking into her physical wounds.

"We?"

"Kestrel," Rei said. "He uh... offered to go down with me. Just in case. We were going to hang out, afterwards. But uh... yeah."

Aria's face shifted in a way Rei didn't quite understand. But she smiled all the same, a small but happy look.

"Oh?" A devious smirk crossed her mother's lips. "Rei, did you get into a fist fight on your first date?"

"Wh-*MOM*, come on!"

"No, no, I understand. Why, when I was your age-"

Despite the stinging, despite the dried blood on her cheek, Rei sputtered into a belly laugh.

"M-Mom! Quit it! I... it wasn't a *date*, I just... was going to hang out with him. Then maybe walk him home. And get his number."

She blushed. "Okay maybe it *would* have been a date. But then we beat up some losers! That's definitely not a date."

Aria rolled her eyes, and patted Rei on the head gently.

"If you say so, little bell. Now, that all being said..." her tone went back to serious, and Rei could *feel* it.

"Rei, I don't mind you being late... but that really was a dangerous thing you did Rei, even if I'd have done the same at your age! It's not that I don't trust you, you're a brave, strong, wonderful little girl. But make sure you've got friends with you- like Kestrel. Things could have turned out so, so much worse if he wasn't there, you realize that, right?"

"Yeah, I know Mom," Rei said. It wasn't exactly what she expected to hear, but... it felt nice to know her mother would have done the same. A small bit of validation that, danger or not, it was the right decision.

"Good. But you know what's coming next. I'm your mother, sweetheart. I can't *not* punish you, a little. Alright?"

Rei nodded. She didn't mind getting punished. Necessary or not, lying to Aria just felt wrong, and it was a reminder that sometimes *normal* things happened to her.

Aria nodded in return and cleared her throat. "Okay. First off... no more games after school. For at least a couple days. You *can* still go to that tournament of yours, but otherwise no."

Somehow, that stung harder than some of the punches she'd taken. Rei wasn't entirely sure she was up to snuff, not least of which because of all the distractions going on. All that really meant is she'd have to focus even harder.

"I'm also imposing a curfew. I need you home by eight at the latest. In bed by ten. I realize it's harsh, but it'll help your injuries and give me some peace of mind. Is that okay?"

Rei nodded again. There wasn't much she could say in protest, her mother was right.

Aria smiled, and kissed Rei on the forehead. "Good. Now go wash up. I'll get tonight's supper ready. It'll have to be heated up, but... we've got some roast chicken and mashed potatoes tonight. How's that sound?"

Rei's stomach growled before she could answer, and they both laughed. But as Rei went to leave, Aria stopped her with one more question.

"So, Rei... that boy you beat, he punched you in the eye, right? How badly did you leave him?"

Rei felt a smile creeping onto her face. "I broke his nose."

Aria gave her a thumbs up, and Rei bounded up the stairs. It was nice to know, when push came to shove, her mother would always have her back.

###

Rei sat at her computer and cracked her knuckles. After a relaxing bath had been movie night, much to Rei's surprise. She figured after everything that had happened, her mother might want to rest. The film was the expected fare, but something stuck out in Rei's mind that distracted her.

Aria seemed way less concerned about it than Rei expected. It wasn't even necessarily a bad thing, just an oddity. She'd also- jokingly- admitted to getting into fights herself, and said she'd have done the same thing at Rei's age. Supportive yes, but was it true...? Seeing her mother almost yawn during a graphic, suspense filled horror film two nights in a row made her unsure.

Of course, thinking about *that* lead her down the winding path of weird stuff that had happened. Sparks on her palm and burn marks on a door was one thing; punching a man backwards six feet was another thing entirely. Every so often Rei took a glance at her knuckles to make sure they weren't literally on fire. They had certainly *felt* on fire during the fight at least.

By the time the movie ended, it was nearly time for bed. So little time left, and no games allowed. What she had to do next was obvious; finally do some searching online about what Gamma's deal was.

Step one was obvious. Search for him. Someone must've seen him somewhere. Her fingers tip-typed away, entering in [Shirtless black-haired guy].

In retrospect she should have expected what popped up.

Face a little flushed, she backspaced and tried typing in something else. [Weird red creature].

Nada. She saw the article she'd read the other day of a red bone being found and dissolving into ash, and that... definitely *seemed* the same, but a quick re-read told her nothing new.

Next, she tried [red puppet]. All that popped up was a strategy guide for an RPG. She filed that away for later use, then typed away at the only other thing she could think of.

[Mancer]

Mancer. Man-cer. Noun.

Someone with the ability to divine through specified means. From Old Felisian, -*mancier*.

"A dictionary entry," Rei said with a sigh. "How helpful."

Despite the sarcastic remark, she continued reading. It was interesting, and something about it did feel... correct. She wasn't sure what, but there was something here that she wasn't getting. She scrolled down, looking for anything else of note.

She saw it. Sixth link from the top, a page and a half down the search results. A website advertising information on mancers. She clicked it. Unsure what to expect.

The site looked... shoddy. The screen was black, with basic text on it. What graphic design there was looked slapped together in a default paint program and was misaligned. But there *were* photos.

A vacation photo of a young girl lifting her hand up, and a wave rising with it. A lucky news reporter's shot of a firefighter leaving a building, fire parting with a gesture of his axe. A goth kid's selfie, holding a ball of light in their hand.

Rei started laughing. This was ridiculous. She and Verde had edited pictures of themselves like this when they were thirteen. It was hilarious. They were good edits, *really good*, but obviously fake. She scrolled down, wondering what else she'd see.

An image from a security camera. A woman, bleeding from some unknown wound. A crystalline red figure being skewered by branches that were both bending to shield her and attack the puppet.

Rei felt the world drop from under her and scrolled back up to read the website.

"Mancies. According to definition just a form of divination. But what the dictionary tells you is often far from the truth. It is far, far more than that. The ability to command, to *create*. Few have it, fewer are aware they do."

"They are locked to their element, whatever it may be. But each have the ability to control it, to create it from their bodies. It is not magic, as magic must be studied, taught. If a mancer can imagine it, can *feel* it, they can do it."

"This humble site covers only a small part of what I know about mancers. My other sites detailing the rest of this world's secrets are linked below. But know this."

"They are real. And they are out there."

The webpage continued on about the author's theories, and ended with a call for any mancers out there to contact them. There were further pictures, from all around the world, showcasing all sorts of the so-called mancers. Rei's mind reeled. Hand shaking, she hit a link to learn more. She *had* to learn more.

The link was dead, leading to 404 pages and sites taken down for illegal materials.

But this was all she needed. Rei could *feel* it in her veins as she read the words. It all felt so right. The burning in her nerves, the melted metal fence, the hand print burnt into the door, the spark in her hand when Ella did her fortune telling– hell, Ella's fortune telling in general really.

Magic was real. And Rei was a pyromancer.

######

Chapter 7

The next morning, Rei woke up to two unavoidable facts. The first was that, given all that had happened, the thought of heading off to her game tournament today seemed a little... less, than she was expecting.

The second was that violence hurt. A lot.

"*Aaah*! Why does that sting so much?" Rei asked, between bites of her breakfast- *pain doré* with powdered sugar and jam- and pulses of pain.

"Well Rei, it's *probably* because you got punched in the face," Aria said, pressing the warm, wet rag to her Rei's face. "I don't know, call it a hunch."

Rei grumbled, but let it happen all the same. "Alright, jeez. I get it. Why are you doing this anyway?"

"To help get rid of the bruises. Maybe help you heal. I *imagine* you don't want to go around town looking all swollen, right little bell?"

The way Aria sounded, it felt more like an instruction than a question. Rei sighed and gave her a quick nod. She *did* have a point, and it reminded Rei of the times her mother would come running to her rescue when she'd hurt herself at the park, or if she'd taken a bad fall.

Of course, with what she'd read online last night, questions she'd never thought to ask came to mind. As far as Rei could remember, a little motherly love and a warm cloth was enough to wash away most of her bruises. But that couldn't be right, could it?

Soon Aria had finished, and walked off to pour herself some coffee. Rei watched her the entire time, and soon came to a conclusion; if she was magic, she was damn good at hiding it.

Rei put it out of her mind. With so many mysteries popping up she was running the risk of worrying herself into an absolute mess. She needed a distraction, something to focus on until it was time to actually meet up with her friends and try to return to *some* sort of normalcy.

"Hey, Mom? Do we have any like, cool jackets or whatever? Nothing too bulky, I mean."

Aria thought for a moment, sipping at her coffee. "I... don't *believe* so. Why, little bell?"

"I wanna look cool! For the game tournament," Rei said. Her face flushed as she realized how... decidedly less cool it sounded to say it out loud.

Aria's poorly suppressed laugh only cemented the fact.

"Okay Rei. I... think we *might* have a summer jacket somewhere in the closet near the front door. That might be cool. Just, don't make a mess little bell."

"I won't!" Rei said, quickly finishing the last scrap of breakfast and rushing off to the closet in question.

It was only after a brief struggle of opening the closet's folding door did Rei remember that they hadn't really looked inside here since last winter. It was an absolute mess, stuffed to the brim with raggedy old snow-pants, mismatched mittens, and thread-bare scarves. Not a single jacket was hung up where it should be, and underneath it all was sure to be a trunk of further, older clothes.

Rei cracked her knuckles, immediately regretted it given they were still sore, and went to work.

Rei rummaged through the trunk, tossing another hole-ridden tuque over her shoulder into the ever-growing pile that she was absolutely going to clean up. She'd been searching for what had to have been an hour, and her knees were starting to hurt on top of the rest of her body.

The distinct sound of Aria coughing caught her attention, and she slowly turned her head to great her.

"Oh, hey Mom. I uh... haven't found anything yet."

"You *are* going to clean this up, right?"

Rei nodded, absentmindedly reaching for more. "Y-yeah, I will. Don't worry

I've got time, the tournament's not for another... hour or so. I think. I should get a watch."

Aria stifled a laugh with her coffee cup. "Good. Though from the looks of it you've basically emptied the whole thing out. We should probably donate some of this..."

Rei sighed. *Mom's right, I can't find anything! We've got a ton of WINTER jackets, but that'd be way too hot to wear. Maybe I can make a quick stop at a clothes store or something? But no, it's almost winter. They're not gonna have anything light. Maybe I should just give... up?*

Her train of thought immediately derailed as she felt something smooth and plastic against her fingers, vaguely shaped like a dome. With some amount of tugging, she freed it from the small pile of clothing it was still wedged under.

What Rei had found was a mask. A smooth, black mask with a cartoon-y skull painted on the front. A felt mesh hung from it along with a leather looped belt, cushioning for wearing it and the strap to keep it on respectively.

"Uh, Mom. Why do you have a skull mask?"

Rei wasn't sure, but for a second it seemed like her mother had frozen in place.

"Wh-what? Oh, that old thing. That... it was a joke gift. Your father's idea. He felt it suited me," Aria answered.

Rei gave her a side-eyed glare. Something about her answer seemed off, but she couldn't place it. It was probably nothing. But then again... after last night, Rei couldn't be sure.

"He... you know he really was such a goofball," Aria continued. "He gave it to me after he first saw me in court. Said I reminded him of a grim reaper. He got me a *proper* birthday gift later."

Despite her suspicion, Rei laughed. "Oh, like what? A scythe, maybe?"

Aria gave Rei a sarcastic grin and ruffled her hair.

"You, my little bell. Now, any luck with the jacket?"

Rei took one last look in the closet, then back to her mother.

"No. But...," a smirk crossed her face, "how about the mask?"

Aria laughed, taking a moment to sip her coffee in thought.

Finally, she put her free hand on her hip and said "Well, why the hell not.

See if it fits, at least."

Rei took a deep breath and slipped it over her face. The first thing she noticed was that while there were no eye-holes that she could find on the smooth surface, she could see almost perfectly. The only slight obstruction was the border of the skull image itself, and only then on the edge of her vision. It was like it was a skull shaped one-way mirror. It was rad as hell.

Less so was the second thing she noticed; a musty and ancient rust-like stench that Rei immediately recognized. Gamma's infected wound was stronger by far, and age had dulled the smell, but it was unmistakable.

"O-oh... oh god Mom. When was the last time you *washed* this?" Rei pulled the mask off, hair frizzled up and twisty from static just from the few seconds she had it on. "It uh... it smells like blood. I think."

"Oh?... oh! Yes, yes, I remember now. The last time I wore it, it was, well it was cold out. I slipped on some ice and landed face first. Busted my nose up something fierce." Aria said.

Rei narrowed her eyes. "Wait... the *last time* you wore it? I'm pretty sure that means you wore it *multiple* times."

Rei *saw* it, the small shift a person made when caught out. Her mother hesitated, for just a moment.

"Oh, alright Rei. You got me," Aria said with an exaggerated sigh. "I... may or may not have wore it, on occasion. It *is* a pretty cool mask, after all."

"Mom I'm pretty sure you were twenty-five when he got you this."

"Shush. Kids these days just don't know anything about style," Aria swiftly snatched the mask from Rei.

Rei pouted. "Oh, come on Mom. I didn't say I *wouldn't* wear it."

Aria shook her head. "Unfortunately, this thing *clearly* needs to be washed out. And looking at the time... you should probably be heading off. Don't want to miss your tournament now, right?"

"Oh, right! Thanks Mom!" Rei shouted, hopping to her feet. She'd been so distracted looking for something cool to wear, she hadn't even realized how much time had passed.

She threw out a wave to Aria. "Um, sorry Mom please clean up after me bye!" then ran off, a skip in her step.

Rei dashed her way down the streets, Laketown's decorative flowers starting to fade as the cold reality of winter began to settle in. The air was crisp and cold, not enough to call snow but enough to be what out-of-towners would consider 'nippy'. For Rei it was nothing, and the brief realization that her resistance to cold might be due to her being a pyromancer flew across her mind as she arrived at the local combination game store slash arcade, creatively named 'Neon City'.

The sign attached to the building was, ironically, lit by regular bulbs, and had gone out when Rei was only six, leaving only 'N City' visibly glowing at night. By day it was just a gaudy, light-less box with only the impression of letters. Ugly to look at, but an excellent landmark.

Verde and Ella both were waiting for her at the entrance, Ella still carting around her shopping bag from the previous day, though it didn't hang nearly as low in her arm. The number of chocolate bars had been substantially diminished.

Verde, meanwhile, had her hands hidden behind her back, concealed by the gargantuan sweater she was wearing. The both of them were standing off to the side from the door to let the scarce few others on the street make their way inside.

"Hey guys! You're early," Rei said with a wave. "Hope you didn't have any trouble finding the place."

"From the looks of it, Miss Rei, you're early as well," Ella said with a curt, polite wave in return. "Are you sure we're not... *too* early? Barely anyone is here."

Verde laughed. "Oh, don't worry, we're right on time, for once. She's barely on time for anything *but* coming here."

"I mean what else is important enough to wake up for on the weekend?" Rei said with an exaggerated shrug.

"I can think of a few things myself," Verde said. "So, Rei. I've got a surprise for you."

She thrust her hands out from behind her back, a small rectangular device in her hands. It took Rei half a second to realize what it was.

"Holy *shit* Verde is that a video camera?"

Verde smirked, eyes shining behind her glasses.

"Hell yeah it is. ONY's newest model. I won't bore you with the technical info but rest assured; it's the good shit. You *did* want to film this, right?"

"Aaaah... you little goblin, that's what you and Ella were busy with yesterday!"

"Oh, absolutely, Miss Rei," Ella said. "She's been showing me how to use it all morning."

Verde gave the both of them a cocky, if flustered, grin.

"Hey, what can I say. You're my best bud Rei. I wanna keep this memory as much as you do."

Rei blushed in return, and pumped a fist triumphantly. "Hell yeah! I'm ready to kick some ass, let's get going!"

With an air of excitement about them, Rei led them in. Standees littered the floor, cardboard cut outs of knights advertising new games and faux-neon signs giving directions every which way; a much-appreciated necessity. 'Neon City' was split between two buildings, a ploy by the arcade's owner to keep his business running that had worked out fairly well. For Rei, it was about the closest she'd ever had to a taste of the big city.

She told them- primarily Ella truthfully- as much as they approached the stage at the far end of the arcade section. The 'stage' was really more of a ten-foot flat of wood with a shag carpet thrown over it, space enough for three televisions, a console hooked up to each, and a mixture of poofy bean-bag chairs and stiff, over-designed computer chairs on the edges.

It wasn't large, or special, or even all that well-presented. Laketown was one of the smaller northern communities and it showed. But for Rei, this was *it*. Sure, the last two days had shown her just how big the world could be, but this was *different*. For Rei this was the epitome of her normal life. Nothing could ever really surpass that, and everything else fell away as she focused on that one thought. This was something she was good at, something she *chose* to do. This was her *time*. She approached the stage, ready to take her place.

And up on the stage was Chloe, looking for a place to sit.

"Why the hell is Chloe here?"

The words felt dull. Rei hadn't even realized she was the one who said them.

Chloe spotted Rei and ran up to her with a short wave. "Oh, hello Rei. I suspected as much that *you'd* be the next to arrive."

Chloe was smiling. A happy smile. She sounded... pleasant, almost musical.

And it was all wrong. That wasn't what Chloe was like at all. She wasn't even dressed right; Chloe would never be caught in trousers and sunglasses. Rei *knew* that.

"You know, I took a look at everyone who's signed up for this silly little game. Between you and me, none of them can hold a candle to the two of us. Surprised we're not seeded."

Rei blinked, shook her head, did everything she could to try and force reality to make sense. Somehow this was more unbelievable then what she'd learned last night.

"Chloe, what are you doing here?"

Chloe tilted her head to the side. "Well, why else, stupid. I'm here to win."

Rei felt her hands start to curl into fists. Her palms were starting to sweat.

"W-what?! What makes you think you can just... waltz in here and do this?!" she asked.

Louder than expected. An employee turned their way, Ella and Verde doing their best to wave them off as though everything was fine.

"Do what, Rei?" Chloe asked. Then a spark of realization crossed her face. "Oh, I get it. You can't have Kestrel, so this easy win is to cheer you up. Well, unfortunately Rei... this won't be as easy as you think."

Rei tried to scoff, but it came out as a strangled laugh. "Oh, *really* Chloe? You think you can beat me? *You?* Have you ever done anything harder than flip people off? Those dainty little fingers of yours are going to snap off."

She shouldn't be trash talking like this. She was *better* than this. But just seeing Chloe here, *here*, was pissing her off to no end. Chloe hated games. Chloe hated *her*.

And worst of all, Chloe was right.

Chloe's expression soured. "You have no *idea* what I can do, Rei. Care to put your money where your mouth is?"

Rei wanted nothing more to repeat what she said. Of course, she had no *idea* how to use her pyromancy- and truthfully, no actual proof beyond a lot of arguably circumstantial evidence- but at that moment, the idea of scaring her with a burst of flame was *so* appealing. But calmer thoughts prevailed; as much as sinking to Chloe's level would be fun, she wanted to beat her *her* way.

Rei had an idea. A stupid one, but it was worth a shot.

"Sure thing, *Chloe.* What do you want? What could I possibly give the great *Chloe* if, IF, I lose? Because I know what *I* want. I want you to leave me the hell alone. I want you to tell me what your *damn problem is!*"

That would show her. When it came to bets, Chloe always had too much pride to back down. If Rei won, Chloe would finally leave her alone. She'd be too embarrassed not to, losing to a 'loser' like her.

To Rei's surprise and satisfaction, Chloe's expression wavered. She looked hurt.

But her response was typical. "Hmph. In that case, *when* I win, I want *you.* You hang out with me, and *only* me, for a week."

Rei shuddered. That would be torture. A part of her wondered why she'd want that, but another side screamed the answer. Chloe wanted her as a servant for a week.

That was how little Chloe thought of her. Rei thrust out her hand to accept the terms, and when Chloe grabbed it, Rei squeezed. Hard.

"Let the best woman win," Chloe said.

"I will," Rei returned.

Chloe walked off in a huff, back to a seat on the stage. Rei just stood there, silently fuming.

"Er... Miss Rei, are you alright?" Ella asked.

"God, what an asshole. Kick her ass, girl." Verde said.

Ella's bit her lip in concern, and Verde's face had scrunched up into a snarl behind her glasses.

Rei tried to laugh it off. "Hah, I'm fine. And I'll try, Verde. I doubt that idiot's going to get past round one. The only sad thing is, I won't get to see her face when she loses."

The building's door 'ding'ed as more attendees and a few competitors arrived. They had been for a while, but Rei had been entirely oblivious to it all. Emotions swirled as anger made way for a pang of nerves; playing in front of even a decent amount of people picked at her brain and left chicken skin on her arms. But after a deep breath, she knew she was ready.

Rei gave her friends a thumbs up. "Wish me luck guys."

The two cheered her on, and Rei approached the stage. A wide smirk started to creep along her face. A part of her realized she wanted Chloe to somehow get to the finale, just so she could watch her fall.

In a small place like Laketown, there was rarely that much to do. So, when the opportunity presented itself to watch a bunch of teens play a fighting game, even the least interested could get a little invested. The ebb and flow of a game like 'Knights of the Stars' was easy to see after a few fights; two characters in a 2D arena made to fight to catchy Kaigan pop-music. Intense skill and timing was a must, and even the unsavvy audience members could see it on display. They watched with rapt attention as the eight competitors duked it out in best-of-three matches in order to advance up the ladder.

Rei focused on her fights, tearing through her foes like a wild beast. The raw anger Chloe had instilled in her had thrown her off her game, but also fueled the aggressive play style she was known for online. A few mistakes here and there, a dropped combo or mistimed parry, but as she played rage gave way to elation. She was the most skilled here by far; her opponents didn't stand a chance.

With only one match left, there was a short break to rest and drink water. Rei glanced over to Verde and Ella, the latter holding the video camera in one hand and her umbrella in the other. She was looking tired, clearly not expecting the camera to weigh so much.

Verde meanwhile was cheering wildly, standing out even with her height. It warmed Rei's heart in a way winning probably never would to see her friend so excited. It got her blood pumping for the final match.

Who IS the final going to be against? God, I haven't been paying attention to any of the other fights… not that it matters, this has been a cake walk. Can't wait to see the video!

A haughty voice broke her train of thought as easily as- and with the impact of- a rock through a plate glass window.

"So, you've made it to the finals. As expected, of course," she said.

It was Chloe. She'd taken the sunglasses off, her face an unreadable mask of smug satisfaction. She was even smiling again. "Congrats, really. You've earned that second-place win."

"… second place? Who's going to beat *me*?" Rei asked.

Chloe's smile twisted into a devilish smirk. She leaned in, close.

"*Me*. We're the only ones left, idiot. Just you and me."

Her words struck like an icy chill down her spine. "Wh-what, how did you get this far?"

Chloe chuckled. "Oh, don't be surprised, Rei. I learned from the best. *You*. I hope you're ready… I spent most of my matches imagining what *fun* we'll have together."

…me? What is she talking about? Rei thought. It echoed in her head. All emotion, all other thought, all focus, all of it fell like a pit had opened up in her brain. This was impossible. Chloe hated games, Chloe… no, she didn't.

Memory washed over her. Five years ago, the two playing games together. They were laughing, the both of them. Having fun. The memories stung, worse than a fist to the face.

Before she could linger on the thought, there was a whistle. The match was about to begin. Rei picked up her controller and tried to focus.

It was time to get to work.

######

Chapter 8

Any question Rei had of how Chloe got to the finale were immediately answered in the opening round. Chloe had picked a tricky, high skill character the emphasized control and defense, keeping her opponent at bay with damaging traps that littered the 2D arena and shut down an aggressive play style. It was Rei's worst match up, but the character was so skill intensive she rarely had to worry about it.

Rei's typical strategy was a full-on assault, quick moves and quick reflexes. Her opponents would block and parry in an attempt to space their two characters apart. To get *some* breathing room to respond. But there was only so much you could do if you only held your ground, and Rei's aggressive style of play demanded they answer her with an offensive of their own or be left in the dust. Or, present a perfect defense Rei couldn't crack.

In that opening round, Chloe did just that. She parried every strike, dodged every unblockable move, and slowly but surely whittled Rei's life-bar down with light punches and aggro-punishing traps Rei only barely avoided. Frustration grew as they traded blows, none quite able to surpass the other. In terms of skill, it was like Rei was facing a warped mirror. Every weakness Rei had was Chloe's strength, and vice versa.

The in-game timer buzzed, the first round over. Chloe had won by time out, though only just. She taunted Rei, enjoying her brief shining victory before the second round begun.

The second round went much the same as the first, the two of them struggling to eke out a win against the other. Chloe only seemed to be getting better, but as adrenaline and heat pumped through Rei's veins, she could feel her focus tightening. Her inner ear rumbled like a roaring flame.

The match approached time out, Rei's life-bar a fraction more than Chloe's. But Rei's own stubborn pride demanded she *win*. She pushed harder, faster, surrendered every thought of defense for pure, raw offense. At this level of skill, overextending this much could spell certain death, but if it pushed Chloe hard enough to slip then she'd be able to end it.

It worked. Chloe's defense slipped, a single mistimed parry that left her open. Rei struck her foe down with the most basic of jabs; it was all Rei could manage in that brief window.

Round two was hers. The next would win it.

The game's digitized voice called out the start of the last round. Chloe was taunting, shouting, trying to psych her out. Rei stayed stone silent, focusing on the game. She took a breath, and focused on the game, letting her instincts flow.

The sword-master dashed forward, an aggressive start. Her foe, a wiry mage, swung her staff to keep her blade at bay. She ducked into a half-step forward, raising the edge of her sword to strike at an opening. The mage danced backwards in a shower of magic dust, evading the sword-master's strike as easy as a fly evades a child's grasping hand.

A growl escaped her lips and she charged forward- right into an ambush! Magic symbols appeared around her, traps the mage had left in the wake of her retreat. The sword-master was caught, and only a split-second dodge could save her.

But she couldn't move. Her legs were frozen. It was no attack, none that she could see. The explosions rocked her body, tearing through armour and flesh both. Her foe smirked. She shot forward, intending to finish it here and-

And then the game paused, and Rei's imaginings slammed to a halt, catapulting her back into reality. The judge's whistle blared loud and sharp, calling a time out.

Chloe nearly screamed in frustration, and Rei had to blink, hard. Her eyes were dry, her hands were clammy, and she smelt smoke. Of all things, *smoke*. Rei looked down at her controller.

The hard-plastic case was warped and sticky, the softer plastic starting to melt in her hands. Rei gawked at the sight of it; it was even cracked in places, steam rising from where the batteries where. The entire controller was dead. No wonder she couldn't dodge the traps.

The judges discussed among themselves, the crowd growing restless. Rei wondered how it must all look to them; controllers didn't just *explode*, especially not in the way Rei's did. Chloe's was grumbling in the venomous tone Rei was familiar with as they waited with bated breath.

Finally, one of the judges called out his call; Rei's controller had a faulty battery pack, and the extensive use and intensity of play had caused it to overheat. A reasonable explanation, though the tingling in Rei's hands made her doubt it. A five-minute break was called to set up and test a new controller, then they'd reset the round.

Rei wasn't sure how well that would go. Her brow was drenched with sweat, and she was starting to get hungry- far hungrier than she expected. Her arms were sore from stiffness and yesterday's injuries. But as soon as the new round began, it was clear which of the two had been affected worst.

Chloe had lost her flow entirely, had been forcibly ripped from the game and made to wait five minutes, and she just couldn't recover. Rei finished her off with a showy special move, winning the round, match, and the personal victory of digitally slicing her enemy to ribbons.

Chloe grit her teeth, almost loud enough that Rei could hear them grinding.

Despite that, she stuck out her hand. "Good game, Rei," she said. It didn't feel as virulent as Chloe always sounded, but Rei could sense the venom in it. At least, she was sure she could.

"Good game, Chloe. I guess the better girl won."

Chloe's face twisted in defeat. It felt great to see her so defeated for once. She'd put up a good fight, sure, but ultimately Rei couldn't lose to some faux-rich haughty prick. Rei was flying high, and nothing could bring her down.

"Thank you. I... suppose she did. I guess I'll, I'll see you later. At school. I... I don't want to talk about it here," Chloe said simply.

The bet. In truth Rei had almost forgotten it in the excitement. Before Rei could respond, Chloe left, slipping her sunglasses back on. She was quickly lost in the crowd. But as she left, a lingering thought dug its way through the euphoria of victory.

Chloe had looked sad. All at once, the raw emotion riled up by competition faded and Rei felt a cold pit in her stomach. It'd been so long since she saw Chloe act genuine for once... and in a way it had felt nice.

One of the judges handed Rei over her reward, a hundred-dollar coupon for the store.

But suddenly, her victory tasted sour and she didn't know why.

"You were *amazing* up there, Rei!" Verde said. She was pumping one fist in the air, the other holding the video camera Ella had passed off to her when the tournament finished.

The three had left the store once the crowd had started dispersing, and out on the open sidewalk Verde had immediately gone into a play by play of Rei's victory, striking dramatic poses and shouting excitedly as they walked together. It wasn't often that Verde got like this, and it brought a smile to Rei's face and a warm blush to her cheek.

It also helped stem the tide of thoughts digging into her brain.

"I uh, hope it wasn't *too* boring for you Ella," Rei said, once Verde had finally started to calm down.

Ella shook her head. "Oh, not at all Miss Rei. I'm glad my fortune came true; you won your fight, even if it got a little heated."

Something clicked in Rei's head. "Uh, about that. Yesterday when I went to Gold Row I ended up in a fist fight."

The other two stopped dead in their tracks.

"Holy shit, really?" Verde said.

Ella dropped her bag and umbrella to the sidewalk and grabbed Rei by the shoulders.

"Rei! I told you not to do anything *reckless*! D-do I need to explain what *reckless means?!*"

Rei laughed as Ella shook her back and forth, all but throttling her. "H-hey, don't worry about it! I'm fine, see! Hardly any injuries!"

"*HARDLY ANY-*"

Ella sputtered, barely able to continue.

"Wait does this mean- how did the date with Kestrel go? Girl, tell me *everything*."

"Oh uh," Rei blushed. "First off, not a date. Not really. Second, uh... three losers were bragging about breaking into houses so I kicked their asses... with Kestrel's help. After that, he..."

She remembered back to how Kestrel stood there, bloody pipe in hand. Not a very heroic image to share her friend. Better to leave it aside.

"After that I told him I needed to get home. We didn't even really talk."

Verde groaned, shaking her head. "Dude comes to the rescue and doesn't even offer to take you home. *Again.* Romance is dead in Dulace."

Ella collapsed to the sidewalk next to her discarded umbrella and bag of sweets. "Y-you... you fought... three people. Is anyone hurt? *Did anyone die?*"

Rei shrugged. "I mean, we kinda messed them up. Kestrel uh... he didn't really hold back. I got beat up but like, nothing serious. Do I look messed up?"

"Now that you mention it... you're a little bruised, in the whole uh... face, area," Verde said. "Nothing I would have noticed if I wasn't looking for it, but still. Hope you got'em back good."

Rei pumped her fist. "Hell yeah. I punched one guy back like, seven feet. It ruled!"

"Mi-Miss Rei..." Ella murmured, still on the ground. "M... wuh... why even get a fortune... if you don't... listen to it..."

The poor girl looked like a statue, and Rei laughed despite herself. "Hey, I mean, if I was gonna get in an actual *fight* you could have warned me."

"Come on Rei. You remember, 'it's not magic' and all that. Right Ella?"

Verde held a hand out to her, and that was enough to break Ella from her shocked misery. With a polite cough and Verde's assistance, she got back up to her feet, umbrella firmly under her arm and bag of chocolates in her hand.

"I had no idea you'd be in a brawl with... with *ruffians*. All I saw was that you're very skilled, and that if you did something reckless... terrible things could happen! But as Miss Verde said... it isn't magic. Not really, anyway."

"Well, don't worry about it Ella," Rei put a hand on her shoulder and flashed the most confident smile she could muster. "I'll take your advice *now*. No more reckless stuff."

Like I figured, Rei thought to herself. *Ella's not actually magic, she's just... got a good head for people. She's not wrong, I definitely could have gotten my ass kicked- or worse. God, I don't want to think about it...*

Her thoughts where interrupted by Verde's hand squeezing hers, hard.

"Hey, Rei? You okay? You're uh... starting to look pale."

Rei let out her breath, not realizing she'd been holding it. "Y-yeah, I'm fine. Just... man, I'm *starving*. Wanna get some lunch?"

"Hell yeah, let's get some *grub*. Standing around all day is tiring work."

"Of course, Miss Rei. And, er... perhaps, next time you have horrible, frightening news you can wait until we've had a seat first?"

Rei and Verde laughed, but Ella just pouted... till she couldn't resist the infectious joy of her friends.

"Yeah just a second, I need to phone my mom, tell her I wo-"

Her phone wasn't here. Obviously.

Verde smirked. "Forgot your phone again?"

Rei chuckled, playing it off as cool as someone in her predicament could. "N-no, I just, just gotta use the bathroom. Feeling a bit... off. I'll be right back, I promise!"

The two looked at her, concern clear across their faces. Rei just hoped it was for the right reasons. Without waiting for a response, she dashed off.

As Rei made her way down Gold Row, she thought of how best explain herself to her friends. Verde had clearly noticed something was up, and Ella had made it more than clear that her safety was a priority. She'd need to think of something to tell them. A part of her considered telling them all the truth. It'd make things so much easier.

It'd also probably hurt them. Assuming they *believed* her, assuming they didn't think she'd gone crazy, they would have to live with the same information Rei had. They'd have to handle that, knowing that the supernatural, that *magic*, was all real.

85

As Rei hopped the fence around the condemned, burnt-out building for the third time in as many days, she reflected on just how well *she* had been handling the revelation.

Yeah, I'm not gonna put that on anyone if I can help it, Rei thought to herself.

She climbed through the window and whistled.

No response.

"H-hey, Gamma?" Rei said. "I'm uh... just checking in. Sorry I didn't come by yesterday, I got... it's a long story. Are you dead? Please don't be dead."

This time, she got her answer.

"Gr... who is- is that... you, the girl. Why does everything hurt?"

He sat up from the floor. Judging from the blood red ash nearby he'd fallen asleep right where she'd left him and hadn't moved since. And judging from his voice, he was recovering... mostly.

"I told you. I'm Rei. And, well Gamma, I'd imagine it's because you look like someone ran you over," Rei answered. She started rummaging through the puppet's ashes, chill to the touch. Her phone must have dropped somewhere around here.

He grumbled at her joke, cringing as he sat up. "I wasn't run over. I was beaten. And stabbed. It should've stopped hurting by now... what are you looking for?"

"Yeah, I know," Rei said, ignoring him. "And I'm looking for my phone. I dropped it when that thing attacked me."

Finally, she found it; buried beneath linoleum rubble and red ash.

The screen was cracked, and battery acid had started leaking from its back. Near she could tell, it was utterly destroyed.

"Oh, come *on*. That's the last thing I needed right now."

She collapsed to her knees with a sigh, letting the phone drop with a sullen thud.

"Having a rough day?" Gamma asked.

The sight of this boy, bloody bandage plastered to his side, covered in healing bruises, asking if *she* was okay, was the last straw.

Rei started laughing, hard. "Hahaha, man, I don't... I don't even *know*. I barely know where to even *begin*," she sat down, elbows on her knees and chin in her hands.

"Two days ago, the world made sense. It was a stupid kinda sense, I was obsessing over a crush and upset because of a stupid bully and just, having fun. It was dumb but it made *sense*."

To her surprise, Gamma nodded. She wasn't sure if he understood, but it felt like he did and that was all that mattered.

She continued. "Then I met you, and you saved my life from that creepy ass crystal thing. Yesterday I get in a *fist fight* with some dudes and it was super scary, but I handled it super well and now- now, I'm rambling. To the shirtless hobo that saved my life. And that's not even the weirdest thing! I, I go to this game tournament, and *Chloe* is there. And she's, she's just completely different."

"Who's Chloe?" Gamma asked.

"She's an old friend of mine. Or was, anyway. I don't know what I did to piss her off, but she hates me now. Or at least I *think* she does. I didn't remember her being so good at games. Maybe, maybe I just forgot it? I had no *idea* she was so good."

Gamma nodded again. "I see. She's an enemy then. Did you beat her?"

The question briefly jolted Rei out of her rant. "I-well, I mean yeah, I did. She sounded kinda sad when she left, though..." her words trailed off into the dark.

A minute of awkward silence later, Rei spoke up again.

"Hey, look, uh... Gamma. I'm sorry. For bothering you with this. You've got more important stuff to worry about."

He shook his head. "Yeah. But *you* saved my life as well, girl. It's the least I can do, until I've recovered my strength at least."

"Well, thanks Gamma. It's nice to know I've got you in my corner," Rei said with a nod.

It *had* felt good to let some of that out. And with the clarity of venting, a weight seemed to lift from some of the questions plaguing her mind.

Rei chuckled to herself. "So... you called me something. A mancer. Are you one?"

Even in the dark, Rei could see his expression harden.

"It's none of your concern, girl. And besides, I was mistaken. You're no mancer. Not one I'd know, anyway. The pain had simply dulled my senses."

Rei stood up; eyebrow raised. "Really? I guess that'd explain it... save me one minute, try to push me back the next. I guess in your case, a mancer would be *your* enemy, then?"

Gamma grumbled, as though thinking of an answer. "Something like that. But it's n-"

"I know, I know. It's 'not my concern'" she put on her best imitation of his gravelly voice. "And you're gonna tell me to leave next, right? Well, I'm not, Gamma. You listened to me cry about my problems and I had to touch your blood, far as I'm concerned that makes us friends."

There was silence, for a moment. Finally, he spoke up.

"Yes, a mancer is my enemy. But when I tell you it's not your concern, it's for your own safety. You don't *know*, you've made that pretty clear. It's safer for you to not get involved."

"Hey, I know some stuff. I read a website on mancers. And I'm pretty sure I *am* one, actually. The website said the first sign of a mancer waking up their abilities is things going weird around them. I've got *more* than my fair share of that."

Further silence from Gamma. Not expected, but something about it felt off... like he was anticipating something. Rei shook off the feeling and continued.

"I mean, like a week ago I set the science lab on fire. Totally ruined a table. And, whenever I'm trying to cook stuff, if I start to panic everything gets burnt. I'm seeing signs of it everywhere- I punched a guy like six feet or something. Hell, just like, five minutes ago I *melted* a controller! With my bare hands!"

Rei could feel that same heat building now as she spoke. Old memories she'd thought nothing of put in a new light. She *knew* she was onto something, she had to be.

"And, and recently another friend, Ella, she said she can read fortunes. It's not legit but, when she did it, I saw flames. Just... I mean, a little spark the first time, really. That's what started all this, seeing that little spark. It's what brought me here in the first place! This place was burnt down by *something* and I can *feel* it. I can feel... this *place*. It's this subtle sick *haze* at the back of my head that I can't-"

A voice cut her off.

"Okay Ella, you first. Then pull me up."

It was Verde. It came from the window. They must have been looking for her. Rei looked to the window, and saw Ella hop down from the window frame. She was looking around, as if her eyes were trying to adjust to the dark.

A sound like a sudden crack ripped through the air. Rei's head turned towards the source.

Gamma had also looked towards the window. And all around him, faint in the dark, something moved. Something dark and amorphous, swirling around him. She almost thought it was her mind playing tricks on her. The shadows of the burnt-out club were dancing.

But then the dark moved. It flitted across the ground, stretching like shadows only... more. It held a weight to it, like it had been given physicality. It grew, lifting from the ground, small threads of inky darkness sticking to it like strands of glue. It split like a budding flower, petals turning into an array of claws. Four hooked fingers and one gnarled thumb, each razor sharp and shimmering with a dark glow.

It was heading towards Ella. She couldn't see it approach, she had turned her back and was helping Verde in through the window. Rei doubted she would have seen it even if she *had* been looking. Darkness reaching out from a black void, poised to strike.

Rei only realized mid stride that she was running as fast as she could. She turned on her heel and threw herself between the claw of shadow and her friends, just as Ella turned to watch. Just as Verde looked into the dark.

"Verde, Ella, get *BACK*!"

Her voice echoed through the condemned building. The shadows, both Gamma's encroaching darkness and the heavy gloom of the dance club were burnt away by a bright, burning light.

Rei's right hand was wreathed in a cherry-red flame that crackled and sparked with energy.

######

Chapter 9

Rei could scarcely believe what she saw. It was one thing to mentally know something, to believe in a truth. It was another thing altogether to see it proven true. And in that single instance two things had proven themselves irrevocably true.

"G-Gamma! St... stop, you don't have to attack them! They're my friends!"

Her voice was wavering. From the intensity of the fire on her hand, so bright she had trouble seeing. From the inky darkness that had, and was still, surrounding Gamma. From the fear of what would have happened if she didn't step in.

"R-REI! What is... what's going on!?"

It was Verde. Her voice was cracking. Ella seemed frozen in place, though she was holding herself between Rei and Verde.

"I'll answer later, just... just stay behind me!" Rei shouted.

She glared at Gamma. He was just standing there, a dark glow in his right hand like faint, black smoke. Further tendrils had risen up in the air, some topped with claws and others with sharpened tips.

Then, all at once, the shadows dispersed. They receded back into the ground around him, becoming one with his own actual shadow.

And then he laughed. A short, curt chuckle that felt more than a little unsettling, especially given what had just happened.

"Sorry. I was... testing you. Intense emotions can awaken these abilities, so I, well, I was going to attack *you*. Then those two showed up and I sensed *something* and-"

"WHAT!" she shouted. Any fear she'd had fell away. Rei stomped over to

Gamma, hand still alight. "You... you attacked random people to *see if I had powers?* You were *going to pretend to attack me?!*"

"I-I told you. I sensed something, and... well, I-" Gamma said.

Rei punched him in the gut, hard.

He doubled over in pain, gurgling out what remained of his apology. He tried to straighten up, but simply collapsed on the dance floor with a thud.

The silence afterward was deafening. Rei looked over to her friends, panic clear across their faces.

"Hey guys! Um, sorry I was late," Rei said. She waved at them.

Her hand was still on fire. "O-oh, um... hey. I'm still on fire. That's uh, that's not normal, right?"

She kicked at Gamma's arm. "Hey, *asshole.* Th... this is supposed to go away right? I'd like to stop being on fire now. It's, it's kinda scary, honestly."

Gamma didn't respond, beyond further grimacing. His eyes had gone white, and the pink of his bandages had started going dark red.

...ah shit. Oops.

"H-hey, Verde, Ella, you got... got any bandages! I think I went a little too far!"

###

It took Ella five minutes to find and purchase the medical supplies they needed. Rei, cautiously and with Ella's assistance, replaced the bloodied bandages wrapped snugly around Gamma's torso. The disinfectant had helped, it didn't smell nearly as rotten as before, but the wound was still raw. Rei could see where mending flesh had torn and felt a tinge of guilt.

The newly forming burn marks on his torso made her feel even worse. And to top it all off, Rei's hand wouldn't go out. Ella ended up doing most of the medical work.

Rei forced the painkillers down Gamma's throat then sat on the dance floor, exhausted. With some caution she touched some wooden rubble, setting alight a makeshift campfire so that they wouldn't need to rely on her burning hand to see.

Ella and Verde sat across from her, the former's hands and arms stained with blood, umbrella cast aside. The poor girl was shaking.

Verde was just staring at Rei... no, past her, to her hand.

"...so. I should probably start at the beginning?" Rei asked.

"I... I-I told you... you *promised*-I... Miss Rei this is a *lot* to handle." Ella asked in return. There was a desperation to her voice Rei had never heard before.

Verde took off her glasses, wiped them clean on her sweater, and put them back on.

"Just so we're clear I'm dreaming, right? This isn't real? Any minute now I'm gonna wake up and tell you both about this weird ass dream where *a magic hobo* tried to kill me and R- Rei saved us both, by setting her hand on fire."

"I mean he didn't... *try* to kill you. It was an accident," Rei said.

Even she had to admit that didn't sound convincing.

"Oh, that makes it *so* much better, Dream Rei. Manslaughter's just water under the bridge!"

"This is like, *ten times* worse than a fist fight!"

The concerned chorus of her friends was growing louder by the minute. Rei tried to ease them the best she could.

"C-come on... it's okay. Calm breaths everyone, calm breaths. This isn't a dream, it's um, real. It's very real. I swear it makes sense. Really, it does. Mostly."

Rei took a deep breath and tried to calm herself as well. As if on cue, the flames on her right hand died away, leaving a few smoldering embers in its wake.

"Okay, look, see. Fire's gone. I'm not on fire anymore. It uh, it didn't even hurt. No, wait, being on fire is supposed to hurt, right? Um... okay. Is everyone okay?"

Shockingly, it seemed to work. Rei didn't know if it was the burst of adrenaline finally subsiding or what, but Verde and Ella had seemed to calm down a fraction or two.

"O-Okay, okay, so... this isn't a dream. I'm awake. And that guy," Verde pointed over to Gamma, who was either still reeling from the pain or passed out. "That guy tried to kill us. By mistake."

"N-... I mean, I don't know. Probably? I did... *kinda* punch him before he could finish explaining."

"Wh... what was that, by the way? The uh, the hand thing. The fire hand thing. And... I mean I guess the thing *he* did. You... you seem like you know what it is."

Rei nodded. "Yeah, I do. Well, I mostly do. Like I said, I should..."

Rei thought about how they'd react to knowing monsters like that puppet existed.

"Yeah we'll save that for later. That fire hand thing was... me. That was me. I can do that. Cause I'm a pyromancer."

To emphasize her point, Rei snapped her fingers.

Nothing.

Rei grumbled, starting to snap her fingers multiple times. "... oh, come on... do... do the thing. Do the thing."

The makeshift campfire in front of them roared, a gout of flame rising up from it. All three girls jumped in place, Ella actually rising to her feet and taking half a step back.

"I... Miss Rei, when I was telling your fortune, you *saw* this, didn't you? *This* is what you were talking about, wasn't it?" Ella asked.

Rei looked at her hand. Tiny little burns littered her palm, scorch marks that would no doubt heal away by the end of the day, just as the first one hand.

"Y-yeah... I did. That's what started this. My interest in it, anyway."

Verde shook her head, hair getting tangled, glasses starting to slip down her nose. "So... so let me get this straight. That was real. It's, I mean everything you were rambling on about, t-the fortune telling, that's all real magic?"

A groan came out from the darkness.

"Not... magic. Shadowmancy"

"No one asked you! You dang-... -*magic hobo*!"

"No, he's right. I uh... I read up on a website about it. Mancies, that's what they're called, they're not magic. They're more of a talent, I think? Besides, Ella's not either of those things, she couldn't predict my fist fight- or this, actually. It was just like, reading people."

Ella was nodding in agreement so hard Rei was sure her head might come flying off.

"Yeah, that's about right," Gamma said with a pained sigh. He pulled himself closer to the fire, Verde and Ella edging away as much as possible.

He looked like an absolute mess. Some of the more superficial wounds Rei had noticed were healing, but... this was the first time she'd ever seen him in actual light.

His skin was sickly pale, and though he was muscled and lean there was a shallowness to it, like he was wasting away.

"Holy shit, are you okay Gamma?"

"I'm... fine. It's none of-"

Then he pitched forward, hand over his side. It wasn't bleeding, but... something was clearly wrong. He grit his teeth in pain.

Then they heard it. A deep rumbling tremor, coming from his stomach.

"...god, he's *hungry.* Right he can barely move. Ella, Verde, do you uh... have any food?" Rei asked.

Verde looked over to Ella, who had finally sat back down. Ella nodded, and Verde pulled a bag out from her sweater. It was marked with the unsettling, submarine-sandwich faced logo of 'Smile's Subs', one of the few chain-restaurants willing to go that far north.

"We... picked up some food while you were gone. Figured we could eat it when you got back. You really gonna give it to this guy?" Verde gave Gamma a glare.

Rei took the bag from her. "No. I mean, not all of it. Just mine."

"Give him mine too, Miss Rei. I don't think I can *eat* right now anyway..." Ella added. "Though... please, if you can, pass the napkins."

###

Gamma devoured Rei's foot long sub in seconds, an almost feral gleam in his eyes. Then he immediately tore into Ella's, though at a slower pace, as though savoring it.

"Mm... my *god.* I've, mmmf, never eaten anything so good before," Gamma said between mouthfuls. "I've never eaten *anything* before but, mff, I imagine it's still true."

Verde gave Rei a sideways glance, scooting ever closer to her friend.

"You uh... sure this guy is alright? He doesn't exactly strike me as..."

Gamma started licking his hands clean of the sandwich sauce and the meat's greasy leavings.

"... human."

"No. I'm human. You'd have noticed if I wasn't. Trust me on that one."

"... what the hell does that mean?" Verde asked, more to Rei than anyone else.

"The website I read mentioned *something*, but it was mostly all dead ends. I've got no idea."

"It sounds a little suspect to me," Ella said, having finally returned from cleaning her hands and arms. She dumped the armful of bloody napkins and formerly wet wipes in the fire.

"Though I suppose, given what else we've seen, that sounds a bit presumptuous of me to say."

Gamma wiped the rest of the mess of food off his face with the back of his hand. "That'd be right. There's... urp, far more to this world than any of you know."

"Yeah. I uh... when I first came here. Like, *into* here, I ran into something," Rei said. This felt a good a time as any to bring it up. "It... was this weird crystal skeleton looking thing. You called it a puppet, right Gamma?"

He nodded. "Yup. Puppet. Not... exactly what I was talking about though. Those are magic constructs, not *people*."

"Wait, so magic *does* exist? And your mancy shit or whatever, that's not magic?"

"Yeah, that's what it seems like anyway," Rei said. "The website I read said mancies and magic are *supernatural*, but otherwise there's no real connection between the two. Compared it to... being naturally fast, and training to run a marathon. That sound right, Gamma?"

He nodded again.

Verde blinked. "Well. Good to know then. So... what *were* you talking about anyway?"

"It might be better if I showed you," Gamma answered.

He extended his hands over the fire, fingers hooked like claws. Slowly, tendrils of shadow lifted out from around them, blooming like flowers into strange, twisted shapes. Inky dark figures formed, like shadow puppets pulled on a string. They looked... unsettlingly alive.

One looked nearly human. A woman in a lab coat, but she had no ears, at least where they'd except them. Rising from her head were two dog ears, and from her backside came a fluffy dog tail, just below the waist. It was almost cute, in a way.

The other looked horrifying. A massive humanoid *thing*, eight feet tall with a lithe body of what looked to be chitinous plating. Its head looked like the cross between a lizard's and a beetle's, horned and scaled but with an all too human maw full of gnashing teeth. Its fingers were segmented like insect legs. It was also wearing a lab coat, which somehow made it worse.

"This is what I meant. There are three types of 'humanity'. Beastmen, demons, and of course... humans."

It was Verde who managed to speak first.

"Wh... what are they? I mean, you said they're a type of humanity but what does that *mean*?"

As Gamma spoke, the shadowy figures seemed to move, a mock imitation of life before the flames. "They're what I said. They're people, like you and me. Forgotten by history."

"How'd we forget something like... like *this*?" Rei asked.

"What I've been *told* is that something happened long ago to decimate their populations. They went into hiding to survive... and then fell into myth and legend, few of which are actually accurate."

"They... hide? How exactly do you *hide* that?" Rei gestured towards the demonic shadow puppet for emphasis.

With the flick of Gamma's wrist, the demon's shape changed. Chitin faded away, horn shrunk, wings tucked themselves into its back. When it had finished, all that remained was a bald-headed scientist in a lab coat. The dog woman had changed as well, though only the ears and tail had vanished.

"With beastmen, they typically use a magical glamour, disguising their more noticeable parts. With demons, it's more natural. Each demon has a human form they can take, but on the inside they're the same as their true form. With both, if you look closely... you can see little imperfections, that show the truth."

"What kinds of imperfections?" Ella asked. "I... that sounds important!"

He flicked his hand again, and the bald scientist knelt down and stretched his hand out above the fire.

His fingers were boney, the joints visible. They almost looked segmented, just like in his true form.

"Huh. So... th-that's it, huh? They could ju-just be some guy. Huh." Verde said. "I'm uh... I'm gonna need to lay down. Think about this for the next oh... entire rest of my life."

She flopped down on the dance floor, poofy sweater dampening most of the thud.

Ella had just gone silent, staring intently at the shadow-made fingers.

Rei scratched the back of her head. "H-hey, look on the bright side guys... I figured I'd have to keep this a secret. Now we all know together. That's good, right?"

Before anyone could respond, Gamma started coughing. The shadows dispersed back into the darkness.

"As... much as I'd love to continue this, I think it's time you all left. I need to rest."

Rei hopped up to her feet. "Yeah, yeah that's fair, Gamma. I uh... I guess we'll come back tomorrow. I mean, if you guys want to."

Ella was the first to fully recover. She stood up, dusted off her skirt, and picked up her umbrella.

"Well... I suppose there's no *real* harm to it. The fortune, it appears, has passed."

Despite her calm demeanor, Rei could see the white-knuckled intensity with which she held her umbrella.

Verde slowly rose to her feet. "Yeah, sure. I've got like, a thousand questions buzzing around in my head and I don't think I'm going to sleep tonight, or ever really, so I might as well commit to coming back. What's the worst that could happen."

"I mean you could die," Rei said, patting her friend on the shoulder. "I almost did."

Verde shuddered. "Yeah, that's... thanks, for that mental image."

As they left, Rei turned to Gamma. He was lying next to the still burning fire, its light casting a dark shadow across his face.

"Hey, we'll be sure to bring some more food tomorrow. At least enough for a few days. See you then, Gamma!"

Gamma stared into the flames, light flitting across his wounded form.

Wounded. The word felt good to think about. Not injured, not dying. *Wounded.* He was healing. Healing slower than he was used to, but faster than expected considering the situation.

He had food, shelter, and protection. Life was good.

The girls were a nuisance of course, though useful. They'd patched him up and fed him. He'd let them get close, but the instant things got bad he'd cut them off. No point in getting his saviors hurt, especially Rei.

Yes, that was it. The instant things got hairy he'd push them away. For their safety.

Easier said than done. Though he'd never admit it, he realized... they were people he could trust.

######

Chapter 10

The three squinted and cringed as the noonday sun shone overhead. Even with the makeshift campfire, they'd become accustomed to the dark. They began to head back towards the commercial district.

"So... that *did* happen, right? That wasn't a dream?" Verde asked.

"Verde you know me. If we were in a dream there'd be a lot more fire." Rei answered.

"I me-Rei, there was a *lot* more fire than is normal, even for dreams."

"...really?"

The two laughed at Rei's confusion. "M-Miss Rei, you don't... mean your dreams are always on fire, right?"

Rei looked at her hand. The burn marks had faded away already, just as she suspected. "Yeah, they are. I just never mentioned it. I... thought that was normal?"

Ella's stride hitched half a step and she started mumbling "... oh my god she dreams about fire *all the time*," under her breath.

Verde punched Rei in the hip as she joined in on the laughter. "You... god, no wonder you fell for all that supernatural shit online."

"Verde *it was right* I don't think you can fault me for that now!"

"Just because that's *true* doesn't mean I can't tease you, girl."

"Look just for that I'm gonna look up more of this 'supernatural' shit on my-"

Right. The reason Rei had left the two in the first place. Her phone.

"Piss, my phone broke. That stupid puppet fell on it or something... god this is gonna suck. I can't call Mom, I can't-"

Verde patted her friend on the back. "Don't worry about it, Rei. *I* have a phone, remember. I called your mom already."

Relief washed over her. And then realization.

Rei held her head in her hands. "Oh my *god* I could have avoided all of this! I left to get my phone to call my *mom* and- uuugh, I've really gotta learn to focus!"

Verde doubled over laughing.

Above Verde's laughter, Ella said. "You seemed to focus well during your tournament. Maybe you just need to think of the world as one big fight?"

"Yeah but that's different. It's gotta be like, adrenaline pumping. I feel that heat and I just... vwoom, focus. It was like that back when I took boxing too... you know thinking about it that might be a pyromancer thing?"

Verde hurried to catch up with the two, who had kept walking as she laughed. "That sounds legit, but I don't have a clue how any of this magic shit works so don't take my word for it."

Remembering the tournament brought back memories of Chloe, and how she'd acted. How the both of them had acted, really.

Rei shook her head, trying and failing to rid herself of the nagging thoughts in her head. "Hey, I'm *starved* and for some reason only Verde had a sub. Let's get something and gloat about how fresh ours is compared to hers."

"H-hey! You can't just-" Verde said.

Rei stuck out her tongue and ran off before she could protest further. Verde cursed and ran after, this time Ella hanging back to laugh before composing herself and walking after them at an even pace.

After their late lunch, the three girls spent the rest of their afternoon hanging out around town. Ella was still fairly new to the place, and now that their weekend was free the girls felt it was their duty to show her around what little there was to see.

They hit the library first, one of the larger buildings in town, and Verde took great pride in showing off how she'd managed to memorize the sorting system. An hour was spent just roaming the calm, quiet shelves. Not one of the three could find any books related to the day's revelations, though Verde did manage to find some interesting history and geography books.

Afterwards, Rei dragged them back to 'Neon City', though after all of the day's excitement, she found herself completely burnt out. Even *Ella* could beat her at the arcade version of 'Knights of the Stars'. No matter what game they played, Rei found she couldn't quite build up the focus that she normally could. She also realized that, even after pounding back an entire foot long sub, she was still starving.

Ella insisted her own victory had been simply luck, then went to play some skee-ball while the other two bought some snacks and milkshakes.

Rei and Verde sat by the side of the road, watching cars drive by and sharing potato chips. It felt... wonderfully grounded, to Rei.

But still, the lingering thought plagued her mind.

"Hey, Verde?" Rei asked.

"Yeah Rei?" Verde answered between handfuls of chips.

"I... think I did something bad today."

Verde laughed. "I mean... you *did* punch a guy with a stab wound in the stomach."

Rei shook her head. "No, I mean at the tournament. Chloe, she wasn't being her usual self. I got aggressive, and she kinda... I don't know. Maybe I'm imagining things."

"Huh" Verde thought for a moment. "You know she did come off a little weird. We don't know her as much as you do, I imagine, but the Chloe *I* know wouldn't be caught playing video games."

"Yeah! But like... thinking on it, we used to play games all the time! It's just I don't really remember when we *stopped*, you know?"

Verde took a sip of her milkshake. "Eh, don't worry about it. I'm sure she did something nasty to you, so you've just blocked it out or something."

Rei looked up at the sky. It was just beginning to take on that amber hue of the sun setting. She'd probably want to get home soon. She sighed.

"I guess you're right. I just, it feels bad, you know?"

A fluffy, plush moth suddenly pushed itself against Rei's face.

"Oh, don't fret Rei-*chan*. Your friends are here to help pick you up," Ella said in a goofy, cartoonish voice. "And if you're unsure, you could just ask the wonderfully talented Ella Umbra to do a love fortune for the two of you."

The three girls laughed, scraps of fluff coming from the plush moth cutting Rei's short.

"I- I... come on Ella, I'm not in *love* with her," Rei said. "And where did you get that thing anyway!"

"Arcade prize. And just because you're friends doesn't mean a love fortune wouldn't work. There are other kinds of love, you know."

Rei rolled her eyes. "I *guess*. But can we do that later? I don't want my hand to burst into flame again. Besides, I, uh, might not like the answer."

They laughed harder, Verde having to brace herself lest she spit up her milkshake. As the laughter subsided, she spoke up.

"Rei, if you're serious about this, try and make up with her. I'm telling you this as your friend, girl. You're not gonna feel better unless you at least try."

"Wow, Verde. Given how much of a jerk she is at school that's real big of you to say."

Rei felt a devilish grin force itself onto her face. It took them a second.

Verde snorted, trying not to laugh. "Yo-you did not just make a *height joke*. Damn it Rei I'm trying to be serious!"

"I know, I know! I just, I won't be able to do it till Monday anyway. She's busy with singing lessons all weekend... aside from when she came to the tournament, I guess. Don't worry, I'm taking it seriously."

Despite the jokes, it was true. When Verde had brought it up, her heart skipped a beat.

Rei had to make up with Chloe. Or had to *try*, at the very least. When Chloe fulfilled her side of the bet- and Rei was sure she would- she would respond positively. She'd face whatever problems Chloe had with her head-on. It was the proper thing to do.

The proper thing to do was also, unfortunately, get going. Rei stood up, stretching her arms.

"Well guys, it's getting late. *This* prize-winning intellect forgot to mention she was grounded, because I got distracted almost dying to a weird skeleton monster thing. And because I broke a dude's nose. So, I've gotta get home before my mom decides to follow me into the condemned building and gets attacked by the weirdo whose life I saved."

Verde snickered. "That's pretty specific girl. And really, given your busted phone... you're d-o-a."

"Oh *god* you're right. I'm so dead. Think of me often, friends, for this may be the last time I see you."

The three laughed at her over-dramatic flair and wished her well.

Rei took a deep breath, and walked home.

Much to Rei's surprise, she got home five minutes early. Further to her surprise, Aria was waiting for her by the door with a warm smile on her face. Not a scrap of old winter clothing remained in the entry way.

"Welcome home, little bell. How was your tournament?" she asked, giving her daughter a hug.

Rei hugged her back, hard. A part of her wishing the still lingering concerns about Chloe, her powers- everything really, could be squished away.

"It was great. I won the whole thing. Verde bought a camera and Ella filmed it, so I can show it to you later!"

"Oh, that sounds wonderful! I do have a question though..." Aria's eyes took on a sharp glint to them. "Why did *Verde* call me to say you wouldn't be home for lunch? I take it you didn't find your phone?"

Rei scratched the back of her head nervously. "I uh... yeah. It's completely busted. A car ran over it. Sorry, Mom."

She handed over the phone. "Well, thank you for telling the truth Rei. It means a lot. And don't worry, you wouldn't have gotten in trouble. I figured you were going to have lunch with your friends afterwards anyway."

Her mother gave Rei a wink. "We can let *some* things slide, you know."

Rei laughed, suddenly feeling a lot better. "Y- yeah, I guess so. So, what's for supper?"

"I'm roasting us up a chicken. You're a little early, actually, so it's not *quite* done yet. I'll call you when it's done."

Rei nodded. "Thanks Mom. I'm gonna go watch some TV. If that's okay, I mean."

"It is. But go up to your room, first. I got you something. Consider it an early birthday present."

"Awe... thanks Mom. I bet I know what it is."

Aria simply smiled and headed off into the kitchen. "You'll see, my little bell."

Rei let out a deep sigh of relief when she walked into her room. She was finally home, after what felt like forever. Between the tournament, Gamma, and hanging out with her friends, she had next to no energy.

Now that she was safe in her room, she could finally let the weight crash down on her.

She dragged herself over to her bed and flopped down on it. On her pillow was small, simple package which she lazily ripped open.

It wasn't the skull mask she'd found in the closet. Instead it was a book, bound in faux leather dyed red. A golden embroidery along the spine, front, and back that made it look far fancier than it actually was. Flipping through it, Rei found that all the pages were blank.

And then a note fell out from the book and directly on her face.

'To my beloved little bell, Rei,

I know, at times, things can be hard. School was a mess for me, though I don't like to say it, and I have to imagine it's a mess for you too. Whenever you're feeling down, or feeling stressed, or just have something interesting you want to remember, use this.

I realize a journal isn't the most exciting gift in the world, but a good friend of mine gave me one once, and that year was the most exciting one I ever had. I met your father. I made YOU. And if I didn't have my own... I doubt I'd have been able to remember it all. So please, accept this gift for what it is. A sign that I hope your life is as exciting as mine, and perhaps a little less messy.

Love, Mom

P.S. If you come home on time tomorrow, consider your punishment finished. I trust in you, my little bell.'

Rei smiled, a soft warmth running through her body. She felt tears sizzle at the edges of her eyes. She put the note on her bedside table and grabbed a pen from her computer desk.

She had a lot to write about.

Chloe pressed her back against the building wall and took a deep, long drag of her cigarette. The ashen taste soured her tongue, but after today she'd more than needed it. She'd faked having a sore throat, even purchased *sunglasses*, all so she could sneak out and go to the game tournament.

And for what? Sure, she'd had a blast playing, even if it most of her opponents had been mindless chaff as far as her skills were concerned, but Rei...

Leave me the hell alone.

Tell me what your damn problem is.

Her words had echoed in Chloe's mind for the rest of the day. After she'd returned home, she'd thrown her disguise in the corner and flopped on her bed in thought. What did Rei mean? Why did she want her to leave her alone, after they'd been friends for so long? What *problem* was she talking about? Sure, they'd fought in the past, but... what had changed in her?

The stress of worrying had struck Chloe hard, and she'd snuck out again that night, when Mother and Father had gone to sleep, to sneak a cigarette or three. Anything to stop her shaking hands and the words reverberating in her brain.

Her phone dinged. She'd received a text message. She wondered if it was her brother, telling her about his schooling down in Center City.

[Yo shithead, where were U 2day?]

It was Clarissa, messaging her directly in a chat room with the rest of her gang of friends, Diane and Heather. They'd promised to hang out on the weekend.

At least, the three of them had. Chloe had told them she had singing lessons this weekend. Reminded them that she alternated weekends between free time and lessons.

[Singing. Father wants me to be an idol, remember?]

It didn't take long for the others to chime in.

[lol really you can barely sing]

[Really, U give up cruisin' wit the SQUAD for daddy?]

[Come on guys, cut her some slack. It's the only thing she's good at, let her have it.]

Chloe rolled her eyes, and typed back to them, cigarette poised between two fingers of her free hand.

[Ah, you bunch of assholes. I know you all came to my recital a week ago. It was lovely.]

There was a pause before the next response.

[no we didn't idiot]

[We don't got time 4 that dumb shit.]

[I mean I went, but I left with the usher.]

A flurry of texts popped up, the other two asking for details. Chloe sighed, cloying smoke mingling with the night air to create a sickening, chilly smog.

[Speaking of which, I think I'm going to seal the deal with Kestrel.]

A lie of course. She hadn't even talked to him; he'd spent almost all of that first day latched to Rei and she just couldn't find the guy otherwise. But it'd draw her friends' attention.

[U wish, skank! WE rootin' 4 U!]

[send the deets what did you say to him]

[Ooh, good to hear. Don't let the little red-haired loser sink her fangs in.]

[as if shed ever try lol stupid moron]

[Yeah. He's too much for her anyway.]

That last text had been her own. Chloe felt a pang of guilt stab into her heart, but quickly pushed it aside. It was just a joke, it wasn't like Chloe or her friends actually *believed* all that, it was just harmless fun. Besides, it was *true*; poor little Rei would have been dumped after he got what he wanted from her.

That's how these things just went.

She didn't even really *care* that much, but when Heather overheard Rei and Verde talking... she'd *insisted* over text Chloe assert herself when she got in. 'Someone as handsome as Kestrel couldn't date someone like Rei', she had sent her. So, Chloe did what she had to.

And Rei'd been okay with it. She politely accepted and after Chloe had walked off, started laughing at her jokes. Her best friend was happy, her *group* was happy. It was all good.

But then why were Rei's words eating away at her?

Another ding on her phone.

[Where are you anyway? Your bedroom light's off.]

[you know shes snogging kestrel]

[Yeah rite. Picz, loser!]

[Girls please, it's nearly midnight. She's probably slumming it at Gold Row looking for a quick bang before the main course.]

Chloe laughed to herself. It was kinda true, in a sense. The border between Gold Row and the regular commercial district was a favorite place of hers, a place where sidewalk only just started to twist into a crooked mess, where brightly coloured storefront faded into dull, drab, peeling walls. No one lingered here for long, at the point where new met old.

A perfect spot to be alone.

[Hell yeah. I'm *starving*.]

It felt good to play up the lie. The three of them texted back a variety of insults, congratulations, and demands for her to prove it. Chloe felt content, the support of her friends always good to read.

She just wished it didn't hurt as much as it did.

Chloe was about to feed into it more when something caught her eye. She gasped, cigarette dropping from her lips. She quickly crushed it beneath her heel.

"H–hey, Kestrel. What brings you out here so late?"

He was just a few feet from her, walking down to Gold Row. At this distance, she could almost see what the others had said about his looks. His piercing gaze felt more like he was looking through her than at her. It was almost intimidating.

"Oh, just out for a jog. What about you?"

"Oh, *I'm* just enjoying the night air, dear Kestrel. Though, you may walk me home if you wish."

Chloe's answer left her mouth so quickly she'd almost forgotten to speak properly. Heather had taught her the proper way to address people; with a rich, refined aura that felt ever so slightly condescending. All in good fun, of course.

"No, I'm still busy. I... wait, you're Chloe, aren't you? From school. I've got a question for you."

Chloe felt blood rush to her face. If he asked what she thought he would... she'd be able to write off this entire garbage day as a success. Her friends would be so proud.

"Do you know Rei? I saw you talking with her at school the other day."

Chloe's hopes, however minor they were, shattered all the same.

"I-I... yes, I do know of her. She's a friend," Chloe said. Saying it out loud felt good, the last time she did Clarissa had poked her in the side with a ruler.

"Good. Where does she usually hang out? I need to ask her something, and I haven't been able to find her all day."

Chloe resisted inquiring, worried what it might be "Well, there's 'Smile's Subs', a sandwich shop, down the block. She goes there all the time. I don't know where she could vanish off to though..."

He smiled, and it seemed to light up the night sky. "Thanks. Do you... can you tell me anything about her? Just to help me get an idea of who she is."

"She's a darling. Oh, but you didn't hear it from me," Chloe said, momentarily forgetting herself. "She's cute, and funny, and smart. And so nice, too. She'd never so much as hurt a fly."

"Thank you," he nodded, and looked over into the dark. The look in his eyes held a wistful glimmer. Chloe wondered what it was like, to see someone look at you like that.

"You know, she's actually my best friend. I can... introduce you, if you'd like."

He waved her off. "No, that's fine. She's already asked me out herself. I just haven't had time for it."

"But-" Chloe felt something rise to the back of her throat. The imagery of the two dating made her sick.

"And... I can see what you're doing. I'm not oblivious. You and those other harpies want me for something." Kestrel turned away. "My eyes are on Rei, and Rei alone. I don't even know who you are."

Before she could say anything, Kestrel left, heading off into the darkness of Gold Row.

A ding from her phone.

[Hey trashbag. Have you screwed Kestrel yet? We're waiting.]

Chloe slid her phone back into her pocket, ignoring Heather's text.

Looking at it made her hate herself, and she didn't know why.

######

Chapter 11

For the first time in what felt like her entire life, Rei woke at the crack of dawn. She could feel energy running through her veins, like liquid fire running up her arms and down her spine.

Rei had decided it last night, between bites of roast chicken.

She was going to ask Gamma to train her. His mancy had been so impressive, and all she'd ever managed to do, aware of her abilities or not, was accidentally set things on fire.

Rei hurried through breakfast, wished her mom a good day, and ran off to meet with Verde and Ella so they could do some shopping for Gamma.

The two waved as she approached, the later bundling up in a slightly thicker skirt and an elegantly embroidered vest. The first drifting flakes of snow were coming, Rei could feel it in the air.

"You know, since Ella came here, I don't think I've seen you two apart for very long. I know you're ace, but is there something I should know about, or...?" Rei said, voice trailing off as a smirk came to her face.

The two laughed. "Oh no, Miss Rei. It just so happens that we live next door to each other. Makes it quite easy to meet up."

Verde rolled her eyes. "Mostly, anyway. She sleeps in more than you do. She's just faster."

Rei joined the laughter, and the three began to walk toward the commercial district.

"So, you brought the books, right?" Rei asked.

"Yeah," Verde patted the slight bulge on her back. "Backpacks here. Why'd you want me to bring this stuff anyway?"

"Well, when I first met him Gamma said he doesn't know where he is. So, I figured I could help him with that," Rei answered.

"Honestly, it's a good thing you came by, I'm uh... not too good at geography. Or history for that matter. That's more your thing Verde."

Verde's pace quickened at her words. "Well then, let's get some food for the guy and get to it! I've been looking for a way to show off!"

"Ah, don't run too quickly. I... I think the ground is starting to get icy," Ella said.

"Don't worry about it, Ella. Just one step at a time," Rei said. "Oh, also, we need to pick up some candles. I don't wanna set the dance club on fire. Poor buildings been through enough."

They laughed again, even Ella, as they made their way down the street.

The three girls piled in through the window, each carrying at least one bag of groceries.

"Yo, Gamma! We're home! You dead?" Verde asked, shouting into the darkness. The fire had worn itself out, the bloody smell of bandages replaced by ash.

He groaned. "No. Not dead yet."

"Good to hear. Watch your eyes guys," Rei said. "You get the food out. I'm gonna set things up"

The three got to work, Rei rummaging through the bag for the wax candles and utility lighter they'd bought, the others setting out tin cans and other non-perishables.

"Hey, you know how to read, right dude?" Verde asked.

"Yes. Obviously," Gamma grumbled. He looked at the can, studying it.

He cringed as Rei lit the candles, setting them up so that everyone could properly see.

"Is that... necessary. I can see better in the dark."

"Yeah, and we can't. We can't teach you stuff if we can't *see*," Rei said.

With the food properly placed in a distant corner of the dance club, it was actually starting to look like a home. A burned, ashen, dusty, warped in places home that still smelt vaguely of death, but a home nonetheless.

"... man, we should get some furniture," Rei said.

"Hell *no* Rei!" Verde shouted. "We could barely afford this stuff as it is, sorry man but you can sleep on the floor."

"What's furniture?"

The three looked at him, Rei speaking up. "You know how to read but don't know what furniture is? No offense, but where were you raised?"

Gamma shrugged. "In a tube, mostly."

Verde sighed, and dug out the books she'd borrowed from the library. "Alright, fine. I'll accept that, I guess. Not like it's important anyway. We got... stuff, to lay on. Probably."

Ella walked over to where they had made their makeshift campfire yesterday and started building a more proper one with some of the dance club's charred tables.

"There we are. Now we can cook your food, Mr Gamma."

She looked over at the small tower of cans in the corner. Some of them already had bite marks.

"If... you want, of course."

"I still don't know why you're doing all this. I saved Rei's life, so I understand that, but what do you all owe me?" Gamma asked.

It was a piercing question, putting a stop to all but Rei's activity; currently checking Gamma's bandages.

"A moral imperative," Ella said simply. "You're someone who needs help, and I can do so. So, I will. Besides, we're her friends. I've only really known Miss Rei a few days and I'm sure I could trust her with almost anything."

Verde rolled her eyes. "Yeah, same here. Though I'm not gonna be that altruistic. You're gonna answer every question I have about all this supernatural shit."

"I'll answer what I can," Gamma said. "But... you really shouldn't involve yourselves in this. It's too dangerous."

Rei poked Gamma in the side, gently. "Too bad. You saved my life, and my friends apparently think I'm smart enough to make good decisions, so you're stuck with us. Your wounds are looking good. Might want to change out the bandage and gauze, but otherwise it looks like you're healing nicely."

He nodded. "I feel better, yeah. I think that food helped. Can I have... more. Of that sandwich, I mean."

"Uh, we didn't pick up any. I figured we were gonna cook some canned ravioli or whatever. Should we get some?"

Ella answered the question. "Yes, I do believe you should. It'll take some time to cook, and *something* tells me our friend here is hungry."

"Yeah that makes sense. Okay guys I'll be right back with some grub," Rei said.

She could hear Verde calling to her as she climbed through the window. "Oh, yes, please leave us with the half-naked guy covered with horrible wounds. That's what we want."

The only response Rei could think of was to laugh, as she dashed off to the sandwich shop.

She had intended to be quick about it, but two things had slowed her down. First, 'Smile's Subs' was packed. Orders were backed up; it'd take a while for the subs to actually finish.

Secondly, Kestrel was there. He was waiting for his own order, and it hadn't taken much more than a happy wave to get Rei to sit down with him. He sat across from her, a slim smile on his face. His eyes still held that wistful depth to them, and Rei noticed a beauty in them she hadn't noticed before.

Her heart was pounding in her chest. All the excitement she'd been through the past few days had put her feelings for him by the wayside, but seeing him again brought it all up to the surface. It felt like her skin was on fire. A couple times, she actually checked to be sure it wasn't.

"So, how's the weekend treating you?" Kestrel asked.

"I-oh, my weekend has been great. I've uh, been hanging out with my friends, mostly. What've you been up to?"

"Jogging. Now that I've got a better idea of the place, it's just for fun," was his answer.

"Cool. Uh... what brings you here, Kestrel? Other than lunch, I mean."

He stared at her, briefly confused at the notion you'd do anything at a chain restaurant *other* than to buy food.

Oh cool I'm dying. Come on Rei, get yourself together! Rei thought, echoing through her mind.

"Eh, just joking with you. You picked a good place! Really. I know it's a chain, but they make some good food."

"Ah, I see. And I know, I love their shawarma. Reminds me of home... whenever we had an especially good day, Father would treat us all to some."

He laughed, that smooth calm laugh that made Rei's skin tingle. It was clear this was developing into more than just a childish attraction.

"That sounds... really nice. I guess your family doesn't do fancy food much. You said the soup reminded you of home too."

He nodded. "Yeah, we usually go for the cheaper option. It's not that we need it, necessarily, it's just..."

"I get it, I get it. It's part of your parents' job, right?"

He smirked. "Oh, you remembered. Yeah, they think living frugally will help them understand the best way to sell things. I do love them, but it can be a bit frustrating."

Rei thought of her mom and couldn't help but relate. She smiled back. "I hear you Kestrel. Parents can be like that sometimes."

"Oh, how was your tournament by the way?" He asked suddenly "From what I did see, I imagine you won?"

"It uh... it went real good, and-wait, what you saw?"

He laughed again. "Yeah. I was jogging across the street and I saw you and your uh, other friends hanging out by the curb. You seemed pretty happy. I would have come over but, well, I didn't want to come off as rude."

"O-oh wow, really? I mean, you wouldn't have seemed rude. You're... you're a friend of mine too, I would have loved to hang out."

She had hesitated, slightly. If he had hung out, he would have been dragged into everything as well. Maybe it was for the best he didn't approach them.

"Well, thanks Rei. I'm glad to hear I'm your friend. Truth be told... it's been harder adjusting than I thought. So, I'm glad I've got someone in my corner. You all seem... really close. Especially, Verde, was it?"

Rei felt her face heat up, cheeks burning red. "I'm glad to hear it Kestrel. And yeah, Verde's like, my best friend. She's fantastic... if a little rough around the edges."

"Tell me about her. How'd you two meet?"

The memory played like clockwork. Rei took a deep breath.

"Well... she was a transfer student too. Five years ago or so, actually. I uh... was in a bit of a bad place back then. I don't remember why."

He nodded, wordlessly urging her to continue.

"Verde... the day she arrived, during recess, I was off to myself. Probably crying, honestly. Then she approached me. And she just hugged me, with those big poofy sleeves of hers. And she asked me if I was okay. We talked a bit, and... well, that's it. We've been friends ever since."

Kestrel smiled. "That's a good story, Rei. I can tell she means a lot to you."

Simple words, but they hit true. Rei really did care about her. She nodded, and the two sat there for a moment.

Then Kestrel spoke up again. "So, Rei. I've been thinking. About what you asked me."

He reached out a hand, gently put it over hers.

"I uh... sure. I'd like to go out with you. When're you next free?"

Rei could feel the beginning rumble of fire in her ears.

"O-oh, I'm uh, I'm free Monday! But, um, my birthday is Wednesday. If you wanna come to that," Rei asked.

She could barely get the words out. He had said yes. It took him awhile, but *he had said yes.*

Kestrel smiled, his sharp grin sending goosebumps up Rei's arm. "Wednesday could work. I'm busy Monday, but... maybe Tuesday? I was hoping we could have a date first, before I met your parents."

All her words caught in her throat. Her feelings crashed against the side of her head.

The... day before my birthday. Right, was all that remained in her mind.

"N... sorry, but Tuesday's not gonna work out. I've got... something important to do, on Tuesday."

Never in her life did she expect to be turning down someone she had a crush on... but there it was.

There was a slight look of disappointment in his eyes. He nodded. "I understand. I'd love to come to your party though. Can I see your phone?"

Another knife to the heart. "Agh... shit. My phone's broken, sorry. I... if you give me your number, I'll phone you when I get a new one. Or, or we could talk in class."

To her surprise, he smiled again. "That sounds fine by me. I'll write up my number for you."

He did so, just as the sandwiches Rei'd ordered finished. She pocketed the number and grabbed her sandwiches.

"Thanks, Kestrel. I'll call you as soon as I can."

"Any time. Truth be told, knowing you might call me at any moment is pretty exciting. I'll make sure to pick up straight away."

Rei blushed. "Y-yeah. Anyway, see you later Kestrel!" she waved.

He waved back, and Rei rushed off, barely able to contain herself.

"What took you so long?" Verde asked, as Rei finally came back in through the window.

"Kestrel asked me out on a date," she answered. She sounded dumbstruck and out of breath.

Verde hopped up from where she was sitting. "W-wait, really?!"

"Oh, Miss Rei, that's wonderful news."

"What's a date?"

Rei fell onto her knees, a smile spreading across her face. "Oh... oh my god, he really said yes. I've got a *date*. For my *birthday*."

The other girls cheered. Gamma just looked around, confused.

"What's a birthday? And why is she doing it with some sort of predatory bird?"

Gamma's baffling question kicked the feet out from under her. "Wh...

Gamma you know obscure birds but you don't know what a date or a birthday is?"

"One of my caretakers was a bird watcher. He wouldn't shut up about them." Gamma didn't elaborate further.

Rei blinked once, twice. "Wu-... alright, sure. Anyway hey, sandwiches are here. How's the teaching going?"

Verde rolled her eyes, taking the sandwich bag and handing them out. "Oh, you would not *believe* it. There's so many gaps in what he knows, it's ridiculous."

"It's not ridiculous. I was only taught important things."

Verde threw Gamma's sandwich at him, knocking him flat onto his back.

"Dude, *history* is important. Geography is important!"

Rei managed to pick herself up and sat down next to the fire. "So, what *does* he know?"

"Biology, mostly," Ella answered with a shudder. "A *frightening* amount of biology."

Gamma shrugged, prying his mouth away from his sandwich. "What? Knowing how to twist an arm so it tears off at the elbow is *vital* information."

The three cringed, and Gamma just shook his head. "You know, you don't *have* to do this. Just leave the books here, I'll read through them."

Verde pointed at him, face stern. "Yeah, you're not getting out of this that easy. You still owe me some answers."

Ella sat next to Rei, chewing on her sandwich as the other two bickered.

"Have uh... they been like this the whole time Ella?"

"Unfortunately. Miss Verde asked him about magic, and, well-"

"I don't *know* any magic. I can tell you how it's done, but that's about it."

Verde grumbled, sitting down next to Rei and Ella. "Eggh, fine. How *do* you do magic?"

He took a deep breath, setting his sandwich- or what remained of it- aside. "Magic is done through ritual. You study things, you learn their patterns. Nature has a shape to it, if you look hard enough. Then you draw out a circle, write in the patterns you studied, concentrate, and speak the spell. Then it goes off, fueled by your stamina."

As he spoke, Verde pulled out a notebook and started taking notes. "Yeah, yeah, go on?"

"That's basically it. You can draw the magic circle out of anything. According to what I learned, accomplished mages can just etch it in the air with their finger, bleeding stamina out like a light. Other than that... I know if you don't draw it perfectly, the spell can backfire, or worse. That's *it*. All I know."

Verde sighed. "Well... what about mancies? Can you teach those?"

He shook his head. "No, not the way you're thinking. Mancies are natural born. Like Rei said, a talent. Once you awaken it, all you need to do is practice and it'll get better. A spell will always be the same spell, but a mancer can manipulate their element however they choose, whenever they choose. Spell casters can do anything if they study long enough, but the narrow versatility of a mancer is hard to beat. And again, it's a *part* of you. If you have it, you've always had it. And if you don't... you never will."

Verde kept writing, but she had gone silent.

Rei cleared her throat. "Uh, not to interrupt, but why do you care about it so much, Verde?"

She looked away for a moment, face buried into her sweater.

"I... no reason. I just figured it was something we should know about."

It was an obvious lie. Rei felt an itch run up her arms.

She wouldn't push the question.

"Hey, I've got an idea. How about... you teach Gamma more history and stuff, and he can show me how to actually use my powers. Does that sound fun?"

For a moment, there was nothing. Worry started to form, a buzzing spark up her neck.

But then Verde answered with a smile. "Yeah, that... that sounds like a good idea."

######

118

Chapter 12

"Sway your arms like this. Your movements must be fluid," Gamma instructed. He stepped across the dance floor with surprising grace. As he moved, twin trails of shadows swirled in the air, tracing the path of his arms. With a sudden movement, like a dancer turning on his heel, one of the trails lanced out and struck at the empty sandwich bag, punching a perfect round hole in the plastic.

Rei tried her best to imitate him. The instant her feet crossed she stumbled over herself, falling face first on the warped flooring. The others cringed.

She'd been going at it for four hours, and not even a spark. The closest she'd gotten was feeling a warmth through her arms and even then, she wasn't sure if it was from heat or from typical exercise.

"You okay, Rei?" Verde asked, flipping through her history book.

Rei grumbled, picking herself up off the floor. Her clothes were filthy, and she was pretty sure the still healing cut on her cheek had started bleeding again.

"Bleeegh," was the only answer she could manage.

Ella handed her a small container of wet wipes. "Here you go. Don't worry Miss Rei, I believe in you."

Rei started to clean herself off. "Man, there's gotta be something wrong. It... it feels like it comes so easily when I *don't* want it, but when I do... nothing."

"Hmm..." Gamma said. His arms were crossed, a pair of shadowy arms imitating him with such ease that Rei started to feel an altogether different sort of fire.

"I'll think on it. This method always works for me...."

Rei sighed and laid out on the floor. "Eeeh, let's leave it for now. I'm getting tired. It's not like I *need* to be able to use it anyway."

Rei bit her lip. That wasn't exactly true. It went unsaid, and she wasn't sure if the others had realized it, but... someone *had* attacked Gamma. Another mancer. She didn't know why, and Gamma sure as hell wasn't talking about it, so she was at a loss. Rei figured learning how to use it would mean she could fight.

And realizing she *wanted* to fight, made fireworks go off in her mind. She could be a hero if she wanted. She had the power. She just needed to learn how to use it.

"You know, here's a thought. Do you think the government knows?" Verde asked.

The others looked at each other, Verde's question lingering in the air.

"I mean, think about it. The government's basically everywhere. There's like, thirty million people in this country. *Somebody* in the government has to know about this stuff, right?"

Rei thought on it a moment. "It... doesn't really make sense. If they knew, wouldn't they bring it up? If they could control how we learned it, that might make things easier to understand."

To their surprise, Ella spoke up. "No, I don't imagine so. Humans are notoriously superstitious at times. Suddenly telling them every myth they'd ever heard was true, but not the way they think, would be far too dangerous. Er, at least, that's what it sounds like to me."

"Huh. That's a good point. Hey, maybe the uh... what's his name, the president of ONY knows. They build a bunch of tech stuff, that's basically magic, right?"

"ONY?" Gamma asked.

There was a sharpness to his voice, one Rei hadn't heard since he saved her life.

"Yeah, they're this manufacturing company. I talked about them while Rei was getting the food, they're the guys who sold all the weapons to the Felisian's," Verde said. She pushed her glasses up slightly and hopped to her feet.

"With their advanced weaponry, the Felisian government defeated the combined forces of Exova and Trestaria, bringing an end to the south-eastern civil war. They named themselves the Felisian Hub, and declared that the defeated Exovan-Trestarian Alliance, as well as Dulace and Kaiga who had already been free nations who waited out the war be made provinces of the country we now know as Felis. For their help, the at the time president of ONY Manufacturing was named a 'personification of the Felisian state' in the constitution."

Verde took a little bow, her recital of the knowledge done. Ella clapped, though everyone was impressed.

"Wow, I knew like... some of that. Kinda. That's what you meant by the president running the country, right?"

Verde shrugged. "More or less. The prime minister is supposed to be the real power, and the president's gotta go through his general manager to do anything, but according to my mom the president does all the real work. Dude's even got his own army, though he calls it the 'ONY Security Force' or something."

"What's his name?"

There was something... off, about the way Gamma asked that question. His shadows, still under his control, were starting to twist and churn.

Verde held a hand to her face, tapping away at her cheek in thought. "It's uh... hm. Oro Yamata."

The shadows stopped, but there was a tension in the air. Rei could taste it, bitter against her tongue. It made her feel sick, a hazy smog in her head.

Gamma coughed. "Thanks. I was just... curious."

After a moment of silence that weighed down on them all like a sack of bricks, Rei picked herself up off the floor.

"Well, I uh, think it's about time for me to get going. How about you guys?"

Verde went back to flipping through her history book. "You know, I *think* I'm gonna stick around. Maybe bother Gamma until he breaks something."

"You can't have any of my food," he grumbled. Verde just laughed at her own joke.

"Yeah, okay. You can keep your campfire spaghetti or whatever. I'm gonna head home too."

Ella raised her hand. "I, um... will be going to the library, if anyone would care to join me. I realized there was a book I meant to pick up."

She looked to Rei, then Verde, but both shrugged.

"Well, guess it's just you and me tonight Verde. Let's get going. See you later, Gamma!"

As the two walked home, Rei told her everything that had happened at the sandwich store. It hadn't been a long conversation, but she lingered on every detail of it. She'd even let it slip that she'd told Kestrel how the two of them had met.

Verde's response had been an attempted smack in the back that only led to the two laughing harder.

Finally, they reached Rei's home.

"Okay Verde, I'm off. Have a good one. I'll see you tomorrow!"

"I'll see you tomorrow too, lovebird," Verde said, a teasing grin on her face.

"And don't worry about Gamma. I had the... pleasure, of explaining what school is. He knows we might not show up."

Rei hopped the fence, not bothering to open the gate. "Well, that's a relief. But uh, not so loud. I don't want Mom to know."

"Oh, you *don't* want your mom to know you've spent the last two days hanging out with a shirtless, blood covered, emo-hair weirdo with shadow powers?"

Rei laughed so hard she almost fell to her knees. "H-hey, come on. He's not that bad. Is he?"

Verde nodded with a laugh and headed off without answering the question.

Rei took a deep breath and headed inside. It had been a wonderful weekend, but now it was time for some rest. She'd write down the good news in her journal, and even take the time to tell her Mom about it.

That was the plan, anyway.

As Rei entered the house, she knew something was wrong. The television was on, turned to a news channel, the volume too low to make out. Her mom rarely listened to the news at this time of day, especially when she was cooking.

Rei carefully walked into the living room and found Aria in her chair.

Her face was twisted in a serious glare, the type Rei had only ever seen when peeping in at her office while she worked; the expression of her mother dealing with an unruly client, and making it clear just where they stood.

The news report was already in progress. "-nd now, an update to our top story. A caution, this may be graphic for younger audiences. Tragedy has struck, along the streets of the historic Gold Row district of Laketown last night. It is now confirmed that Officer Emmanuel Grant, friend to the community, has been killed. Reports say that Officer Grant had been out doing his nightly rounds when an unknown assailant approached him. An altercation ensued, in which Officer Grant was fatally injured with a stabbing weapon that police believe at this time to have been a knife. While no explicit motive has been announced, law enforcement is urging inhabitants to avoid going down Gold Row if possible, especially at night."

The report continued, detailing the officer's history, but Rei could barely hear it. A tinge of fear itched across the back of her neck like a boney finger. Fear, not just for herself, but for Gamma.

But what scared Rei the most was her mother's reaction. It grew harder, sharper, and she could have sworn her eyes flickered with fire.

"H-hey Mom. Are you alright?" she asked. Anything to break the silence.

"Oh, Rei! My darling little bell, you're home early!" Aria said. Her voice cracked a little, like she'd been caught off guard. Her expression immediately softened, and she gave Rei a warm, if tired, smile.

"Yeah, I am. Is everything alright? I heard the news, and..."

Aria got up from her chair and immediately pulled her in for a hug. "No, don't worry, it's fine. Your old mother just... the news can be intense, sometimes. And it's been so long since something like this has happened here. That's all, Rei."

The reassuring tone and the warm hug helped wash away most of her fears. Most of them.

"I... I know, Mom. I love you," Rei hugged her back, hard. Memories of the crystalline puppet flooded back. Its smooth, emotionless face, entirely blank.

She shuddered, and Aria held her tighter. She could feel it.

"I love you too, little bell. I'm here, and as long as I am you don't have anything to fear."

Rei wondered how true that was. Her mother didn't know anything about what had happened. She didn't know how close she'd come to death, truthfully Rei hadn't really processed it until just now.

Gamma's words echoed in her head. *I don't want you to get involved.*

It was because of this. It had to be. Whoever was hunting him was getting closer. The street toughs she and Kestrel roughed up where nasty, but not like this.

Rei needed to learn how to use her powers. It was the only way she could protect Gamma, protect her friends, protect *herself*, even.

The only way she could protect her mom.

Rei was all Aria had anymore.

Realization hit her. There was something she could tell her. Something that might take her mind off this.

"Oh uh, Mom... I've got a date. Another date, I mean, with Kestrel."

Her mother smiled, ear to ear. "Oh, how *wonderful* Rei!"

She turned the television off, and sat on the couch, patting the seat gently.

"Now, come on. Tell your mother all about your new boyfriend."

Rei stammered. "H-he's not my boyfriend. At least, not yet. I mean I don't, I don't think so, anyway. He'd... he'd be my first, so I wouldn't really know how to tell, I guess?"

Aria nodded her head sagely. "Oh, little bell. When you know, you know."

"When did you know? With... Dad, I mean."

The question came out before she could even think it.

"Oh, why do you want to hear such a silly story as th-"

Rei smirked, laughing under her breath as she sat next to her mother.

Aria grumbled in half-hearted protest. "Ah. The letter. I knew that'd come back to bite me. So... you want to hear how I first fell in love with your father, do you?"

Rei nodded. In truth she was a little nervous to hear it. She'd never really heard many stories about her father.

"Okay. Well, way back, almost eighteen years ago if you can believe it, I actually used to live in Center City. The both of us did. One of the head lawyers, he'd tasked me with a specific case, which I handled *beautifully*. The old bastard was so happy, he took the whole firm out drinking."

Aria swished her hand as she spoke, as if drawing a picture with her words. She sounded wistful, as though remembering days long since passed that felt more like fairy tales now than truth.

"Now, I'm not much of a drinker. But your father, *he* put away just about two bottles of the stuff. One of the other office assistants challenged him to a game of darts, and of *course* he accepted. And the crazy, drunk fool tears his tie off, grabs four darts at once, one between each finger, and thwip thwip thwip, four bullseyes!"

Aria laughed, remembering old times. Rei could see the subtle crease in her mother's brow. Telling this story was hard.

"... you know, I think that was one less thwip then it sho-no, it doesn't matter. Anyway, the point. The point is he looked so different, at that moment. He was my personal assistant, and... really, I treated him as a glorified secretary more than anything else,"

Aria paused, then took a deep breath. "Until that night, I don't think I ever really *saw* him. He always seemed like such a mess, over concerned and panicked about everything. Very... reserved, otherwise. Like you. But when I saw him land those bullseyes, there was this fierceness in his eyes. I knew, then. He had a fire in him, a passion I couldn't turn away from. No matter how hot it could get."

Rei listened, quietly, until the whole story was done. She could almost see it happen in her mind; just the way Aria told it. Her father seemed... fantastic.

She wondered what advice he'd give her, now. The thought hit her far harder than she'd expected.

Then Aria kissed her daughter on the forehead, holding her tight.

"And now, little bell, that fire is you. Though *I* got to name you," she said, bopping Rei on the nose with a teasing grin on her face.

Rei laughed, and swung for her mother's nose, but to no avail. She was far too quick.

"Now then! I hope you enjoyed that story, Rei, and I hope with your boyfriend you can make a story just as romantic."

Rei felt her cheeks flush as red as her hair. "T-thanks, Mom. Really. It was... a beautiful story."

A thin, happy smile crossed her Mom's face. "Now then... I believe we've got ooone last movie to push our way through. Shall we..." she reached back and pulled out the case of another chintzy horror flick. "Get *spooked*?"

The faux watercolour painting on the cover used a bloody hook as the number two. To both Aria and Rei's surprise, Rei laughed.

"Sure thing Mom! I think I can handle it this time."

Rei smirked. After the past couple days, she doubted a horror film would be much problem now.

###

Verde peeled off her sweater and threw it aside. She did love the thing, but after a while it got itchy and irritating. It was worth it to keep her small frame from freezing in the cold... the thought of the coming snow sent a chill up her back. She sighed, stepped over her dusty toolbox, and inspected the space heater.

The thing was all but busted. They'd got it when they first moved to this frozen shithole, and Verde had insisted they keep it once it started to crap out. She'd even said she'd fix it herself.

And to her credit, she'd managed it. After two months of cuts and burns, Verde got it running.

But, like always, it wasn't enough. It was *never* enough. Never quite smart enough, never quite skilled enough. So, she moved on to the next bright idea, the next challenge she wanted to try. The half-finished model kits lining her shelves, and the instrument case her space heater sat on were a testament to how well that had gone.

Verde had had no idea *what* to focus on after that. It felt like she'd tried everything, like nothing could catch her attention. Then all of a sudden, she got a little bug-bite of curiosity.

It started the day after Rei's freak out at Ella's fortune telling. Verde had caved in and asked the girl to tell her fortune, just a small one. Nothing had seemed out of the ordinary at the time, but the experience had sparked something that finally caught her attention. She'd spent hours searching online for information after that.

Only to find nothing, of course. Verde sighed, and flopped on her bed.

Then the weekend happened, and everything Verde knew was flipped upside down. It was like the world was *taunting* her.

Verde didn't resent Rei, who somehow seemed to coast above it all, who seemed blessed with talent. That was just the way things were. But she couldn't deny that there was a jealousy there. She tried to hide it, but–

There was a knocking on her window. She looked up, wondering what it could be.

It was Ella. She'd snuck into their backyard and was trying to get her attention.

She had a book in hand. Leather bound, a deep forest green.

Verde opened the window.

"Ella, what the *hell* are you doing here?" she asked, voice barely a whisper. Her mother was sleeping upstairs and would kill her if she was woken up by anything less than an emergency call from the hospital.

Ella thrust the book forward. "I–I found it. In the library. I... think it might be magic. And I, well, I noticed you were interested, and, well.... "

Her cheeks turned red, bright against her pale skin.

"I guess, seeing you always supporting Miss Rei, I felt I should do the same for you."

Verde took the tome, flipping through the pages. It was in Exovan, though she could make out some of the words from her own attempts at learning the language.

"What makes you think this is actually *legit*, anyway?"

A fair question, Verde felt. Rei was confident Ella's fortune telling wasn't real, but Verde wasn't sure yet herself. Proving a negative like that after they'd just learned supernatural shit was real felt like an impossible task.

"Oh, well..." Ella hesitated a moment, drumming her fingers on the windowsill. "I read it. I'm fluent in Exovan, I just have some issues with speaking it. Turn to the cover page and say the word there. You'll see."

Verde did as she said, flipping back to the start. The cover page had a large circle on it, inked with a green pen. Intricate geometric shapes filled the circle, and at its center was a stylized gust of wind. At the top of it was the word Ella told her to say. Verde took a breath.

"*Windzauber...*"

Verde felt a faint tug at her arm. A calm breeze blew across her hands, and the book *glowed*. She smiled so hard Ella could see all her teeth.

"This... this is fantastic! How did you find it?"

She looked away, a shy expression on her face. "I... well, I remembered how the library ordered things- thanks to you I might add- and searched through every shelf."

A rush of emotions flooded through Verde. But there was a problem. With a solution of course, but... Verde cleared her throat.

"So, Ella. Do you wanna come in. Help me study." Verde wiggled the book at her for emphasis. "I can't read even a quarter of this shit... I need you, girl."

Ella blushed again and clambered through the window.

"Of course, Miss Verde," Ella said, situating herself on Verde's tiny bed. "Where do you wanna start? I've already read through the entire thing."

"Wow, really?" Verde asked. The book looked to be like, two hundred pages at least.

"Like I said. I like reading."

Verde thought a moment. "Magical theory. Tell me everything you can."

"Well," Ella started, "there's a lot of technical stuff, stuff even I have some difficulty understanding- not that that's unusual of course. But the way it works is... think of it this way."

Ella poked Verde in the chest. "Mancies come from here. You feel it, like a part of your body" then poked her in the forehead "and magic comes from here. Conceptually, anyway. You think about a cool breeze, about its ebb and flow, how cold it is and how it feels on your skin, and you think about it, down to its every like... concept. And what you think up, that mental image, is a pattern. You draw it as a magic circle, and that's the spell."

"Don't poke me," Verde deadpanned. A bit of humour to try and calm the storm currently exploding in her head. "Magic is thinky, mancies are feely, got it. Now explain the *actual* hard stuff."

Ella laughed and started flipping through the book, reading off the more complex theories and explanations of the inner workings of magic.

It was a lot to take in at once. Verde's mind already felt close to bursting trying to understand most of her schoolwork. This almost seemed impossible.

But as Verde looked around at the various scattered failures in her room, her attempts at doing something she probably couldn't do, she couldn't help but feel that familiar desire well up in her chest.

Maybe she couldn't repair a space heater. Maybe she was barely passing her classes due to the assistance of a friend. Maybe she couldn't film that best friend winning a tournament with such ease it made her mind *boil*.

Who cares? Difficult things were worth doing.

######

Chapter 13

The next morning, Rei was brimming with confidence. She had managed to watch the horror film last night without averting her eyes.

Now, that had been a *mistake*, but she had done it. That mattered. And she'd only had a *little* nightmare, and it didn't even use any of the legitimately horrifying information she knew was real, so as far as she was concerned it was a net gain for her.

And truthfully, she felt she needed it. Today, she was going to try and make up with Chloe.

The only problem of course was Chloe.

"Wh... what was that again?" Verde asked, yawning.

"I *said*, it seems like Chloe's... avoiding me. She's not even here for lunch. I'm going to get a better look."

Rei stood up on her seat, eyes darting this way and that. The lunch hall was a large room all the high school students ate in, and each grade was sectioned off into designated areas. There was some overlap of course, but typically everyone sat where they always sat. Chloe and her sycophantic clique always sat near one of the school window's, to bask in the sunlight. But Chloe wasn't there today.

Rei briefly considered just walking up and asking them where she was, but the thought of talking to *three* Chloe's worth of person exhausted her. She sat down in her seat with a sigh.

Verde yawned again, lazily chomping down on a sandwich. "So, any luck?"

"Hey, enough about me for a bit...you okay Verde? You seem... worn down."

Verde stretched, and rubbed the sleep from her eyes. Her right hand was bandaged.

"Yeah, yeah, I'm good, girl. Just a little tired... after all the fun we had on the weekend, I think I exhausted myself."

It felt like a deflection. Ideas started to swarm in her head. But she didn't say anything. Verde... was stronger than Rei was. She felt that wholeheartedly. If Verde needed help, she'd say so. Digging would just make her close in.

Finally, Ella arrived with a smorgasbord of food. A bright, sunny smile plastered across her face.

"Miss Rei, Miss Verde... did you know the cafeteria changes menu every week? I feel as though I'm in heaven."

Her eyes were sparkling. The other two laughed, Ella's good humour infectious.

When it had finally died down, Verde spoke up.

"You know, if she's not *here*... she might just be leaving for lunch today? You could catch her at her locker or something. Might make your love confession easier."

"N-not a love confession, Verde. But uh, that's a *great* idea!"

Rei leapt up from her seat. "Wish me luck guys. If um, things go well I'll bring her back here for lunch?"

"Oh, that would be lovely Miss Rei," Ella answered. Verde gagged, but nodded all the same.

Rei let out a sigh of relief. She doubted anything like that would happen, but it was better to make sure. Every time she thought of how this conversation would go... her mind turned towards something hopeful.

"Okay. See you in a bit guys!" and with that, Rei was off.

As she walked, Rei could feel her heart pounding in her chest. The school hall was empty, teachers in their classrooms or the staff lounge, students in the lunch hall or already long gone. Rei's steps echoed slightly, measuring her pace by inches. Chloe's locker would be right where it always was.

How can I even remember that? It feels like it was so long ago... god, why am I so concerned about this!? the thought danced across her mind. A part of Rei, however small it might be, hoped that she'd be late. That Chloe had already gone, and she could avoid this. That she wouldn't have to swallow whatever issues Chloe had with her and at least *try.*

But there she was, in the same sea-blue ensemble she always wore. Chloe was fiddling with her lock, so focused on it she was dead to the world. Not that there was anything to focus on, beyond the two of them.

Rei cleared her throat. "Uh... Chloe? How're... how're you doing today?"

Chloe jumped in place, turning to see her. What expression she'd had on before, Rei couldn't tell, but she had put on the haughty look she always had on.

But this time, something about it felt off.

"Um, I'm... doing well. And it's Miss Chloe, to you. Please," she said. Her face looked the part, but her tone was anything but. Her voice was almost melodic, the notes going sour with forced venom. "What do you want, Rei?"

Rei resisted the urge to roll her eyes. "Well, uh, *Miss* Chloe. I ju-well, I wanted... I know we made a deal, that if I'd won, you'd tell me what your, your problem was, and that you'd leave me alone, but I was wondering... maybe, we could forget that last part. After we talk, we could be friends again?"

"...we aren't?"

Chloe said it so matter-of-factly it was like running into a brick wall.

"Wh-what? What do you *mean?*" Rei asked. Her voice, and confidence, were starting to waver.

"All that 'MISS Chloe' stuff, all that... the rude shit, and you really think we're friends? Really? You told me I couldn't *date* Kestrel, because I'm...I'm just worthless, compared to you, and you think we're still friends?"

Chloe's lip quivered, as if she'd been hurt. "I mean, of course I do Rei! We've known each other since grade school. We stopped... stopped hanging out, but I mean we're still friends, we just grew apart a little. You've always been my best friend."

Rei felt her skin start to itch, sweat and nerves in equal measure. "I... I-I... Chloe, the last time we talked to each other that wasn't you being an asshole was *five years ago.* Ever since you've been a stuck-up brat! It's crazy! Every time you *deigned* to talk to me, it was to insult me."

She took a step back, lip quivering more noticeably now. "I... Rei, those are just... just jokes. That's just how all my friends talk."

Rei grit her teeth, hands tightening into fists. "Well, then they sound like pretty *garbage* friends. I noticed they didn't come to cheer you on at the tournament you *lost*. Let me guess... they insult you about that too."

Chloe's eyes went wide. She looked around, then snarled a whisper at her.

"I-don't you *dare* bring up that game. I, I have to keep up *appearances*. That is my one, my *only* bit of levity. If they, if they find out, they'll-"

Rei knew what she had to say. She knew what the right thing was to say. But years of insults, years of disrespect, years of Chloe being so *dismissive*, flooded up to the surface.

The fuse was already lit.

"They'll *what*? Insult you? Make *fun* of you? I thought all your friends *do* that, Chloe. Maybe I was right. Maybe they're not your friends. Maybe, you're afraid they'll stop being your friend, since your *best* friend hates you."

Something in Chloe flipped like a switch. She glared at Rei, lips curling in rage.

"Th-that's what this is, isn't it? You're going to blackmail me. Make me a laughingstock in front of my friends! You're going to push them away from me, because you're jealous, like you've always been! You couldn't... you couldn't handle me being better looking, better at that stupid little game, me being, being more *popular*. You're going to tear down my life!"

She took in a sharp breath, and her snarl turned into a smirk.

"But I... I know a secret too! Your friends, th-they don't... they don't like you either. That little rat in the sweater, she's just using you. I've seen her copying your notes. That pasty-faced weirdo, she's so blissed out on whatever occult nonsense she's taking that I doubt she even knows who you *are*."

That was the breaking point.

Rei grabbed Chloe by the shirt and glared at her, eyes twitching. She wanted her to burst into flames. She wanted to beat her face in. She almost did.

Instead she spoke, loud and clear.

"Those two have been better friends than you've *ever* been. Fuck off, bitch!"

It wasn't until she heard the echo that Rei realized she had screamed it.

She let go and turned to leave.

Stars exploded in Rei's eyes before she realized what happened. She stumbled backward, head ringing and legs weak. She fell to her knees, a cool wet feeling running down her face that only now began to sting. Somehow, the cut on her cheek had opened up again.

Chloe stood above her, the knuckles on her left hand smeared crimson red. She had punched Rei directly in the face, as hard as she could.

Chloe was hyperventilating, expression twisting. Her skin had gone pale as snow, her eyes had lost their luster. She was babbling, barely able to string together a sentence.

"Oh... ohnononono... oh shit. Shit! Rei, I... oh god Rei, I'm sorry. I'm so sorry, I-"

Chloe started to cry. Her hands went to her head, as though she was the one who'd been punched in the face.

Rei managed to mumble a response. "I... I'll be fine, Chloe. God..."

The impact had drained all the fire from her. Or maybe it had been the shouting. Rei wasn't sure herself.

"A... oh god, oh shit. I do–don't, I don't know what came over me. Rei, I'm sorry, I..." realization hit, like a bullet. Her knees shook. "I really am as bad as you said. I-I... I need a smoke."

Chloe fumbled for her cigarettes, dropping all but one on the floor. Seeing her like this felt... bad. Rei hadn't wanted it to get this far, right? She'd gotten mad, but this... Chloe was a mess. She really hadn't understood what was going on.

Chloe put the cigarette between her lips and took out her lighter.

Rei smelt it first. Her nose twitched at the scent; gas. There was a faint wet mark on Chloe's dress shirt, where she always kept her lighter. Where Rei had grabbed her.

The lighter was leaking. It was warped and twisted from heat. *Her* heat.

Rei knew something was wrong and said nothing all the same.

It happened in an instant. Chloe sparked the light with her right hand, and the entire thing burst into a shower of metal and light pink plastic. The lighter fluid coated her arm, sprayed across her face, and little chunks of the former lighter embedded themselves in her hand.

The spark of cherry-red flame that had caused the explosion had already begun to ignite the fluid.

Flames lit across Chloe's right side. Jacket, shirt, skin and hair burned bright. Chloe screamed, as loud as her lungs allowed. Rei rose to her feet and reached out, ripping Chloe's burning jacket off, but the fire lingered on her body. Rei focused, tried to douse the flames, but they refused. She couldn't control them.

The fire alarm rang, the sprinkler system coating both girls in lifesaving water. The both of them fell, Rei to a sitting position and Chloe to her knees.

Chloe's entire right arm was a disgusting mass of burnt skin, rose red and bleeding all over. The right side of her face was worse. Rei couldn't even tell if she still had both eyes. In the distance, people shouted. A dull sound that barely penetrated either of them.

The smell was horrifying. Rei felt her hands tremble, small burns on her fingers.

Chloe was crying, and Rei realized she was too.

Rei could still hear the ambulance sirens echoing in her mind. Her cheek still stung, the bandage replaced, but... it seemed like such a meaningless pain, now.

Chloe had been sent to the hospital, the poor school nurse vomiting when she saw what had happened to her. The school questioned Rei on what happened, rigorously, but all she could tell them was that Chloe had tried to light a cigarette. They'd been talking, and Chloe lit up a cigarette and... then it happened.

She left out how they had been fighting. Any hate Rei had, at that moment, had gone up in smoke. The nightmarish scene flashed past her eyes in slow motion every time she so much as blinked.

School let the students leave early that day. There was little else they could do.

Ella and Verde were waiting for her. Without a word they hugged her close, and it was all Rei could do to hold them in return. So much hesitance in a single act, to hold her friends.

She was afraid of what might happen if she did.

Before Rei could really realize it, the two of them had dragged her half way across town, to 'Smile's Subs'. Verde sat beside her, holding her hand in a death grip.

It was Ella who finally spoke first.

"Is... everything alright, Rei? What happened?"

Rei looked at her right hand.

How can I answer that question?

The thought smoldered inside her like an errant ember that refused to go out. Rei knew, she *knew*. She saw how the lighter was leaking. Saw how it was warped. Could feel it, on the precipice of exploding, and *she'd let it happen.* Even if Rei couldn't fully control her abilities, she may as well have set a torch to Chloe with her own hand.

Chloe's scream still echoed in her head. There wasn't any going back from this.

"I... it's my fault. I set Chloe on fire."

Silence. She didn't blame them. How could she? She'd hate herself after this too.

"It was... an accident. I tried to, to talk to her. She, what she told me made me so mad. I yelled at her, she yelled at me. It was just another argument. But I was, I was just so furious, I... I *wanted* to hurt her. I didn't, really, but..."

Rei couldn't finish it. Her voice hitched, like the last straining cry of a dam about to burst. She started sobbing, her body shaking. Rei collapsed face first on the table and felt every last bit of misplaced hate and meaningless anger round back on her.

Verde held her close. Rei's hand started to hurt with how tight she held it.

There was little either of her friends could say to help her. But feeling them close like this, knowing they cared... it calmed her. It wouldn't staunch the bleeding guilt carved into her, but it gave her frame of mind enough to come to a conclusion. What she *had* to do.

Rei took a deep breath. "I... need to learn how to control this. I-I can't, can't risk this happening again."

"It won't," Verde said. There was a surety in her voice Rei had never heard before. "I *know* you Rei. When you put your mind to something, you don't fail."

"She's right, Miss Rei. And for as long as I've known you, I can say for sure there is a gentleness in your soul that shines bright. You didn't... you didn't do this on purpose."

Kind words, words she wasn't sure she deserved.

Rei closed her eyes and saw it all play out again. When her eyes next opened, she was ready.

"Thanks, guys. It... means a lot. It really does. Verde, could you... call my mom for me. Say I'm hanging out with you for a bit."

Rei clenched her free fist, hard. She felt her fingernails dig into her palm until it started to bleed.

"I'm not going home until I master this."

"Again!" Gamma shouted. Rei imitated the moves, feet moving with only half the elegance he had, arms stiff at the elbows. She finished with a clumsy flick of her wrist.

Nothing. The campfire didn't so much as flicker.

"Damn it!" Rei shouted. It echoed through the dance club.

Rei had been at it for three hours. School was over now- or would have been had they not excused everyone early. Sweat clung to her brow, her hands clammy to the touch.

But it was all from exertion, not the heat of her inner flame.

"How do you expect to control it if you don't focus?" Gamma asked.

When they'd come to him, three hours ago, he was more than willing to assist. But now, there was a cold edge to his voice. He wasn't angry, not really, just... frustrated, the same as they were.

"I *am* focusing! It's... it's just not going!"

Rei kicked an empty can of ravioli, sending it clattering off into the dark.

"Maybe you should take a break? You've been going at it for a while," Verde suggested

She was sitting off to the side on some burned seat cushions she'd finally decided to pull over to make some sort of soft place to sit. A green book was in her lap, and she was lazily flipping through it as Rei struggled.

Rei growled. "It... I don't *want* to take a break. I *have* to get this *done*!"

Rei realized she was panting, and not just from grief-fueled exhaustion. She was hungry, too, as though her failed attempts at harnessing her pyromancy burnt out her insides. She tried to imitate Gamma's dance again, only to stumble and fall flat on her face.

Rei didn't bother getting up.

Gamma sighed. "Yeah, you need a break. I'll be right back, going to get some food. Even if you're not using it, all this effort you're putting into getting it working is going to work up an appetite."

He stomped off, toward his small forest of non-perishable food.

"Fine... maybe you're right. I need to rest. Maybe... clearing my head will help."

Easier said than done Rei thought, letting out a frustrated grumble. She almost didn't *want* to clear her mind, as if trying to put away what happened would make her lose clarity of purpose or something.

Ella patted her gently on the back and helped her up to a sitting position.

"Don't worry, Miss Rei. You'll get this. If... if I could help, I would. Just... try to think about something else. I've found it helps."

The pat on the back and kind words helped, as much as could be expected. But she could still feel a weakness in her legs, like they'd refuse to get up if she didn't let them rest longer. An unavoidable sign that what she'd seen, what she *caused*, had worn her down.

Rei sighed. They were right. So, she'd have to try and put it aside. There was only so much grief you could handle before it consumed you.

"Thanks, Ella. Really, thanks. So, Verde, what've you got there anyway?"

Verde hopped up from her seat, smiling wide. She put the book aside, and rummaged through her backpack, finally drawing out a piece of paper.

"Oh, just some language studies stuff. Just because school let out early today doesn't mean I don't have schoolwork. Hey uh, Ella? Could you help me with some of this?"

Ella nodded. "Y-yes, of course Miss Verde. If you'll excuse me, Miss Rei."

As they worked, Gamma came over with a can of ravioli, holding it over the campfire with a claw made of shadows.

"So, why do you even care about this anyway?" Gamma asked. "I understand wanting to control it, but why the sudden rush?"

Rei's answer was immediate. That bandage was already torn off. "I hurt a friend of mine. I got angry and ended up burning her, badly. I never want that to happen again. *Ever.*"

She took a breath, and for the first time in hours something else came to mind. "And... another thing. You probably didn't see it, but a cop got knifed around here yesterday, and I just can't shake that it's related to whoever's after you. I don't want to hurt anyone, but I have to learn how to fight to protect you."

The room went silent. Even the crackling flame was hushed.

"I'm sorry *what*?!" Verde shouted.

"D-do you not watch the news Verde?"

"Do I w-Rei, no! I'm busy! With recovering from the shock of... of *this*!" she gestured to the entire dance club.

Ella shivered. "Y-you mean someone was... was -*killed* here? Do you think it's..."

"What, no," Rei said. She knew exactly what Ella was getting at. "There's no way Gamma would *kill* someone."

Once she said it, Rei realized how unsure she really was of it.

Before the others could respond, Gamma stood up with a start.

"The three of you need to leave. I know what she's talking about... this wasn't just a regular stabbing."

If they'd wanted to run at the news, his words had frozen them in place.

"What do you mean, Gamma?" Rei asked.

He grumbled, clearly wondering if he should talk. As though he realized reacting the way he did was somehow a mistake.

Finally, he relented. "It... I heard sirens and went to investigate. There were doctors and policemen around, but I saw the body. There was an eight-inch spike jutting from his chest, twisted and red."

Ella retched. Verde's face had gone pale. But all Rei could do was wonder what it meant.

"I've... seen something like it before," he placed a hand on his bandaged side. "The man who was hunting me, he's a ferromancer. Iron. If he touches you, he can even manipulate the traces of it in your blood. He was only trying to *capture* me, so I was lucky."

Rei cracked her knuckles. "Well, that proves it then. I *need* to master this stuff."

Not just for Chloe's sake, but Gamma's too.

Gamma glowered at her, and the can in his shadowy grip crunched slightly. "Absolutely not. You don't understand what he's-"

To the surprise of everyone- herself most of all- Rei scowled back. "You're right. I don't understand. I don't understand anything about mancies or magic or any of this supernatural shit. Someone almost died because I didn't understand."

She took a deep breath and continued. "And maybe I'm only speaking for myself, but I *want* to understand. You're my friend, and I just learned someone is out there trying to... to capture you or kill you or *whatever*. I'm not letting a friend of mine get hurt *again*! If you want us to understand, tell us. Tell us what happened to you."

For a moment, no one moved. Then Verde nodded.

"She's right. We... I can't do anything to help, but if Rei wants to help you then I'm in. Someone needs to be able to pull her out of the fire. Probably literally."

It was hesitant, but Ella nodded as well. "I... I don't... I will stand by you both."

Gamma's eyes crossed all three of them. He sighed and took a deep breath.

######

Chapter 14

Shadows danced along the inner shell of his home, an inky darkness that swallowed everything. Swirling black, enveloping all within like a horrid swamp of decay. Night solidified on a knife's edge, pulling itself free from its silhouetted form, trails of black hanging off like glue. Thick and dark, it swarmed around him, caressing him, pumping through his body.

He sank deeper into it, shadows coating the inside of his throat. He wanted to scream, but nothing left his mouth save bubbles of air...

Gamma awoke, as he always did, inside the tube. A smooth pane of glass surrounding him from the front, a solid white wall behind him. The lab was outstretched before him, empty save for his tube and the monitoring stations attached to it. Everything was tinted green, as it ever was, the unpleasant chill of artificial amniotic fluid enveloping him.

It made his dreams into twisted nightmares and filled his lungs with a disgusting, acidic taste. But it kept him alive, kept him strong. The doctors had told him that between testing. One of the few concessions they gave him.

A likewise unpleasant feeling were the shackles on his wrists, keeping his arms up above his head. They were bolted to the wall so any attempt to move was fruitless.

Still, he tried. Oh, how he tried. He remembered the few times he'd actually gotten out. The *freedom* it had given him. That was why they had the shackles now. They were to keep *them* alive, though no one had need to tell him. He knew that fact quite well.

But today was different. He had noticed the tests were growing more frequent, though in truth he could never truly be sure. The tube and its loathsome fluid kept him alive, yes, but it also kept him sedated. He only woke when they needed him. He did not know how long it was between sleeps and could measure it only by the faces peering at him through the glass.

All that would change today. He'd come to the conclusion a week ago, or at least what he decided was a week ago. Today was to be the final test.

This would be the day he let them kill him.

Finally, the chamber he called home started to drain. Gravity asserted itself and he fell to his knees, arms burning from the strain. He was slick with emerald liquid, tattered jeans clinging to his legs. His long black hair was slick and matted against his face. With his eyes no longer exposed to the stinging contents of the tube, he jammed them shut. He would face death his way.

The doctors and their guards unshackled him, placing him upon a medical gurney for transport.

"He's quite docile today. Has been for the last week or so," one of the doctors said. Gamma could recognize him even in his 'morning' haze.

Dr. Ingram, the facility lead. A fancy red pip on the shoulder of his white leather coat that he wore over his medical scrubs marked him as such. The bald fool loved his jacket. All the doctors wore the same identical outfits of course, but his subordinates were stuck with soft, muted grays.

He was shouting, the gurney wheel's echoing with an ear-splitting squeak as they wheeled him to the test chamber. Both sounds overlapped into a swirling pit of hate in Gamma's stomach, but he pushed it down. He could not get mad. He had to let it happen.

A second doctor spoke, this one a woman. "Yes, I'm... concerned. We're getting close to the deadline here. All the other Projects..."

Of the faces Gamma remembered from this place hers was the clearest in his mind. A soft, gentle face, warm and loving. Light brown hair and smooth, kind features. A pair of dog ears and a tail, giving her the perfect appearance of a playful, beautiful woman. She was Dr. Carter and was the woman who designed Gamma's tests.

Not one person in the whole facility was as cruel as she was.

"It's okay. Our lord has given us ample time. Do not worry about the *other* Projects," Ingram said, frustration evident. At least the wheels were an indiscriminate pain.

"Besides, his docility is a boon."

There was a murmur of agreement. Gamma picked out the sharp voices of two other scientists he did not recognize, and around five of the near emotionless guards that escorted them. Each in identical black combat jackets, padded armour underneath that implied far more danger than a medical facility could promise. Each also wore a black helmet with a shining white face plate that concealed their appearances entirely and muffled their voices.

Gamma doubted they were even living but given the chill voices of the doctors it seemed an unfair comparison.

They finally arrived at the test chamber entrance, the guards directing the four doctors up to the monitoring area. A rote thing, they'd all memorized the steps long ago.

"Do be careful," Dr. Ingram said. "Lack of characteristic flare-ups or not, he is still *quite* dangerous."

"Give it a rest, doctor," Dr. Carter added with a sigh. Her voice was dripping with annoyance. "If these fools hadn't tried to stave his head in, we wouldn't need this level of protection in the first place."

"Oh, he's fine. He's a tough boy," while Gamma couldn't see it, his tone made it clear he was rolling his eyes.

"Besides, if there is any brain damage it will give us a chance to test if we can recover that as well."

The doctors talking so plainly about his abuse sent shivers of rage through him. Memories of his skull splitting, blood pouring through his hair, his tube turning red as the wound struggled to heal. He felt his muscles tense, could envision the straps snapping under his strength, but he bit his lip and stopped himself.

There was no point to this, to any of it. Let it happen.

The guards undid his restrains and roughly shoved him into the test chamber, and he cooperated only enough to avoid being thrown into the room by force.

It was a large, wide cube of space, thirty feet in both width and height. Two windows of frosted glass graced one of the walls, the distorted figures of four scientists behind them. That aside, the room was utterly empty and fiercely white. Not even a seam of the padding could be seen.

After a brief wait the voice of Dr. Ingram rang out, warbling over the intercom.

"Start recording. Beginning test number one-two-four, in period two-one for Project Gamma. The Project has been docile as of late, as noted in previous reports. All incidents of aggression have ceased after the passing of Security Force member one-zero, during an escape attempt during test number one-zero-four in period two-one. As such, it is unclear if we are providing suitable... stimuli to achieve awakening."

The minor pause infuriated him. As though all that information justified the blood and bruises. Gamma swallowed it, burning like black tar in the back of his throat.

Dr. Ingram continued, tone steady and calm as a professional should be.

"Doctor Carter is presiding over today's test, as are Professor Hunter and Doctor South. Doctor Carter, you have the floor."

"Yes. Today, we will be conducting our standard battery of tests. However," she said, and Gamma could feel her eyes on him through distorted glass. Her voice truly was full of joy as she described the way in which they'd break him.

"Today, we will not be using the Model X-Five riot suppression puppet we have been using up to this point. Our benefactor has provided us with a new prototype, the Model X-Six. Our lord suggested it as a joint exorcise, one that we think will incite awakening."

A third voice interjected. "Really? I'd have thought our benefactor was done with joint tasks when the mnemonic puppet program conclu-"

"Please keep irrelevant comments until after the test, Professor," a fourth voice said. "Health read outs are all within acceptable limits, doctor. Brain activity is spiking, though it's all within expected values. He's probably just listening to us."

"Very well. Let us begin," Dr. Carter said. There was a pause, after which a thin line appeared in the wall in front of Gamma.

The wall swung open, and in walked a machine in the shape of a man. Its body was smooth and shiny, covered head to toe in polymer and plastic layered like plated riot gear. Arcane writing was etched upon it, and a magical hum buzzed from within like the whir of electricity. Its face was a stark white gas mask, a soft blue light emanating from where it's eyes would be.

The puppet looked near identical to the other machines they always sent his way. Always a machine of some sort, an artificial mirror of humanity. Always carrying a metal rod or polymer bat with which to beat him until he could not stand, silently demanding he defend himself.

Always the same, day in and day out.

How hard they hit, how often, that was the surprise.

But today he would have the last laugh. When the test concluded he would finally be dead.

He welcomed it really, and as the test began, he felt the tension actually start to wane. It was finally going to come.

His calm thoughts were rattled with an unbelievable intensity as the puppet's metal baton smashed against his skull, dropping him to the ground like a sack of bricks. Blood was already trickling down his forehead, but despite it all he stood up. It would not strike while he was down.

As he rose it struck at his side, a stinging blow that would quickly bruise. He flinched and the riot baton collided with his face, sending him flat on his back.

His body tensed; nerves fired, demanded to be used. He had to rip the thing apart, to defend himself. He bit his tongue and stopped it. He had to let it happen. He *needed* to. Yet despite it all, despite the rain of blows that accompanied his every attempt to stand, he kept his eyes bolted shut. Though he longed for death, as crimson dripped down and stained the pristine white floor, he stood.

He would die, but he would not give them the satisfaction of knowing it scared him.

Another blow, this time against the small of his back. He let out a groan, the first sputtering of words he'd said all day, and fell to his knees. His body was bruised and split, welts and bloodstains poking through his skin.

A sigh dragged itself from the intercom. "Project Gamma. Get up and *fight*.

Save yourself. We won't stop this puppet from killing you. You *will* die," Dr. Ingram said.

They all knew it was empty. Threats like this lost their effect long ago.

The beatings continued until Gamma's body felt raw and hollow.

And still he stood. He rose to meet the blows of his metal and plastic foe, because so long as he could stand the test would continue. They wouldn't let it stop any other way.

So, Gamma rose, and rose again, and each time was struck down.

Then there was a noise. The clear ringing of a phone. The puppet stopped; the beatings with it. Gamma, in some small way, was thankful for the reprieve.

There was a faint beep-click as Dr. Ingram answered the call, on speaker phone. The voice on the other end was silky smooth. Cool and collected, with not even a trace of malice in it.

And yet as he spoke the room itself seemed to tremble.

"Ah. Doctor Ingram. Still working hard on Project Gamma," he said simply. It was not a question, and yet demanded an answer.

"Y-yes, of course, Lord Orochi," the doctor said.

Gamma had never heard him nervous before, the demonic doctor always the epitome of proper behavior and calm demeanor. His voice was shaking, lending credence to the oppressive weight of the voice on the other line. "We're actually getting some decent progress. Brain activity is nearly there, we ju-"

"We just... what, Doctor Ingram? We need more time?" the man on the other line said.

There it was, a minor trace of venom that belayed an ocean of utter contempt.

"Project Delta and Alpha are growing at an exponential rate, and Project Beta is already finished. Why has yours been so delayed? I've given you ample time. You have more than enough resources. I've read your reports...you've hit the appropriate level months ago. But nothing has come of it. I'm shortening the deadline. You have until tomorrow night. I will accept any methods so long as they produce results."

"But sir!" this time it was Dr. Carter shouting over the phone. "If we damage the Project too heavily, it-"

"If you kill the Project in the attempt, then you've done half the thankless task of terminating the project for me. That will make the rest of the job far simpler. And if you succeed... well, all the better. Do I make myself clear?"

The threat was obvious. Their 'benefactor' held their lives within his hands. And, Gamma realized, his life as well.

"... y-yes, Lord Orochi," they said in unison, defeat plain in their voices. A grim, foreboding aura hung over the blood-stained test chamber.

"Good. Now then... return to work," the man said. The line went dead, dial tone playing over the intercom like a dread siren.

"He won't do it. This Project is too vital to terminate," the third observer said. "But the question remains... what'll we do?"

"You're a fool," Dr. Carter said simply. "We succeed or we die with the young man. Simple as that. I'm disabling the puppet's safety mechanism."

Her voice was dead, all emotion drained from her. The truth of who she was now clear to her fellows as it was to Gamma.

"Doctor Carter, are you absolutely sure?" it was Dr. Ingram. His voice was still shaking, but now that the call was over, he was slowly rebuilding his typical confidence.

"Well, doctor, I'd say the lead in charge of Project Epsilon could answer that," she said.

A short, curt laugh escaped her lips. "Of course, you'd have to find him first."

The others were silent. Then there was a beep, and the puppet whirred to life.

"We do what we must to save ourselves, Project Gamma. We only ask you do the same. Endure hell or descend into infamy with us as Epsilon did. Let it end here, one way or another. For Lord Orochi."

Gamma heard the puppet's body jerk and twist with a mechanical squeal. The room grew hotter, heat emanating from the puppet itself. There was a thud of metal, as the casing dropped from its baton to reveal a shining, silver sword underneath. He imagined it rising into the air, falling down upon him. Cleaving flesh and bone, ending his life.

But something dug into the back of his mind and *stuck*.

The man on the other end of that phone call did this to you. Why? What is the

point? All this torture? You've never wondered that before, Gamma. Think about it.
WHY? *Don't you want to know? Don't you want to find this man? Don't you want*
to RIP *him limb from limb?*

The thought echoed in his mind on repeat, over and over again. He felt his
emotions rise, that bubbling, magmatic hate finally boiling over. He did not
truly want to die. He wanted to *live.* Accepting his death so passively... he could
not allow such a thing. The intensity of that voice, that *smug bastard* on the
other line, *ordering* his death, filled him with an undying rage. If he was to die,
he would die on *his own terms.*

He would not die today.

Gamma's eyes shot open, a dark energy filling them. Black smoke and purple
light rose from his hands. Lengths upon lengths of shadow extended out from
around him, tearing the puppet to pieces, rending it limb from limb with
vicious claws. He extended his own arms out, the tendrils following his lead,
impaling the staggering machine through its chest and bursting out the back.

Shadows twisted and rent the head off the puppet's shoulders, knocking it
to the floor with a shallow bounce and sparks of magic and electricity. Gamma
reached out his hand and lifted the broken mechanical skull with a shadowy
claw.

He could feel the weight in his palm. He clenched his hand and the shadows
crushed it, the head shattering. Flaming wires and shimmering runes flew
from the rubble. Through the blood and pain, he smiled. So much raw power,
at the tips of his fingers.

The doctors cheered over the intercom, a distorted shout of jubilation and
excitement. Gamma ignored them and swished his hands in a fluid motion,
watching the shadows dance, feeling his connection to them. He took a
deep breath, extending his senses, wondering just how far he could feel the
darkness.

He saw the limit of his range and smiled wider.

The doctors in their safe little bubble could never comprehend what would
happen if they succeeded. Gamma raised a finger in their direction, and a
subtly thin shadow began to rise within the monitoring room.

It was a weaker strand, disconnected from him, no wider than a child's arm.

But he could feel its weight. It was strong enough. *Sharp* enough. Dr. Ingram was the first, the lead doctor always setting the example for his fellows. Dr. Carter's triumphant cries of success were quickly replaced by screams of abject horror as shadowy razors burst from the bald doctor's chest through his back, the force slamming him against the frosted glass window.

She tried to run, but with a flick of his wrist the slain doctor was flung at her, both collapsing in a heap. Gamma focused on the shadows in the room, feeling the tendrils grow. Feeling them grow stronger as he himself felt a pull at his stomach, sweat budding at his bloodied brow. He pushed through the pain and hunger, eyes wild.

The other two had been frozen solid. Only now as the mass of darkness approached did they scream, distorted by the intercom. Cut short by shadows. Blood spilled, though much to Gamma's chagrin the only bit of it he could see was the splatters and smears across the frosted window.

The shadowmancer let out a deep sigh of satisfaction, despite the wounds that marred his body. Somewhere, sullenly, an alarm rang. He smiled a toothy grin, shadows coiling up around him.

His freedom awaited.

The violence of that day had nearly killed him. He barely escaped with his life, and even then, only because the ferromancer had intended to capture him. To *return* him to his home.

A part of him had even considered it after a fashion. The injuries were so deep, the pain unreal. But willingly imprisoning himself, returning to that blasted tube... it sent convulsions through his legs.

Then he'd met Rei and her strange friends, and they'd saved each other's lives. Only then had he truly felt free, though he was loath to admit it. He owed them, Rei most of all.

Dragging her into this bloody, violent mess would be cruel. He opened his eyes, reminiscing concluded.

Rei's question hung in the air. "So... you going to tell us what happened to you?"

"No. Absolutely not," was his answer.

Their expectant faces melted into a mixture of raw disappointment and anger.

######

Chapter 15

"Oh, come on Gamma! Really?" Rei said. Verde was grumbling curses behind her.

"I-I think it's fine. Everyone has secrets, and... perhaps he's got good reasons for them?" Ella asked.

It was clear she hadn't really wanted to hear whatever sordid details Gamma had for them, and as much as Rei *did*, she couldn't disagree with her point.

Gamma nodded. "She's right. But... I can at least tell you something. They, whoever *they* are, they *made* me. They made me so I can do what I do. I'm human, as much as the rest of you are, but... I'm their experiment. They want me back, at any cost. If you're in danger, run. I'm only training you so that you don't hurt yourself, or worse. Not to fight. Do not die for *me*."

The three nodded solemnly. At this point, there was no backing down.

Rei hopped back to her feet. "Okay Gamma, more training. If we're gonna do this then lets *do this*."

He stood, the shadow holding his now bubbling hot can of ravioli stabbing a hole in the lid. He drank from it like a soda can.

"Okay, Rei. Show me what you can do."

Rei grit her teeth and pumped her fists. She was ready.

This time, it took only ten minutes to fall flat on her face. Rei's scream of frustration echoed through the dance club, and she didn't stand up.

She could overhear the others talking, a mixture of encouragement, concern, and confusion. Why wasn't it working? When Gamma did it, it was perfect, so what did she lack? It was part of why Rei even wanted to hear his story, as though it held some secret. But if he was made to be like this, he just *was*.

Anger overtook her, and she punched the dance floor, hard. It hurt like hell but felt strangely satisfying. After all the constant failure, she just wanted to *break* something, even if she knew it was wrong.

"Yo, Rei, you okay?" Verde asked, running up to her.

Rei looked up at her from the floor. "Yeah, I'm good Verde. Just... picking myself back up."

She hadn't realized her frustration was so obvious. She pulled herself up off the floor, into a sitting position.

And felt sticky, wet plastic pull up with her. Bits of the dance floor had melted under her right hand. There were fresh cracks in the floor where she'd punched.

Rei's mind exploded and she nearly soared to her feet. Verde had to jump back to avoid being knocked down.

"I got it! I figured it out!"

Gamma took a sip of his can, raising an eyebrow. "You did?"

Rei smirked, took a step forward, and punched with all her might towards him.

Nothing. She growled and did it again.

Nothing. There was an awkward shuffling sound of Ella hitching her skirt as she shifted where she sat. Rei took a deep breath, went to punch towards Gamma, but at the last minute spun on her heels and punched towards the campfire.

For the first time since they started hanging out in the burned-out building, they could see every corner of it. The campfire erupted in a torrent of flame, orange fire turning cherry-red. It lasted for only a moment, but in that shining moment Rei could see a smile come to Gamma's face. When it finally faded, Rei's right hand was wreathed in flames.

"Holy shit Rei, I-how did you figure it out?" Verde asked.

"Well, I mean every time something really bad happened involving my powers it... there was some kinda fire or fuel around. Every other time it's just my hands, and it's not nearly as dangerous. An-and, well," Rei gestured at Gamma. "He's surrounded in shadow all the time, I guess, and mancers control their element, so I figured... I just needed to like, aim at a fire or something. But even then, that means what Gamma was trying to teach me *should* have worked, right?"

"It should have," Gamma said.

"Yeah, right! But it didn't! So... I mean, I got mad and punched the ground," she pointed over to where she'd done so. "And it broke and melted a little! So, it-it just came to me. Your methods *don't* work for me. It... I mean, think about it. Your shadows are all goopy and fluid. That's not like fire at all!"

"I mean that's arguable Rei," Verde said.

"It sounds reasonable enough. But I can make far more shadows than there are around, and I don't get substantially stronger at night. I don't think-"

"Exactly! You don't think! That was the thing I realized. You... you said you were made for this. So maybe something they did, they made it like second nature for you? So, so I thought maybe what you do doesn't work for me because... I mean it's obvious, thinking on it, but we're not *the same.* Every time fire's come out, I've been angry or panicked or, or something like that. So, if I can visualize that, if I can hold onto those feelings... I can do it! Watch!"

Before anyone could respond, she twisted and thrust a hand out at one of the nearby candles. Its wick flickered briefly, then exploded in a soft shower of burning wax.

She turned again, swiping her hand at the candle farthest from them. The small light on it died, leaving the candle otherwise intact.

Finally, she turned back to Gamma, smirked, and thrust a single finger out toward him.

The can, so firmly held in one of his shadow claws, started popping like it was in a microwave. The shadow holding it started to boil as well, steam rising up from it. Rei grit her teeth and pointed a second finger at the can.

The shadows dissolved; the can fell to the ground with a wet clunk.

Rei fell to her knees and shouted, pumping her fists and throwing them to the air.

"I did it! I did it on *purpose!* Gamma... Verde, Ella! I did it!"

She looked across the faces of her three friends, expressions equally shocked as they were impressed. She could feel their heat, along with the campfire and the little candles, like little pulses at the edges of her vision. Not truly visible, but 'sensed', like being on the other end of an awkward feeling of being watched. It was like she was seeing for the first time.

"I'm... I'm so proud for you, Miss Rei!" Ella said. She seemed ecstatic, despite her previous fears.

Verde was just looking at her, jaw hanging open. "Y... you actually did it."

Gamma, silent as ever, was just smiling.

Rei flexed her hand repeatedly, the flames dying down and flaring up with a little effort. But soon, as far as she could tell, it would become second nature. She looked at Gamma, passion sparking in her eyes.

"Okay then. Time for part two. Gamma... it's time to train for *real*."

It was immediately obvious what she meant.

"W-what, no! Miss Rei, you're... you're not *fighting* Gamma! He's, he's injured!" Ella said in protest.

"It'll be fine Ella, promise. I actually thought of an idea on how to do this. He holds onto one of the candles, and if I manage to explode it, that's my win," Rei explained.

"And how does *he* win?" Verde asked. "Assuming you last even a second."

Despite her misgivings, Verde was smiling wide. Rei returned the grin, her blood pumping. Verde always knew when she was getting fired up, and Rei could see that her tiny little friend was feeling it too.

"That's easy. Just like with the earlier training... we go until I fall."

Gamma smirked, a dark mist appearing in his hand. Tendrils, not as sharp as usual, lifted up from around him, one snaking towards a nearby candle.

"Finally... now, proj... pyromancer, *begin!*"

Rei ducked and weaved through the flurry of shadows as four tendrils lashed out at her. It was hard for her to believe that just a few days ago, she had been shaking the rust off of her. Now, with Gamma, it was all coming back. It was just like riding a bike.

A bike that constantly bombarded you with stiff, solid blows to the shoulders and chest of course, but still just a bike.

Not that it was easy in any sense. Every time she tried to blast the candle, a thin whip of darkness pulled her hand away, or struck her across the knuckle to disrupt her aim. Her right hand was aflame, but the rest of her was drenched. She hadn't moved this hard in years.

Gamma, for his part, seemed to almost be toying with her. He barely moved save for the five fingers he shifted to twist and twirl his inky black whips. The candle was held in a shadowy claw beside him, a tantalizing target she just couldn't quite strike. It was honestly starting to piss her off.

But inside, Rei was smiling. Getting that mad was part of her plan.

She dodged another blow, feinted right and dashed left. Three tendrils flew past where she'd been going, and she swung her right hand through them. The intensity of her flames sliced them apart, dissolving them into black mist. Gamma's expression changed, for just a moment, to pleasant surprise.

Rei charged forward, swiping through the remaining shadows with her hand. Gamma stepped backward, thicker shadows bursting forth from the ground like a wall. Now he couldn't see her. She couldn't see him, either, but that didn't matter. She knew him.

Gamma was just like Chloe at the game tournament, in a way. A defensive, controlling opponent. Staying in their corner if they can, commanding the battlefield with ranged attacks and traps. If they didn't have to actually fight back to win, they'd probably just play keep away forever, constantly pushing her back.

Rei was hedging her bets, but she expected that was what Gamma would do. She thrust her hand forward, palm open.

A blast of flame spilled forth from her hand, burning a hole through the shield between them. She could see the candle, right there where she expected. She focused, reached out, felt the flicker of the candlelight.

A shadow the size of a man's fist extended out from the wall and into her stomach, knocking her back two feet. Rei coughed, the flame on her hand sputtered out, and after a brief few seconds of trying to stand, she collapsed to her backside.

The shadows receded, and Gamma smirked at her, holding the candle triumphantly. Half of the handle was melted, dripping down onto the claw.

But the wick was still lit.

Rei groaned. "That... was a low blow."

"Well, it was that or lose, Rei. Besides, now we're even," Gamma said with a smirk. He set the candle down.

"I think that's enough for today. How do the rest of you feel?"

Verde and Ella had hidden behind the food cans halfway through their first sparring mission. Newly flame-wrought scars and the occasional crack and break caused by rebounding shadows littered the dance club floor. If not for the friendly banter, it would look like an actual fight had broken out.

Verde nearly knocked over the tower of cans as she rushed out, hurrying over to Rei and helping her to her feet.

"Holy *shit* Rei that was rad as hell. Y... you should have seen it! Ella, next time we're here remind me to bring the camera, we *have* to film this. This *ruled*!"

"Y-y-yes, th... that sounds wonderful." Ella said. She was stammering, holding on to her umbrella so tight it looked like her bones were about to pop out. "I've, uh, never seen a fight quite like *that* before."

"Well, you better get used to it. I wanna go aga... again," Rei said. She felt a sudden pain in her stomach, like for the first time in her life she was really, truly *hungry*.

Gamma laughed, for what Rei was certain was the first time. Short, curt, but... not without joy.

"I can see it in your face. You're starving. It's to be expected... mancers need fuel, and it burns out quickly. Likely faster in your case," he explained, lancing out a shadow to pick up the can of ravioli he'd dropped earlier.

"Magic users have the same issue. The fuel for their spells has to come from somewhere. Go home, girl. Eat and get some rest. You've earned it."

Rei took a deep breath. Despite it all, it really felt like she did.

"Hey, Verde, message my mom for me. Tell her I'm coming home... what time is it, anyway?"

Verde looked at her phone. "It's uh... about six. And from the looks of it she like, sent a *dozen* texts. I probably shouldn't have put this on vibrate huh?"

Rei cringed. *Of course. I should have... called Mom to let her know that I'm okay.*

That I'd be late, that I'd–I'd be alright. Damnit, another person hurt.

"Shit. Uh, yeah, Verde. We should get going. See you later Gamma."

Gamma smirked. "See you later, Rei."

"Actually," Verde said. "I'm... gonna stay here, for a bit. For real, this time."

"Wh... why?" Rei asked. She had noticed it earlier, but Verde clearly had something on her mind. Rei wanted to know, wanted to make sure her friend was alright too... she felt her hand shake, fear of what prying into her friend might destroy *this* time.

Verde pointed a thumb over at Gamma. "The big lug there needs some more basic information. I was so busy with history yesterday, I forgot to show him a modern-day map. Don't worry, I'll get home safe."

Rei hesitated a moment, then nodded. Verde knew what she was doing.

"Okay Verde. See you at school tomorrow."

Verde smirked. "As if. One of those messages is that school's closed for the week."

To all their surprise, it was Ella that spoke up. "Oh, thank heavens. I don't think I'd be able to handle a full day of school after... all this."

They all laughed, and for a moment Rei could forget the underlying pain that it was all her fault.

Her mother's response when she finally got home was an expected one. Aria had hugged Rei close, nearly crushing her in her embrace.

"Oh, my sweet little bell. Are you alright? You're not... not hurt, are you?"

"N-no, no, I'm fine. It... I'm okay. I am," Rei answered.

Her mother looked at her intently, and for the first time Rei saw something akin to weakness in her expression. Her cheeks were wet, her eyes puffy, like she'd been crying.

"I... okay, Rei. I'm just so worried. After that... murder, the other day, to have *this* happen, at your school. I just, it's just too much for my old heart sometimes. You know?"

Rei held her back, tightly. "Don't worry Mom, I'm fine. Really. I... I'm..."

She broke down. Tears flowed down her cheeks in streams.

Rei couldn't tell her the truth. She *couldn't*, not after this. Letting her mother know that, intentional or not, she'd sent a girl to the hospital would kill her. It could kill both of them.

But she could let out what she could.

"It... it's all my *fault*! We got into a fight and sh-she went to light a cigarette and it was *my fault*!!"

Aria simply hugged her tighter, letting Rei bury her sobbing face into her shoulder. She gently patted Rei's back, a soothing warmth amidst an unrelenting storm.

"It's not your fault, little bell. It's not. You didn't-"

"It *is*! If I hadn't... if I didn't... I wanted to know why she *hated* me and I-I just, I got so angry. I wanted to hurt her and then she almost died!"

Aria kissed her on the forehead once, twice, more times than Rei could reasonably count.

"There, there, my little bell..." Aria whispered. She took a deep breath, as if trying to keep herself from crying with her. "Tell me everything. Let it out."

Rei did. About how Chloe had tormented her, and how at the video game tournament Rei finally got her back. And how that had been such a truly terrible mistake. She told her about what Chloe had told her, and how it made Rei so mad. That the person who hated her the most had no idea what she had done.

Aria held her close and didn't speak for some time. Neither of them made a sound, save the occasional cough and breath from Rei.

Finally, her mother pulled away from her. Rei's tears were drying, and she could breathe again.

"It's okay, little bell. It's okay. I called Estelle-Verde's mother. She's the one taking care of Chloe. I called to see if you had... been hurt. So, believe me; Chloe is okay. She'll be okay. And it's not your fault. These-these things, they happen Rei. It wasn't your fault."

It did little to quench the dark feeling inside her, but Rei accepted her mother's words. At least Chloe would be okay.

Rei swallowed the lump in her throat, the words she almost said. "I know

Mom, I know. I uh... tomorrow, when I go... out, I'm also going to stop by the hospital. I doubt Chloe'll be in any mood to see me, or that she'll even be available, but it just–it feels like the right thing to do."

Aria nodded. "I understand, sweetie. I'm... I think tonight we should order a pizza. Or two. How's that sound, little bell?"

Rei took one last breath to steady herself. "Okay. That... that sounds like a plan. Thank you, Mom."

She realized, in her heart, she'd have to tell her eventually. Tell her everything. But for now, Ella had been right. Sometimes people kept secrets for a good reason.

###

Once everyone had gone, Gamma shot a glare over at Verde.

"Okay, Verde. What the hell were you talking about?"

Verde smirked, and started rummaging through her bag.

"Oh, that? That was just a cover. What I *want*..." she pulled out a pile of sheets of paper, along with the book of magic Ella had given her. She laid out one of them before her.

"Is my shot. You and me, right now. Train me like Rei. Train me *harder*."

He sighed, and Verde was shocked by how dismissive it felt. "Train you? I'm sure you've got passion, but what do you intend to-"

Verde didn't bother letting him finish.

"*Klingenluft!*"

At the sound of Verde's voice, the dance club was filled with its second light show that day. Swirling crescents of visible wind, rose out of the paper before her in a cyclone. Dust and detritus lifted up into the air, pulled in to the small twister of magic. Verde's hair fluttered in the breeze, pale green light from the spell flashing over her face like rave lights, the glare on her glasses and her razor-sharp grin making her look to all the world like a hungry wolf.

As the spell faded, the wind that remained swirled about them for some time in lazy currents. A shower of dust drifted down upon them.

Gamma's face twisted in an awkward smirk that Verde figured was meant to be a grin. A shadowy arm slinked over to one of the candles.

"I *see*. Verde... begin the test!"

Verde took a deep breath. If Rei could do it, so could she.

######

Chapter 16

A chill breeze blew that morning, crisp and cold. Winter was finally here, the snow that always preceded her birthday falling as reliably as it ever did. Of course, the chill was worsened by where Rei was. It always felt coldest here, at the edge of town. In the distance she could see fir trees, snow topping them gently.

She cursed the forgetfulness that led to her not bringing a jacket, but at least her abilities kept her blood running hot enough to manage.

As she walked, she did her best to avert her eyes from the rows of tombstones. No one else was here, but it was a courtesy all the same. These stones weren't for her. She took a deep breath, clearing her mind as she finally reached her destination. She was ready.

"Hey... Dad," Rei said.

The grave marker in front of her didn't respond. 'Samson Scios' was engraved upon it, and underneath a date of birth and death. The latter was all too familiar to her.

Tomorrow she'd be eighteen years old. Tomorrow her dad would be eighteen years dead.

Rei sat in front of it, not minding the dirt and snow. "I hope you're doing well."

She brushed the dust and snow off of him, patting the marker gently.

"So... I've been doing well. You know, the usual. That being said..."

Rei looked around, to ensure she was alone. Unsurprisingly, she was.

"The last week has been absolutely chaotic. Two transfer students came in. I uh, crushed on one something hard. Kestrel. He's... coming to my party tomorrow, and I think it might be love! I'm gonna ask him how he feels next chance I get. I think you'd like him."

She blushed, laughing at her own excitement. She wondered how her dad would respond.

"I also won a game tournament recently. It's not uh, that big a deal though, really. But it was fun, and I made a new friend, because of it. You'd uh... probably get along, given what Mom's told me about you. I wrote all about it in my-" she reached behind her for her book bag. Which of course wasn't there.

"Right, yeah... no school. And I left my journal in my bag. Smart thinking, Rei. Ah well, I'll... I'll read it to you later, Dad. Next year. But I can tell you, it um, it was *exciting*."

She took a deep breath and let the breeze wash over her and the headstone.

"I... I learned I'm a pyromancer," she snapped her fingers, a small spark crackling into a cherry-red flame in her palm. "I-I know, right? It's crazy. I've still, uh, got a hard time believing it myself, honestly. My new friend, Gamma- he's a shadowmancer, and he's teaching me. Mostly, anyway."

She imagined what his response would be. He'd probably be as concerned as her mother would be.

"I know, I know. It's scary. A friend of mine... I hurt her, with my fire. Really badly. I didn't... no, at the time I did. I did want to hurt her. But I never wanted it to-to be so *bad*. I never want to hurt someone like that again. I'm going to be going to the hospital today, to see her. I'm uh, really nervous actually. I don't... I have no idea how it's going to go. I nearly *killed* her."

She took a deep breath, felt her voice start to waver "I'm going to be doing my best, to control my powers. So that I never hurt anyone again. But... I might need to. Gamma's in danger, and I want to help him. I'm stuck. I don't want to hurt anyone, but I need to do *something*. I... I want to be a hero. I guess that's what this means."

It was a hard thought to face but talking it out helped. Her mind buzzed, wishing her father could respond, wishing he could tell her what to do. She was at a loss. How could she help anyone with what she'd done? How could she help when the only thing she did was burn?

But she had to try. For the sake of her friends, who'd helped push her forward. For her mother, who was likely worried sick about everything that had happened the last week.

And, Rei realized, for Chloe. To make up for what she did.

She sighed "I... wish you were here, Dad. Mom does too. I wish... I wish I got to know you."

Rei reached out and stroked his grave gently. "I love you, Dad. I-I've... I've got to go."

She stood, dusting herself off. She gave the stone a sad smile. "I'll see you later Dad. Thanks for the advice. Same time next year?"

There was no response. She nodded, turned, and left as tears welled up in her eyes.

The chill, stuffy, stagnant air. The subtle scent of indeterminate medicine and the faint beep of unknown machinery. The clacking sounds of keyboards, the rolling wheels bumping against the gaps between the tiled floors. The identically dressed orderlies buzzing around at whatever business they were tasked with, like machines.

Every second in a hospital felt like an oppressive weight had been placed down on you, and it wouldn't relent until you left. It was like another world altogether. Rei was having none of it.

She twiddled her thumbs nervously as she waited. Ever since she could remember, being in a hospital made her skin feel like it could burst into fire at any moment. Now that she knew that was possible, she didn't like her chances any better.

Rei *hated* hospitals. Whatever reason Gamma had to avoid them, she'd agree one hundred percent.

She tried to calm herself. The nurse had recognized her as a family friend of Doctor Guérisseuse- Verde's mother- and assured her that she could go check on Chloe and see if she wanted visitors. It'd just take a few minutes. Rei could wait a few minutes.

She heard a cough that had to have come from somewhere, but no amount of looking around revealed where it could have come from.

It was going to be a very long few minutes.

Finally, much to her relief, the nurse returned.

"Miss Scios? She's able to see you now. Right this way," she said, in a terse but professional manner. Rei hopped to her feet and followed after, through the winding white hallways of the hospital. It was small, and the only hospital for miles, so Rei was lucky Chloe hadn't needed to get flown out.

They reached the door. Rei took a deep breath, and walked on in.

The stark white room was empty save for Chloe's bed, the medical equipment nearby, a small television, some chairs, and a single garbage can. She was sitting in bed, dressed in the light blue hospital gown they had given her. Her hair, what was left, was a mess, though there was signs she'd tried to comb it properly all the same.

The snapped comb in the garbage can made it clear how well that'd gone.

Her entire right arm was covered in bandages, laid stiff on the bed palm upward. As Rei approached, soft footsteps sounding far, far too loud in the silent room, Chloe turned to look at her.

Chloe's face was gauzed and wrapped, from the top of her forehead to the bottom of her chin and down her neck, into her gown. The burns hadn't pushed back past her ear, but it stretched far across her face. Even with the medical coverings Rei could still see the beginning of pink, raw scars along the bridge of her nose and near the edges of her lips. All told- arm and areas Rei couldn't see aside- a good third of her face was concealed.

A good third of her face was burned.

And yet despite it all, seeing her made Chloe smile. A soft, sad smile that Rei had never seen before.

"O-oh... Rei. It's good to see you," Chloe said.

Her haughty tone had been destroyed, leaving nothing behind but the soft, melodic voice of a sad girl. It was somber, defeated, but it seemed to gain energy as Rei approached, sitting in the nearest chair.

"I'm... glad you came."

"You're welcome. I..." Rei said. She hesitated.

What could she even say here? This was all her fault. No matter how mad she'd gotten at her... this wasn't what she wanted. Not at all.

"I mean, you uh, *are* my best friend, right? Of course I'd come."

Rei laughed awkwardly, Chloe laughing with her till a light cough caught in her throat.

"Hehe... yeah. Other than my family you're the only one to visit. I could use the company," Chloe said. She smiled, a truly genuine smile despite it all.

"Honestly... I'm surprised you came. After I *hit* you, I expected I'd be left alone."

Rei's heart caught in her chest. "W-... what? I mean, why haven't your other friends come?"

Chloe looked away, out the window once more.

"It turns out, getting your face burnt off scares away the 'popular' kids... not that I care. After recovering enough to think, I realized just how right you are. They... they really were just awful. I-I can't believe how stupid I've been."

Rei hesitantly reached out; her hand placed over Chloe's.

"Well *screw* them, then. Once you're out of here, I'll get you some real friends. Verde and Ella and–well, we'll... we'll hang out with you."

It'd be a hard sell. Verde had been the one to recommend they make up, but actually hanging out... that would be difficult. Especially after everything with Gamma. But she had to *try.*

"Thanks, I... I really appreciate it. It'll be nice, to have some real friends for a change. The only thing they really wanted from me was a willing chew-toy."

Chloe shifted in place, trying to get comfortable. A flash of pain tore across her face. Rei held her injured hand softly, and the pain seemed to fade.

"What a bunch of losers. No wonder you had to disguise yourself at the tournament," Rei said. "Man... that really brought back memories, you know? You've gotten a lot better, from what I remember."

Chloe laughed softly. "Oh, I know. If it... weren't for that controller mishap I think I could have won."

Rei cleared her throat, and said "possibly, *Miss* Chloe. But you'll never be as good as me."

She said it in her best impression of Chloe's haughty voice. Chloe tried to hold a deadpan glare, but it quickly fell away to a wide, happy, and somewhat embarrassed grin.

"Oh... oh no, did I really sound like that? Wow, I... how did you tolerate me?"

"I didn't, honestly."

God damnit. The answer came out so easily, so earnestly. *How could I say that? How could I let HER say that? I was just trying to make a stupid joke.*

As though Chloe could see the pain in Rei's mind, she gave her a warm, somber smile. It helped, as much as that sort of thing could, and Rei continued.

"But... I think things'll be better now. At the tournament, I noticed it. You were still being your usual self, but you weren't going into it as hard as usual. It was like seeing the real you again for the first time in years."

Chloe shuddered. "I... I know, Rei. I've been lying to myself, for so long. I guess being surrounded by that stuff reminded me of you. It brought me back, for a bit."

"Well, you know what that means," Rei smirked. "Stick with me, and... soon, it'll really be like old times."

It wouldn't be, of course. Chloe's scream, the aftermath of the fire. It'd stick in Rei's mind forever, she knew that. It mixed with the horrid memory of abuse Chloe had put on her; not a justification or excuse, but just marks that they had left on each other since their relationship fell apart. Scars upon scars.

But scars faded. Rei owed it to Chloe.

She was pulled from her thoughts by a surprising squeeze; Chloe's injured hand holding hers tightly.

"You know, once I'm out you owe me a rematch. If I can beat you when I'm injured, I've proven my superiority!"

There was a soft crackle of passion in her voice, and Rei could feel the energy flowing through her. Rei couldn't help but smile defiantly.

"Sure thing, Chloe. I... yeah. That sounds wonderful. You better bring your best, I won't take it easy on you, you know."

The two stared bullets at each other, and Rei could feel the heat of rivalry burning up in them both. Then she laughed, and Chloe laughed with her. It only stopped when there was a light tap-tapping on the door. It was the nurse, with a tray of crustless ham sandwiches. She slipped in and out with but a whisper, making sure her patient was comfortable.

Chloe held a sandwich out to Rei with her uninjured hand. "Here. I can't finish them all anyway."

Rei took the sandwich, not letting go of Chloe's other hand, and blushed. In this moment, she didn't want to let go. They ate in silence together, and when they'd finished Chloe looked over into Rei's eyes.

She was crying from her one good eye, softly.

"I... I'm sorry, Rei. For what I said. For what I've *been* saying. I... it's not an excuse. I don't have any right to beg forgiveness. I knew in my heart, it was wrong, and just... just did my best to ignore the pain.

Chloe looked away, trying to hide her tears. "I... if I let myself realize how bad it really was, it'd mean I hurt you *so much*. I couldn't handle that. And in the end, I got what I deserved."

Rei took a deep breath, blinked her eyes, tried not to cry with her. Failed, of course.

"I... forgive you, Chloe. I forgive you."

After everything Chloe had been through, how could she not?

"And never say you *deserved* what happened to you. *Ever.* That shouldn't have happened. You almost died. I..."

"Thank you, Rei. That... means a lot." Chloe sniffled, and wiped away the tears with a napkin.

"You know, Rei. I still owe you, for that bet of ours. I didn't actually tell you what was wrong with me."

Rei had genuinely forgotten about that entirely. "W... no, it's okay Chloe. I don't-"

She continued unabated. "Honestly, I'm... a little surprised you don't remember. You were in an awful mood for *days* after what happened. It... I don't think it was until Verde came to school that you'd recovered."

As she spoke, Rei started putting two and two together. Her cheeks flushed even redder.

"Oh...oh my *god*, I remember now. You were over at my place, and while we were playing a game together, you-"

"I said, 'there's a boy in class I like' and you just stood up, and, and you said-"

"I said 'you're not allowed to like him. Because *I* like you'. And-"

They were both stammering, almost shouting over each other. But Chloe's voice won out, despite the pain. She even started to laugh, and as she did, she seemed to shine.

"And I, I tried to explain the difference, and you, *yooou* said you already knew the difference. That's why you *cared*. You told me you liked me that way! That you, well..."

Rei's face couldn't decide on blanching in horror and blushing in embarrassment. It came back like it had happened yesterday, a younger Rei asking a younger Chloe to love her.

"I... yeah. I uh, I remember *that* now. I... also remember your answer."

Chloe's eyed lowered, looking past her more than at her now.

"Yeah, I told you it was... 'gross', for us to like each other that way and we uh, we got in a shouting match. I pushed you down, and you hit the back of your head pretty hard."

Rei rubbed the back of her head, as though remembering a phantom pain from five years ago. *I... wow, I can't believe I forgot all that. Or... tried to, anyway. I didn't* want *to remember it.*

Chloe sighed, and it felt... wistful. "God, it feels like it was yesterday... after I went home, I told Mother and Father about it and they said I wasn't allowed to hang out with you anymore. They introduced me to Heather, and her other friends, and... well, again, it's no real excuse but I ju-just, I wanted to fit in and-"

Rei squeezed her hand, a little harder. Chloe's lip quivered in pain, and Rei cursed inwardly. But it had given Rei an opportunity.

"It's okay, Chloe. I... I get it. I do get it. It wasn't... I don't think that was your fault. I um... Chloe, I want to try again."

It took a moment for Chloe to realize what she was asking. What Rei could see of her face started to blush a soft pink.

"I-I... I'm not... I'm not sure I'm ready for that, yet."

It took a moment for Rei to realize what, exactly, she had said. What she meant by it. Her face went as red as her hair.

"W-wait! No, no I mean... as friends. When you're out, I wanna... start fresh. As much as we can. I'd... I wouldn't *mind* bu-did you really think I wanted to just... jump into it like that?"

Rei's stammering pulled a laugh from Chloe that sounded like twinkling bells. "I... well, I mean, you *are* pretty forward with these things. I just- well, it wouldn't be the first time!"

Rei joined her laughter, and it sounded pure to her. Like for the first time in a long while, Chloe really was herself again. The girl she knew.

It felt good to laugh *with* her again.

But Rei could still feel the nettle in her heart. She had to say something, anything. She took a deep breath.

"Chloe... I'm sorry, too. I... if I had tried to talk to you before, if I'd actually listened, maybe none of this would have happened."

Maybe. The word almost made it worse.

"I'm sorry for hurting you, too."

Rei felt another weak squeeze back from Chloe's bandaged hand.

"Don't beat yourself up, Rei. If I hadn't... hadn't acted the way I did, you might have believed me when I tried to be less, well, a bitch. And there was nothing you could have done about the... the f-fire. You, you tried to *save* me. You could ha-have been hurt too."

As Chloe brought up what happened again, Rei could see the fear in her eye. That nettle in her heart dug deeper down. She should tell her. She *had* to tell her. She, of all people, deserved to know.

But Rei couldn't.

"I... I know, Chloe. But I won't let anything like that happen to you again. I promise."

Chloe blushed, and smiled faintly. "Th... thank you, Rei."

Finally, however, the nurse turned to take away the lunch tray... and to tell Rei it was time to go. No amount of time would have been enough to catch up, but to Chloe it felt so cruelly short. She wanted to talk more.

"Well… it's time to go. I'll see you when you get out, Chloe."

Rei smiled, and Chloe smiled back. She could feel the warmth radiating off of her friend

As Rei went to leave, Chloe took a deep breath.

"I… know it's a day early but, happy birthday, Rei."

She turned, and there were tears budding at her eyes. "Th-thanks… Chloe. I'll uh, miss you, at the party."

Chloe watched her go, a secret promise worming its way into her heart. Her left hand- her uninjured hand, clenched hard. It'd have to wait until she was out of the hospital, but…

Chloe knew what she wanted now, more than ever.

######

Chapter 17

Snow drifted down on Laketown's commercial district, hiding the sidewalk with a soft, sparkling frost that'd eventually become packed down to the cement, giving it all a marbled appearance. A digital clock mounted on the side of a building marked the time as three o clock; the temperature as negative fifteen degrees Celsius. The near empty street more than evidence of that. People rarely walked at that time, at that temperature, opting for the warmth of a car over the chilly winds.

Rei hardly even noticed. She was lost in thought, going over her conversation with Chloe in her head.

Did I say the right things? Obviously yes, she looked so happy. But is that right- and should I be happy too? I'm the one who put her there. It's given us a chance to make up but that's a horrible way of thinking on it! Or-or, or is it? Should I be... glad, for this? And GOD, I can't believe I-I told her that back then, th-that I... I love... Do I really...?

She'd had a handful of crushes over the years. Some guys, some girls- mostly girls, if she was being honest with herself. But none that had ever gone that far. Hell, aside from Kestrel, none who she'd ever even gotten a *chance* with. It was so much to think about at once, another stake slammed into her already overloaded week.

Eventually, she decided a course of action; after her date with Kestrel tomorrow, she'd see how she felt about him. If her feelings for him ran that deep, she'd know. If not... well, she'd play it by ear at that point. Or something, she wasn't sure.

Rei leaned against the outside of a building and sighed. She was exhausted, emotionally and physically, and starting to feel the chill of winter settle on her. It felt like her skin was on fire, nerves twitching and sparking as she mulled it over. It was like she could burst into flame, at a moment's notice. At least it was keeping her warm... as warm as could be expected, anyway.

She wanted nothing more than to get home and crawl into bed until tomorrow.

"Oh. Hey Rei, I didn't think I'd run into you today."

It was Kestrel, jogging down the street. Taking time out to talk with her.

Rei's face flushed red as her brain desperately tried to pull words out of her messed up tangle of a brain.

"H-hey, Kestrel! I'm great! I mean, I'm *doing* great! How're you doing?" she asked.

"I'm doing well, just out for a jog," he smiled that cute, thin smile of his. "What're you doing out in... a t-shirt, of all things. Didn't you say you were busy today?"

She looked away briefly. "Ye... yeah, I did. I finished up sooner than expected."

He scratched the back of his head, averting his eyes as well. "Would you be free to hang out? It doesn't have to be a *date* date, you do look a little... tired, and all."

Rei's heart thudded against her chest. She dared to look in his eyes and saw the far-off stare of someone deep in thought.

"N-no, no it's fine. I'm- yeah, you know what, yeah. I'm up for a date. Where'd you wanna go?"

He smiled again, staring into her eyes. "Well, first let's get something warm to eat. You must be freezing. I know I am, and I'm wearing a hoodie."

Rei nodded, face flushing red. She had been cold, but as they walked to a nearby restaurant, she suddenly started feeling a lot warmer.

###

"So... tell me about yourself," Rei asked, as they waited for their order.

It felt like a weak opening line for her first actual date, but her nerves demanded she say *something*. They'd both been nearly completely silent when looking over the menu, and Kestrel had chosen way before her and started fiddling with his phone while he waited. Rei was starting to get antsy.

It didn't help that she'd never been in this restaurant before; 'The Chez Lounge', a painfully obvious faux-fine dining establishment. The décor was soft cushioned seats and seemingly hand-crafted tables. The paper covered chandelier cast a moody, warm light down on them, and the utensils even had fancy artistic etchings in the handles.

It was chintzy and fake, and Rei could feel it leaving a thin layer of grime on her skin. The seats were vaguely uncomfortable, the lighting was far too dim, and a listless piece of classical music played softly in the back, seemingly on loop and with no end in sight.

Somehow the fact that she was on a date was the least stressful thing about the entire thing. Kestrel, for his part, was stoic as ever.

He smiled as he answered her question. "There really isn't much to tell I haven't told you already. I'm more interested in you, honestly."

Rei blushed but shook it off. "Well, I mean, I do wanna get to know you. Did you have any friends back home? What do you miss about Trestaria? Did you... ever date anyone else?"

"Hm..." she could almost see the gears turning as he thought her questions over. "Well... I suppose I can tell you. I've a friend, Kite, from my last school. Every so often, we'd go out into the dunes to chase after animals. Desert foxes, mostly. It was a stupid waste of time, but he thought it was fun, I guess. We wouldn't hurt them or anything, just take a picture. Prove we'd caught it, then let it go."

"Huh... were you good at it?" Rei asked.

He laughed. "Oh, no. He always won, or mostly anyway. Better at tracking them than I was. But he also got hurt a lot doing it. I never did. He would hound them, like a dog. Me... I'd find their den and wait."

Rei rolled her eyes. "From the sounds of it you just wanted to goof off. That's cute, though. It... I mean, there's probably not a lot to do out there, so I can see why he might see it as fun."

"I'd never tell him, but it was. The last time we did it together though, things got... a little sour. We'd both spotted something rare; a fox with pitch-black fur. I think we chased after it for an hour, and Kite even dragged me into doing it his way. And the thing is... I almost beat him. The one time I tried it his way and I almost get one over on him."

"That's a lot of 'almosts'. I take he caught it first?"

"Heh... no. Kite got in my way. We were so busy arguing over who caught it, that the damn thing got away from us."

Rei sighed and shook her head. "Yikes, that sucks. That sounds like a fight waiting to happen."

"Thankfully, it wasn't. Though if it came down to that... I'd beat him in the end."

Rei grinned, resting her chin in her hands, elbows against the table. "Talk about confident. And I wasn't talking about a *real* fight, you goofball. That's the second time you've made that mistake. That's kinda cute, too."

He blushed from that. An honest to god blush. Rei felt her heart beat faster.

He tried to compose himself as their drinks arrived. "I-uh... yes. I suppose it is, confident. You've got a good memory. I barely remember that first time."

Rei took a sip of her soda, honestly grateful for its cooling taste. "I'll admit, I almost forgot myself. Speaking of forgetting... the other questions?"

Kestrel grinned, a perfect match to the one plastered all over her face. "Ah, right. Uh... no. I haven't dated anyone. Other than you, of course."

She found herself giggling at his answer, as hard as she tried not to. He laughed with her, and it was all Rei could do to avoid falling over in her seat.

"You know," Kestrel started, "I should say... I hope you're okay. Last time we met up didn't exactly go as planned, did it?"

"Well that's a hell of an understatement. I'm uh- I'm good. I'm okay. I hope you didn't get hurt."

He shook his head. "Don't worry, I'm fine. I'm more concerned about you... aside from the first day we met, it feels like you've had a different bandage on your cheek every day. And that's not even counting what happened yesterday..."

Rei touched her cheek and blushed. She'd barely even remembered herself, but she kept on irritating that cut the puppet had given her. Getting punched in the face- twice- and falling down more times than she cared to count.

"Yeah, I guess so. Trouble keeps on coming my way. It's... I'm not gonna lie Kestrel, it's been a lot to deal with. But thank you, for your concern."

"I understand, Rei. I'm here for you."

His hand reached out to hold hers. But before she could take it, the food arrived.

Rei inwardly cursed her luck, but the bog-standard fast-food fries and burger the supposed fancy restaurant served actually looked worth the slight delay in holding his hand.

She had come to a decision. There was something here, something *more*. He was so cool and calm, like a lake in winter. Solid, with a hidden depth. It was drawing her in, and she could feel it. She could probably talk to him about anything, and he'd understand. Her concerns about her relationship with Chloe, all the supernatural stuff she'd gotten into, her powers... the possibility of being more than friends. She'd tell him, after they'd eaten. She was sure of it.

Kestrel, however, broke the silence midway through their meal.

"You know, there is one thing I miss about home. Aside from my friend, I mean."

Rei leaned in a little closer, urging him on.

"I do miss the heat. I knew Dulace would be cold, especially around this time, but nothing had really prepared me for the feel of it. Even with a hoodie on, the chill reaches down to my bones sometimes. I don't know how you manage it."

"Well, because-" Rei started. A small hesitation hitched in her throat. She was *pretty* sure she almost said, 'because I can set myself on fire' and that? That was definitely a concern. She really was opening up to him. She coughed to cover it and continued.

"Because I was born here. Helps build up a resistance to cold. It's only once the snow starts falling that I even wear a jacket."

"Of course, you aren't wearing one now. Must not be *that* cold yet."

Rei blushed and allowed herself a brief shiver. "I can take the cold, but not *that* much. I uh, forgot my coat today."

He smiled. "You could wear my hoodie, if you'd like."

"Wh-what, I mean, no it's fine. I don't want you to go cold because of *me*, Kestrel," Rei said, though the lick of flame down her spine told her just how much she'd enjoy wearing it.

They laughed, and there it was. The perfect moment. A brief lull to slide in her thoughts and ask Kestrel how he really, truly felt for her. If it was the same as how she felt.

"Hey, Kestrel. I... I think I-"

There was a ringing sound. A distinct jingle more like it, the kind ONY used in all their commercials. It was Kestrel's phone, alerting them both to a text message.

"Sorry, Rei. Just a second," he said. After a quick look at his phone, his expression darkened just slightly.

"I'm... really sorry, Rei. It was my parents. They need me to help with something."

Rei felt the bottom fall out from under her heart. "Are... is everything okay?"

"They are," he grumbled. "They just need help moving in the last of the furniture. It shouldn't take more than an hour..."

"I could come with!" Rei almost rocketed from her seat from how sudden she said it.

"N-no, it's alright Rei," Kestrel said. "We're on a date, I can't ask my date to help move a couch. Especially after all you've been through..."

Her face went read. "I... okay. How about we meet up again when you're done then? I'll uh, go to the arcade or something, and then we can uh... continue?"

Kestrel smiled, that same subtle smile that made Rei's face get even redder.

"That sounds good. We'll meet up, you can show me your uh, fighting game, and then we can get some dessert. Maybe after that, we can go home and... warm up?"

Rei almost exploded. "Y-yeah, that sounds like a plan!"

One last smile between the two, and then he left, stopping only to pay their bill. Rei watched him the whole way through. It had sucked, not being able to tell him how she felt, to ask if he felt the same way, but... they had time. They had all the time in the world. Rei let herself daydream of what it'd be like, going to his home, curling up together, and getting nice and war-

Oh piss. Shit. Gamma.

This time, Rei *did* rocket from her seat.

As Rei dashed down the sidewalk, shopping bag flailing from her right hand, a strange thought crossed her mind; she'd never really looked deeper into the story of the dance club's fire. Not since she learned all that supernatural stuff was real. Too much stuff on her mind to care about such a small detail.

She realized, whoever was responsible for it was a pyromancer like her. That'd explain why she had felt drawn to it, probably. Strange, what things came to mind in a crisis.

As she leapt over the useless barricade fence and clambered in through the window, she made a mental note to read up on it later.

"H-hey! Gamma! How you doing?" she shouted. *Please don't be frozen to death.*

He was sitting by his campfire, as close as possible. At the very least, he'd gotten it going. He would no doubt deny it, but he was obviously shivering.

"I'm f-fine," he answered, grumbling.

"Yeah, you look it," Rei rolled her eyes and threw the shopping bag at him. "Here, put these on."

"W-why? And why are you in s-such a ru-rush," Gamma asked.

"Because I'm a total idiot. I completely forgot about you. I had, had stuff to do today, and after it I was gonna pick you up some clothing cause it's winter and I didn't want you to die after I spent all that time making sure you wouldn't and..." she paused to catch her breath. "And I uh... I forgot. And ran all the way here after getting you some clothes, a-and a blanket."

Rei plopped down next to the campfire as he rummaged through the bag. In the light Rei could see he wasn't frostbitten, but if she'd been late... she tried not to think about it.

Gamma pulled out two fresh pairs of sweatpants and a white long sleeve shirt out of the bag. He inspected them with a level of caution she hadn't expected, placing the pants aside... and then tossing the shirt into the fire.

"Wh-what are you doing?!" Rei shouted. She hopped to her feet, almost falling. Her legs were screaming at her from the sudden, long-distance sprint they'd had to go through.

Gamma gave her a deadpan stare. "No shirts. Too restraining, not enough protection. I can't fight like that."

His hands brushed his wrists, fingers twitching softly. Rei wondered if Gamma noticed what he'd done, how much he'd told her without even saying a word.

She sat down with a sigh. "Yeah... guess that's my bad. You don't have to *burn* it though, some of these are kinda cute. I can take them as an early birthday present."

"I won't burn them, then. What is a birthday? You never actually explained that."

Rei blinked twice, then shook her head. "God, right we did forget didn't we. Sorry about that. It's... I mean it's the day you were born. Every year you get a little older, and all your friends come over for a party and cake and shit."

"Can I come?" Gamma asked.

"Er... I'm not sure how my mom would feel about that. You'd uh, need to wear a shirt for one. I could ask her though. And you wouldn't have to bring a present. I don't... really know how you'd be able to get me one in the first place."

Gamma thought for a moment, then shrugged. "Yeah, if I have to wear a shirt, that's not happening," he said.

He started digging through the bag again, then suddenly stopped. "What is... this?"

Gamma pulled out a black, faux-leather jacket with a low-cut collar. In the light of the fire, it seemed to shine.

"That, Gamma, is your *style*. I uh, I mean I think so. I don't really know. If you don't want it jus-"

Gamma had it on before she could even finish. It hung off his shoulders, barely even covering his chest. It did however cover the healing gash in his side.

He rotated his shoulders, moving his arms back and forth, getting a feel for it. He swished his hands, and shadows danced through the fire. He took a deep breath and smiled.

"This... this is good. I *like* this. It's... quite warm and padded. It's light, but clearly durable. Worth the sacrifice in arm movement. ... this is perfect. It's like it's made for fighting. Where did you find this?"

"Well... I have my ways," Rei said, stifling a smile.

The fact that it was a woman's jacket, designed for maximum comfort as opposed to anything else, was a secret she would probably take to the grave. Of course, she wasn't sure Gamma would mind... and given how well he pulled off the look maybe he was made for *this* too.

"Check the pockets. There's something else."

He did so, pulling out a tiny black comb. 'Unbreakable' was embossed along the length of it, no doubt a misnomer.

"What is... this?"

"It's a comb, Gamma. You know, for your hair? It's a mess... I imagine with this and a little..." she sniffed the air, realizing with horror how easily she'd gotten used to the stench. "And with a *lot* of showering, you might actually clean up nice. And I mean hey... if they don't recognize you, they can't find you, right?"

Gamma pulled the comb through his hair, cringing as it got stuck in its unruly tangle. But he kept at it all the same. From the looks of it, he cared more about his appearance than he let on, and Rei decided she'd take that secret to her grave too.

"Hm... thanks, Rei. Where we you and the others all day?"

Rei blinked again. "You know, I don't actually know. Since my phone broke, I've just kinda been... doing whatever, I guess. I forgot to ask them yesterday. As for me, I uh, I went to visit Chloe. The person I hurt."

Gamma put the comb away and sat down, closer to her. He didn't say it, but it was a clear invitation to speak.

"It... she's doing good. As good as can be expected, really. I just... you ever regret something, Gamma? Do you know what that's like?"

"No," he said. He stared into the campfire. "Everyone I've killed deserved it."

Despite the warmth of her pyromantic abilities and the flames nearby, Rei shivered.

"I... you've killed people, huh. I guess I, I should have expected that."

Gamma turned to look at her, and for the first time Rei saw a pang of guilt over his face.

"Sorry, I-"

"No, it's... it's okay, I just want to help you, Gamma, but I can't... I don't think I can do that. I can't...k-"

He growled, but it sounded pained. "No. You don't have to. Leave... that, to me."

"Th... thanks, Gamma."

The thought of killing someone with her powers, killing at all really, was... entirely impossible to imagine. It made her sick to her stomach. She'd seen the results firsthand. She'd never do that to anyone again.

Worse, seeing Gamma's reaction, seeing him so casually able to consider it... it sent a shudder down her spine. She wondered what could have caused him to be so willing to take a life- and thought about what could push her to do so, if anything.

No amount of fire could keep that chill from reaching to her soul.

To her surprise, it was Gamma that changed the subject.

"So... you also didn't explain what a date was. I'm going to assume you don't mean the fruit, right?"

Rei could of swore the corner of his mouth twitched, and despite herself she laughed.

"N-no, god, how do you... never mind, a date is when someone you like, a whole lot, hangs out with you. And just you," she explained.

He waited, as if expecting more. Rei tapped her fingers against her knee.

"... oh, that's it? That's just love then, isn't it?"

Rei's face flushed. "Wh-what!? How do you know *anything* about love, Gamma? And... and I mean yeah, that's it, but I mean, I've just got a crush on him, I do-don't... don't think I'm..." her heart pounded, hard. Remembering her date, even though it'd not even been that long ago, was making her face get hotter and hotter.

"I do. I mean, I think I do. Jeez."

Gamma's lips twisted in a smirk. "One of the caretakers that watched over me, she talked endlessly about her family when no one else was watching. So, I picked up the term. She was a monster, so I imagine her idea of love was broken. But... it sounds like yours isn't. That's good."

Rei sighed, trying to cool herself down. "I... yeah, thanks. Thanks, Gamma. You know, it's really good to feel in love. Maybe someday you'll find that feeling."

He shrugged. "Maybe. Someone who loves you would never betray you... would be a good friend in a fight."

Rei rolled her eyes and laughed.

"W-what? It's true."

She laughed harder, and Gamma just grumbled and looked back into the fire.

"So... what's he like? Tell me about this... Kestrel, of yours."

"Well, he's...well he's pretty shy, honestly? Or at least he was, after talking to him a few times he started opening up, and he's really just so sweet. He seems like he's trying to be super serious all the time, but it's pretty easy to catch him off guard and fluster him. It's... it's cute, honestly. He also does martial arts stuff. We beat up some dudes together. He... thought that was cool. I think he said he wanted to spar against me once?"

She laughed, rolling her eyes. "Man, guys are such a trip sometime."

"What's he look like?"

"I mean... nothing special, really," Rei said. She pictured him in her mind. "He's... kinda tall, thin. Probably pretty toned under that hoodie of his, he jogs a lot. He's handsome, I'd say. Has a real soft face, and big brown eyes. They... they look really wistful sometimes. Like he's always thinking of some far-off thought or something."

There was a grumble from Gamma, one that Rei didn't quite understand. Like he was clearing his throat.

"Maybe... you could bring him over."

"I was thinking of it, actually. I'm not sure how he'd react to everything.

All this supernatural crap is uh, pretty hard to take in. But... I think he could, yeah."

Rei got to her feet and stretched. "I'll consider it. In the meantime, I've gotta get going. I'm meeting him for the rest of our date after this. I'm... pretty excited."

He waved her off, and Rei made her way out the window. After talking with Gamma, she was more than sure. She knew exactly what to say, exactly when to say it. Her blood was running hot through her body, fighting back against the cold. Everything was perfect.

She was in love.

As Rei made her way down the street from Gold Row, the snow began to pick up. What had been a simple scattering of flakes was now a constant, if not overbearing, downfall. It seemed to shine in the evening sun, as its last rays of life-giving warmth struggled to wash over the world.

Rei really wished she had brought a jacket or had bought her own the mad dash to ensure Gamma didn't become an ice cube. But at least it was a beautiful cold. There was really only one thing that could happen to make it feel better.

And to her surprise, there he was. Kestrel, standing off to the side against one of the nearby houses, hands in his pockets. His hood was up, to keep the snow off of him as it fell around his shoulders.

She waved to him as she approached. "Uh, hey Kestrel! What're... what're you doing here?"

He gave her a quick, stiff armed wave. "I uh... actually, I wasn't being entirely honest with you."

"Wuh-wait, really? Wh... why?"

Rei was surprised by just how much hearing such a simple thing as that stung.

"It's nothing bad, honest. I... was actually going to pick something up. That I had my parents looking for. I thought- hoped, you'd still be in the area, so I'd be able to catch up. So, I could..."

He blushed, scratching the back of his head with one hand as his other hand left his pocket. A small pink box, about the size of a necklace, rested in the palm of his hand.

"So, I could get you this, as a surprise. Happy birthday."

"Uh... what is it? If you don't mind me asking, anyway."

He took a step forward. "It's... an old thing. A necklace, my father gave to my mother when they... first got together. I felt it was an appropriate sign of my affection."

Rei's heart skipped a beat. It still stung, to hear she had been *lied* to, but... she'd never received a gift like this before. Not from someone she was sweet on, not something so personal it almost hurt to hear. Despite the cold her heart set alight with heat.

"I... that's a lot, Kestrel. Do.... does this mean that you lo-"

Kestrel nodded. "Yes, Rei. I do."

He tried to avoid her eyes, and his cheeks flushed. He scratched the back of his neck.

Rei stared right at him, felt the burning in her cheeks, the tingle up her back. "Aww, Kestrel. That... that means so *much*! I... I-"

She reached for the gift.

And in that instant, it vanished into the air. Rei's eyes reflexively followed it, darting up into the sky along its path. A thousand questions exploded through her mind as it turned, end over end.

What just happened? Did he throw it? Did something hit him? Is it something I did? Is it-

Her thoughts were silenced by the sound of boots crunching in snow. She looked down.

Kestrel had his hand outstretched towards her neck.

######

Chapter 18

In the split second before Kestrel grabbed her, a voice echoed through the snow-filled air.

"GET DOWN!"

Rei took a step back, just barely escaping his grasp. A half second later a blade of darkest night ripped through the air, carving a massive gash between the two.

"Gam- KESTREL, what is-"

She looked from Gamma to Kestrel and back. Gamma's crystal blue eyes were shrouded in black, dark mist rising from his hands. Kestrel... didn't look phased at all.

"Rei, get BACK! He's the *ferromancer!*" Gamma shouted, swishing his hands towards him.

Kestrel shot backwards a full two steps as the shadows swirled and struck at where he was last standing. He placed his hand on the nearby building, as though to brace himself.

And then a mess of iron plumbing blasted out from the building, along with a gush of water. It flew through the shadows, slamming into Gamma's chest. Rei couldn't see if he was okay, couldn't dare take her eyes off Kestrel, but the shadows between them dispersed.

Kestrel dashed towards Rei, shoving his left hand into the hole the pipe made in the building midstride, and ripped out a broken, shattered piece of pipe.

He swung, and Rei stepped back. She felt something wet against her shirt.

The pipe, in an instant, had become a long, slender saber. Despite its iron-grey colour, it still seemed to gleam in the fading light.

The blade's edge was dyed crimson, and only then did Rei realize she'd been sliced across the stomach. It was shallow, only really the tip of the curved blade, but pain rocketed through her body once her nerves had caught up with the rest of her.

Without thinking she shoved both hands upward, a torrent of flame welling up from inside of her and rising with her. Twin pillars of flames caught along the ground, creating a wall of cherry-red fire between her and Kestrel.

It stopped him for the length of a single breath. He leapt through the flames, slashing at her. Rei ducked backward, faint strands of hair drifting down across her vision.

She'd dodged it by inches.

He advanced, raising his saber for a vertical strike. Rei's eyes twitched. Instinct saw the briefest of openings and forced her right hand forward. A blast of fire erupted from her palm, colliding into Kestrel's chest with an explosion.

It singed his hoodie, embers sticking to it faintly. He flinched, enough for Rei to take another step backward, his vertical strike cutting nothing but the air. He stepped back as well, and for the briefest of moments they stood still, regarding each other.

Kestrel's eyes looked blank, as though he was deep in thought. He held his sword out defensively, ready to intercept anything she did. Running, truly turning tail and running as fast as she could, was out of the question. He'd be on her in a second. There was only one option.

Rei put up her fists in a sturdy, if still rusty, boxer's stance. Left fist forward, right fist close to her face, both wreathed in flames.

"G... get back, Kestrel. I... I'll-"

He didn't let her finish. He stepped to her left suddenly, and Rei responded with a right hook. She felt the burn of flame as heat left her knuckles and soared towards where Kestrel was.

Where Kestrel had been. It was a feint. He had ducked to her right, both hands gripping the hilt of his saber, and thrust his sword out to meet her. Rei couldn't stop her forward momentum in time, the fire propelling her. She braced herself for what was sure to be the end of her life.

Black filled her vision. But it was not the embrace of death, but Gamma's back. A second later, grey blossomed out his back along with flecks of red.

He'd thrown himself between them. Kestrel's saber had pierced him through.

Gamma growled, voice thick with pain and blood. "G-Grab... the sword!"

He'd grabbed hold of Kestrel by the shoulders, shadows tangling up the latter's legs. Kestrel was struggling, pulling at the saber, and it was clear he'd win if she didn't act.

An image of Kestrel slicing Gamma open across the chest filled Rei's mind. She could not let it happen. She grabbed the saber's blade, holding it as tight as she could.

There was a shout, a soft voice turned hard, as Rei fed her heat into the blade, burning Kestrel's palms. He let go of his sword hilt and punched Gamma across the face. Gamma's grip loosened, and with his opponent momentarily pushed back, Kestrel leapt backwards.

It was a mistake. Gamma gave him a grim, bloody smirk as he swung his arms forward.

Shadows erupted out from around him, ripping with such force that the sticky trails that momentarily hung from them seemed to sharpen. The tendrils slammed into Kestrel's left arm, twisting and churning around it, digging into his flesh. It started to bend at the elbow.

First there was the popping sound. Then, a strangled gasp from Kestrel. Finally, a sickening sound of wet meat being shorn in half by force.

Gamma's shadows ripped Kestrel's arm off at the elbow, a veritable torrent of blood accompanying it. Rei's skin went cold at the sight, flames dying.

Gamma took a step forward, panting hard, and a wave of shadows pushed out to finish the job.

Blood red spikes, gnarled and jagged, burst out from Kestrel's severed arm and into Gamma's chest. He screamed, coughing blood, and fell to his side.

Before Rei could react, Kestrel pulled something from his belt. There was a brief flash, then nothing but white smoke. Once it faded, he was gone.

The snow continued to drift ever downward upon the two.

###

Rei didn't linger to check Gamma's wounds. She'd be an idiot not to know how serious they were. He needed help, but the hospital was so far away. So, she did the first thing that came to her mind.

Rei wondered what she must look like. A bloody, dying man on her back leaving a trail of crimson life across the snowy sidewalk. By the time she'd reach home, there was a good chance he'd be dead, and it would have been all for naught.

When she threw open the door, tears pouring from her eyes, the last thing Rei was expecting was shouts of "Surprise!". Her mother, Verde and Ella only managed to get half the words out before they were replaced with screams of concern and fear.

"I–Gamma, he... Kestrel!" Rei shouted.

She took a step two steps into her home and collapsed from exhaustion.

###

The instant she'd fallen, Aria had stepped into motion.

"Ella, there's a first aid case in the kitchen. Now! Verde, help me pull him off her," was the order, and both of them acted as quickly as they could. "Careful now, he's lost a lot of blood. Keep that sword in him! If you remove it, he'll bleed out faster. Now check on Rei!"

"Y–yes ma'am!" Verde shouted. Her voice was breaking from panic.

With strength honed from years of lifting her daughter up in her arms, Aria dragged the stranger to the couch. Ella hurried back with the case, sobbing.

"Verde, how is Rei doing?! Is she okay?" Aria shouted. It pained her to ask someone else to check on her daughter, but... Rei had dragged a dying man to their door. It had been for a reason, and she wasn't about to let him die either.

It took a moment for Verde to respond. "She, she's fine! Sh... oh god, she's got a cut on her hand, a–and I think on her body. I ca... I can't tell. There's... there's so much–"

"Deep breaths Verde. Deep breaths. Ella, help Verde bring Rei here, and then get me some water bottles. They're going to need them."

The work went as swiftly as could be expected with two children- teens or not- assisting her. The cold had helped stem the flow of blood, but not enough to avoid nearly killing the young man and covering Rei in dark red life. Aria took a deep breath.

The man's injuries were insane. The sword wound itself could have been fatal, though it looked like it had missed anything vital. The twisted red spikes in his chest were dug in deep and removing them would take a steady hand to avoid damaging him even more. The worst of it was an old gash in his side. It had been healing nicely from the looks of it, but something had torn it open, worse than it had been previously. Too much strain and it'd probably rip him apart.

She popped open the first aid kit. Bandages and gauze, disinfectant and wet wipes for cleaning. Needle and thread for stitching.

This wasn't nearly enough. But she'd handled worse.

With a little luck, she could do this.

"Verde, take some bandages and disinfectant. Help Rei. Ella, you assist. And start running some water, we'll need it to clean our tools. Hurry now!"

Noise thudded against Rei's head like a steady piston threatening to shatter her skull. She had passed out, though she couldn't quite remember why.

As she finally opened her eyes, she remembered. She remembered everything.

Verde and Ella were beside her, the both of them slathered with blood. Hers and Gamma's, no doubt. Verde's face was stained with tears, and Ella was still sobbing. From the pain in her eyes and the wet marks on her face, Rei had been too.

"M-Ma'am! She's awake! Rei's awake!" It was Verde. A strangled noise came from Ella, as though she tried to say something herself.

"I... is he alright?" Rei asked. Her voice sounded gravelly and pained, like she'd just run a marathon with a dead weight strapped to her back. When she was more readily conscious, she'd cringe at the awful realization that she had basically done so.

Her mother's voice rung out, clear and sharp. "He'll be fine. Mostly. It took a lot of work, work I haven't had to worry about in a *long* time, but he'll survive."

Rei managed to sit up and look around, head still thrumming, mind still groggy. Her mother had been wearing a lovely dress, but it was just as stained as the rest of them. That was almost all Rei could focus on.

The living room had been set up as a surprise party, streamers and banners hanging from the entrance way. If it weren't for all the blood, it'd look wonderful.

Verde and Ella hugged her tight, so hard it almost hurt, murmuring words of relief and care that she could barely make out. Aria, pain clear on her creased brow, hugged her a half second after.

"Rei... what *happened?*"

It was Aria asking. Rei was starting to feel awake enough to actually answer.

"Kestrel... tried to-to kill me. He, Gamma... he saved me. Again. I-I tried to fight back, but I wasn't able to."

No response they could muster felt appropriate. They held her tightly, till their tears dried up. When they finally had, Aria let go and took a step back. She took a deep breath.

"Girls... tell me everything. What's been going on here?"

Kestrel dragged himself through the front door of his home. A less than hidden approach, one he'd never have allowed himself in a normal situation.

This was not a normal situation.

The dossier hadn't listed any pyromantic abilities. Some incidents with fire yes, but nothing that wouldn't seem out of the ordinary unless you looked at it sideways, and even then, it could be seen as just idle clumsiness or stupidity. Another mistake- the dossier had been entirely wrong about her address as well.

If Kestrel hadn't already killed the officer who'd gotten it for him, he'd be a dead man walking.

He had expected some resistance of course. Rei was able to defend herself, that was a given, but...but being able to last as long as she did, only really losing out to a feint, it was a sign *he* had gotten sloppy. His chest still stung where the fireball had struck... if she'd actually put effort into it, it could have blown clear through his chest.

And that damn experiment. Rei was so close; he'd opted to capture her first before confirming Project Gamma's status. Kestrel had delivered him a near fatal blow during his escape, but Kite's *idiocy* thoroughly botched the entire endeavor. So, Kestrel had been *sure* the experiment was dead. Then Rei's behavior made him realize she may have contacted the Project, and all too late he had to choose one or the other.

He'd chosen poorly; he could admit that. Project Gamma showed up, so he acted as best he could. He was a known threat, but his main target was *right there.* He let it slide because *she* would be easy prey, something he could have even used to capture Gamma as well.

Such foolishness on his part, assuming this would be *easy.*

"S-sir! Sir, are you alright?"

It was one of the Security Force he'd brought with him. The one pretending to be his mother.

"I'm *fine.* Get me the medic."

He was shocked at how his voice sounded. He was... angry. He hadn't felt angry for a long time. Kestrel felt the emotion sting, and let it fuel him as he dragged himself into the kitchen.

After a moment his 'mother' returned with 'Father', the other Security Force member he'd brought on, the latter fumbling with the med-kit. They likely thought this would be easy too.

"Sir, w... what happened out there?" he asked.

"A minor setback," he answered. It was a growl. "Nothing we can't... handle."

"Sir, with all due respect, your *arm is missing.*"

If he didn't need to hold his right hand against the kitchen wall to stand, he'd have grabbed something and thrown it at her. Slowly, he pulled himself towards a chair to brace himself.

"I said it's a minor setback. Medic, prepare triage... and someone release the damn puppets."

They were getting restless. He could hear them, scratching at the door to their basement, the only place they could contain them. They could smell his blood and *wanted* it.

His 'mother' hurried over to the door. But there was some hesitation. His 'father' opened the med-kit and began cutting away at his sleeve, to get at the bleeding stump where his elbow should have been.

"Sir, we... our lord ordered us not to use the mnemonic puppet's unless absolutely necessary. They're unstable. Dangerous. And we haven't even heard back from the first one-"

"*ENOUGH!* Stop second guessing me and... and open the damn door."

'Mother' took a step back and started following his orders properly. She opened the door, stepping aside.

Two crystalline figures with back-jointed legs scurried out from the basement. Blank, skull like faces peered around the room... till they saw the blood staining the floor. They inspected it, running their claws through it. It was like they were feeding.

"S-sir, I... I'm not second guessing you, but this isn't nearly enough blood to-"

Kestrel grabbed the man's combat knife and pulled it from his belt in a single movement. If it was anyone else the next twist of his arm would have jammed the weapon in his throat. It took every fiber of Kestrel's being not to do just that.

Instead, Kestrel carved a bloody mark across what remained of his left arm. Blood splattered on all of them, but only the puppets seemed to notice in any real sense. Slowly, red mist swirled around them, forming into dark chunks of flesh that clung to their skeletal forms.

There was little Kestrel feared. He feared Lord Orochi's wrath. He feared having to listen to his target rattle on about meaningless drivel he'd have to sift through for weaknesses. He feared mornings when the sun, shining through cloud cover, turned the sky red.

But the mnemonic puppet's forming their protective shell of meat and memory was like something primal had been pulled from his core. The scientists who made them said they pulled memories from the chaos in your blood, whatever that meant, becoming people who you've met. Whoever you had strong attachments toward. You could order them like any other puppet, and they'd listen, but... there was an uneasy intelligence to them. They did not truly live, but the imitation was uncanny.

And for some reason, the two brown skinned people the puppets became pulled at his deadened heart.

"Ah, good evening son. What do you want?" said one. Its tone was pitch perfect to a voice he no longer cared to remember.

The medic began patching up the wounds on his arm. It stung, but not enough to stop his orders.

"Go out into town. Find Rei, you know her. You've seen her in my blood. Capture her if you can... kill anyone who gets in your way, anyone who tries to stop you."

The walking shells of flesh nodded and left without a further word.

"Sir... that seems excessive."

It was his 'mother' again. Kestrel grabbed her by the throat and could feel the iron pulsing in her veins. He made it prickle, enough to sting.

"Enough. Get me every bit of iron you can find. Then suit up. I've got something to attend to."

They told Aria everything. At least, everything they knew. It had come in fits and spurts, Rei mumbling what she could before the shock and adrenaline crash had put her to sleep.

Rei was out cold on the floor now, and Aria hadn't the strength to lift her to her bed.

Ultimately, all she really learned was that Gamma was a friend of theirs, and that they hung out with him at a condemned building. It was nice, if frustrating, that Rei's friends were loyal enough not to spill her every secret. She'd *need* friends like that someday.

Aria sighed, thanked them, and told them to clean up and borrow some of Rei's clothing. Whether they felt they should or not, they'd stay the night here. Aria couldn't risk what might be out there.

Ella had fallen asleep in Aria's favorite chair; the poor girl was exhausted. Even in her dreams she was shaking. Verde had latched onto Rei as she slept and had fallen asleep like that. She was lucky to have taken her sweater off earlier, it had survived Rei's bloody arrival and was now being used as a pillow for the two.

All but two slept. Gamma, and herself.

"You're... her mother, aren't you," Gamma said. It was gruff, but kind. Weakened by his wounds. Aria approached him.

She snapped her fingers, and a pale white flame appeared in her hand.

"Alright, *shadowmancer.* What have you told my daughter?"

######

Chapter 19

Flashes of iron and bursts of fire. Strangling shadows pulled at her arms. A clash within an inferno of heat, blood, and death. She could feel the burning in her soul, feel it melting everything around her. Her heart slammed against her chest as she saw Gamma's face engulfed in cherry-red flames, roasting to ash. She was supposed to help him, and now...

Rei woke with a start, chest pounding. Verde's tiny frame wrapped around her was a welcome sight, if only for a brief moment before memories of last night asserted themselves at the forefront of her mind. All she could do was groan, in a mixture of pain and exhaustion.

Her body was sore, her wounds stung, and everything smelt of overpowering air freshener with the ever so slight undercurrent of rust that just couldn't be removed.

"Good... morning."

It was Gamma. Rei let out a deep breath, not even aware she'd taken one in. He was okay.

He was sitting on their living room couch, a mess of bloody bandages wrapped around his chest. It was the closest she'd seen him come to wearing a shirt since they met.

Rei carefully wiggled out of Verde's arms, trying not to wake her. It brought a smile to her face, despite it all. Verde had always been a hugger.

"I... I guess I really did bring you here, huh. I'm... god, last night was like a nightmare."

Gamma coughed. "It was. I..." he coughed again, unable to continue speaking for long, or just unable to think of what to say.

Rei, however, knew exactly what to say. "Gamma, you almost died because of me. I... you saved my life, again. I don't know how I could ever repay you. Thank you."

If there were any tears left to cry, she'd have done so.

"Don't thank me," he grumbled. He laid out on the couch, cringing at the pain. "I... did what I did of my own will. And even then, I failed. I could have gone for his head."

"Why didn't you," Rei said. Her voice was barely a whisper.

Gamma turned from her, facing the couch. She could see the small hole in his jacket where Kestrel's saber had pierced him through.

"I... I followed you, because I recognized his description as one of my hunters. I wanted to make sure. For a moment, I thought I was wrong. That he couldn't be the ferromancer. If I had been a second late... if I hadn't reacted, you'd be dead."

He took a deep breath, let it linger in the air. "I... do, have regrets, Rei. I'd seen you investigating my home the day we met, saw your flames. I was sure you were an enemy; I was sure I'd have to kill you. I *wanted* to. But when you were attacked, I just acted. Then we spoke, and... I realized I was wrong."

He turned to her. They were small tears, but he was crying faintly.

"You saved my life, and it was the first time anyone had ever done something kind for me. You are my friend and I would die for you a thousand times over, without a second thought. No, now my only regret is that... that I wanted to spare you the sight of someone you loved being killed in front of you by a friend, without understanding why."

Rei felt a sharp pain in her heart. Knowing Gamma cared for her that much, knowing the pain he'd suffered for it, knowing what more he might have to endure... the only thing that hurt more was realizing she agreed with everything he said.

She wished Kestrel had died.

"Gamma... thank you. You've really done enough. Rest, please."

"I will, Rei. You rest too, if you need it. I... don't know what lies ahead, but know I'm with you. And, happy birthday."

He turned away again. It seemed against his words... but Rei could see the subtlety in it. He felt safe here. She took a deep breath, and carefully walked towards the kitchen.

She could smell her mother's cooking.

"Mom?" Rei asked, as she entered the kitchen. A part of her worried she wouldn't even be there.

She was, looking as she always did in the morning, cooking breakfast. It was pancakes today, her favorite.

"Morning, my... my little bell," she said. "How did you sleep."

Rei had never heard her mother sound weak before. There was a shakiness to her voice, like she was replaying the event in her mind and couldn't focus. Rei figured she probably was.

Rei slumped in one of the chairs. "Well enough, considering. Everything... stings. And my clothes are sticky."

Aria turned to her, a wavering smile on her face. Her eyes were bloodshot, and it was clear from her expression she hadn't slept all night. "Well... blood'll do that. It was a brave thing you did, little bell."

"What do you mean?"

"Your friend, on the couch. He told me last night... how you saved his life. Twice, now."

Rei looked at her hand. There were bandages she hadn't noticed– her body too numb to really care– that covered the shallow cut she'd gotten from grabbing Kestrel's sword.

"Yeah... I guess I did, huh? What else did he tell you?"

"Oh, nothing much. Enough, anyway, that I know the gist of what happened. Some... troubled youth attacked him. It's a good thing you took those boxing lessons."

Aria's behavior was obviously put on, and Rei could see in her mother's eyes. She *had* to know‚ to know about her abilities, to know about everything. Someone had to have told her.

And yet somehow, her mom's cheery attitude infected her. Rei laughed.

"I... you know Mom, you're right. It really is. I think I should probably look into picking that up again. Seems like it might be a good idea."

The two laughed together, despite themselves. There was a coldness to it, like they were playing out the motions, but it felt nice all the same.

But she had to break it. Rei took a deep breath. "Mom... do you *know?*"

After some time, she nodded. "I know, little bell. I always knew. I just... I wanted you to live a normal life. A life *I* didn't get to have."

Rei let the words sink in.

"I... understand, Mom. I wish you had told me, though. I could have hurt myself; I *did* hurt someone else, and-"

Aria's face twisted, slightly. A pained expression Rei had only seen once before. When she asked about her father for the first time.

"I *know*, and that... that is *my* fault, Rei. I failed you, and because of it something terrible happened that we... that *I* won't be able to ever fix. And with what I've been through, I could handle it. If it was just me, I *could*. But it... it's you, my darling little bell. If I had told you, this might not have happened."

Rei stood, nearly knocking her chair over with force, and hugged her mom with every ounce of strength she had.

"No, Mom. Even if I had known, if you, you'd trained me or whatever, to control them... I think that would have happened. I got so mad... I just couldn't control it."

In truth, Rei knew her mother was right. It might not have happened. Or, if she'd had control... but got so angry that she lashed out, it could have been even worse. She was feeling that same rage now... and with the level of control she had now, she knew.

She knew what she would have done to Chloe.

Aria hugged her daughter back. "I don't know what to say, my little bell. I don't know what to say."

Rei held her a little tighter, but then pulled back. Even after sleeping, her arms felt tired.

"When were you going to tell me, anyway?" Rei asked.

"Today. I was going to tell... not everything, some secrets need to remain secret, not for your sake but mine. But I'd have told you the truth today."

197

Aria gave her a pained smile, then turned back to her cooking.

"Go wash up, little bell. When you're done, everyone should be up and we... we can have a nice breakfast together. Then, we can talk about what to do next."

Rei nodded, but in her heart, she knew what had to be done. She just wondered if she could manage it.

Chloe stretched, wondering if the old clothes would fit her. It was wonderful to get out of that hospital gown. The doctor had said that as long as she was extra careful, she could wear regular clothing now. She just needed to watch for any wet spots on her bandages where a blister may have broken.

Chloe cautiously looked in the mirror a nurse had given her. Sweatpants and a wool shirt, the latter a fraction of a size larger than she was used to. All that, plus the bandages wrapped along her from hand to head.

She looked like a walking disaster.

But she was an alive- and mostly healthy- disaster. That was truly all she cared about.

Then she heard a noise, like someone had tipped over a cart of medical supplies.

"I... hello, is everything alright?"

No response.

She still didn't feel comfortable leaving her room, not wanting to escape its small comforts and risk hurting herself further, but she approached the door on tip toes.

The door carefully opened, and in walked Kestrel.

Something about his face looked sickly, sunken, as though he was ill. But his brown eyes pierced through her all the same. He had bandages wrapped all the way up his left arm that dripped red as he walked.

"Chloe. Come with me, now. It's urgent."

Such a strident plea, but so little emotion in his voice. Chloe felt a shiver up her spine.

"N-no, I can't. I'm... in the *hospital*, I can't just- is everything okay?"

He grabbed her by the injured hand, hard.

The pain was unimaginable, but below it was an undercurrent of fear. She could suddenly feel every inch of her body tingle and go nearly numb. He glared at her, and for the first time she realized his eyes didn't carry some far-off intelligence, some wistful beauty.

They were dead of all emotion. He had the eyes of a corpse.

"Try to run and I'll break your knees and drag you behind me. Move, now."

Pain and fear intermingled, and she couldn't even shout.

He turned to leave, nearly dragging her along regardless, and kicked open the door to her hospital room.

The first thing Chloe saw were the bodies. Two nurses pierced through the chest by strange twisted spikes. Fear finally won out over pain and she screamed.

It echoed through the hallway, a dull reverberation that was almost more dreadful than the sight before her. The entire place had gone quiet.

Kestrel pulled at her arm harder. Chloe felt something bust in her arm and stumbled, cutting her cry short. The fear that she could fall and be pulled to wherever he wanted her was palpable, and it seemed like Kestrel didn't even notice, marching at a steady pace.

Then as they passed the turned over medical cart, the glimmer of an idea formed. Chloe let her legs give in and fell, falling onto the cart. It was enough to stop his stride, for just a moment.

Kestrel pulled her arm, harder, almost wrenching it from her socket.

"Get -*moving*. You're lucky I need you alive."

She grit her teeth through the agony pulsing up her arm and stood.

And carefully pocketed the scalpel she'd picked up in the fall.

###

Rei rummaged through the dresser in her room, picking out what felt like the best clothes to wear. A pair of forest green sweatpants and a white t-shirt with the image of her favorite character from 'Knights of the Stars' plastered on it.

Leona, a fiery lioness with a bastard sword. She'd won it in a contest that felt like an entire life time ago. It was her favorite shirt, a collectible.

Dying in it would suck, but if she was going to march to her death she might as well dress nice. Rei grabbed her journal and went downstairs.

Everyone was waiting for her, eating away at pancakes. Verde in her light green winter sweater, pulled down around her knees to keep her warm. Ella beside her, already finished eating and grabbing at the hem of her skirt, obviously nervous. Gamma was still on the couch, awkwardly trying to use a fork. His hands were noticeably sticky, and still stained with blood from last night.

And Aria, sitting in her chair, watching the news with that same intense stare Rei hoped she'd never see again.

"H... hey, everyone. I guess it's a bit late, but... thanks, for the surprise party."

Rei was shocked by how hollow she sounded. The shallow cuts on her palm and stomach throbbed, as though in retaliation for trying to speak.

"It was Miss Verde's idea," Ella said. "She invited us all over last morning, while you were... were busy."

Rei took a deep breath and let it out slow. "I... thank you, really. All of you."

She sat down at the living room coffee table, set her journal beside her, and started to eat. Slowly, methodically, trying to savor as much normalcy as she could. The silence was deafening, but Rei didn't want it to end.

But the silence had to break at some point.

"What the hell happened last night?"

It was Verde. Her dry, often sarcastic tone was thick with concern.

"Kestrel attacked me last night. He... we went on a date, he baited me in with some fake gift, and tried to kill me. If it wasn't for Gamma I'd have died. And, if it wasn't for me... he'd be dead, too. Kestrel... he's the one after Gamma. Or at least, he's supposed to be."

Rei looked at her palm, squeezed her hand tight.

"I... he was focusing on me. I think he's after *me*."

"M-Miss Rei, why would... why would he be-?"

"I don't know," Rei said. "I don't *know*. But... I intend to find out."

She looked towards Gamma.

"Gamma... I'm sorry. Tell us everything you can. Who... who made you? Why?"

He sighed, and Rei could see the last glimmer of resistance fade.

"ONY. I'd seen those letters before but didn't know what they meant till I escaped. Till you three. They made me. I was born in an artificial womb, taught a few basics, then... experimented on. I think I was only ever supposed to be a weapon."

He shook his head, as though shaking off old memories. "My caretakers- the doctors called me Project Gamma... and they served someone called Orochi. That boy Kestrel was at the lab, I'd have to guess he works for him too."

The silence returned, save for the sound of Verde's fork clattering to her plate.

"That's... that's *insane*. I knew ONY was big but I- this is *impossible*."

"Believe it or not. I don't have any proof, but... the 'Security Force' you taught me about look identical to the soldiers that guarded my lab."

"They... they control everything," Ella said softly, voice barely a whisper. "If the-they're after Miss Rei, there's nothing we can do but hide, right?"

"I have an idea," Rei said. She took a deep breath.

"If Kestrel is after us, after me and Gamma... we find him, and beat everything he knows out of him. Once we know what ONY or Orochi or whoever *wants*, we'll... have some sort of idea of what to do after that."

"Do you know how to find him?" Gamma said.

"I do. It's... in my journal," Rei opened it up and flipped through the pages.

Her heart flickered like embers once she found the right page; Kestrel's phone number, copied down from the napkin he wrote it on what felt like an eternity ago.

She'd drawn a rough little drawing of the two of them holding hands underneath it. It felt so... childish, knowing what she knew now.

"I... he gave me his phone number. I'll call him. Arrange a meeting or something, I don't know. And then when I find him, I'll force him to tell us everything."

"What the hell is this 'I' shit. We're doing this together," Verde said. There was a force behind it Rei wasn't expecting.

Gamma scowled. "She's right. You're not doing this alone."

"I have to. It..." Rei stood, hands tightening into fists. A small fire started to build in her palm. "Everything is *my fault.* I wasn't strong enough to protect Gamma, I sure as hell won't be able to protect the rest of you. I don't want to see any of you hurt, or worse. And..."

Rei took a deep breath. She had to get it out, the pressure building in her chest. "I... I hurt Chloe. I almost killed her and I think-... I think I did it on purpose. I just got so *mad,* and just... just let it *out.* And if I-I'm not careful, you'll all get caught up in it too. Every time I think of Kestrel, what he did, what he tried to do, I can feel it coming back. I feel like I'm going to *explode!*"

The flame grew, enveloping her hand. Embers started to peak out from her forearm.

"I... no matter what you say or do, I'm going to *go* out there, and I'm gonna *find* Kestrel, find out what he *knows,* and..."

Rei could feel her voice wavering, her heart pounding. The flames were building, and she did her best to stop them. She had to save this rage.

"And I'm going to kill him."

She felt tears roll down her face as she said it. Felt them sizzle on her cheek.

Gamma stood, fighting back pain. "No. No you're not."

"Miss Rei, you... you can't..." Ella was stunned, her fair skin going even paler.

Verde stood too; tiny hands balled into fists. "Like hell you are Rei. If Gamma got as messed up as he did, you *need* help. You need *us.* I'll... we'll keep you in control."

"Guys, no. I have to do this alone. He..." she tried to speak but was overpowered by her own thoughts. Any justification she could think of rang false. But she couldn't endanger them. This was *her* problem. Kestrel was out for blood, and the thought of her friends dying burned itself into her brain. Rei could feel the flames start to ignite within her blood.

There was a sudden thudding sound, as Aria stamped her foot to the floor and stood. A dark look had crossed her face. She took a deep breath and spoke.

"I love you, little bell."

The room seemed to freeze. Rei's heart missed a beat. "W-what?"

Aria sighed, the way only a parent could when they are at the end of their rope.

"I love you. You're my wonderful, darling daughter, and I can't see you tear yourself up like this. Trying to burden yourself for your friend's sake, trying to solve this problem yourself, thinking you'd end up hurting someone you love on *purpose*!"

Her voice was breaking, but she continued. No one could stop her.

"You have such a strong, loving heart, and seeing you hurt yourself like this is so hard. Think about all you've done. You helped Gamma- this *stranger* come back from the brink of death, twice. Because it was the right thing to do. You're stronger than you know Rei, my perfect little bell. But I'm so afraid of you getting hurt!"

It was like someone had let all the tension, all the underlying pain, out of the room. The flames on Rei's arms turned to smoke in an instant, and she ran over to hug her mother harder than she'd ever hugged her before. The both of them cried openly as they held each other.

"I... can see it in your eyes, Rei. That same fiery look, full of fear and deter-mination your father would always get before doing something unbelievably stupid and dangerous for a good reason. And... I have to realize, you're strong. You can *do* this. You're *going* to do this, whether I like it or not. But all I ask; *all* I ask is... please. Rest. For at least a day. And let your friends help you. You'll need it."

It took a moment for Rei to realize what her mother had said to her. When she did, she simply held her tighter.

"I... thank you, Mom. For believing in me. I-no, *we* won't let you down. And you're right, we... we do need to rest. Especially Gamma."

Gamma grumbled, but otherwise said nothing. Ella, however, lifted her hand shakily.

"Are... are we sure this is alright? ONY can probably find us here, right? And what about us? Will... will we be safe?"

"They won't find us here," Aria said. Despite it all, she smirked. "Being a lawyer has its perks. As far as the government cares we live on the other side of town. And don't worry, you can all stay here... I'll make sure your parents are safe too. It's the least I could do, for all you've done my daughter."

Ella let out a sigh of relief and seemed to melt into a puddle. Her nerves where shot.

Rei didn't blame her. They were all exhausted. But things seemed... better, now. Aria's speech, the confidence she put into Rei, seemed to lift their spirits. She broke the hug from her mom, reluctantly, and made her way back to her seat on the floor to continue eating.

"You know Ma'am, that's pretty impressive," Verde said as she picked away at her pancakes. "Tricking the government and all that. I... take it you've have prior experience?"

"Oh, something like that. I was a bit of a rebel at your age. The stories I could tell..." Aria smirked, "oh, but that's for another time. The last thing you girls need is inspiration to do something *reckless*."

"As though running off to get in a fist fight with a madman wasn't reckless enough," Ella grumbled. "At least you'll have protection this time, Miss Rei. Real protection."

"I mean, I guess," Rei said. She'd been mulling it over since they first brought up helping her. "I'm just... you know, not sure what you guys will be able to *do*. No offense, but-"

Verde suddenly flashed Rei a toothy grin and shot from the living room to the entrance and back, flinging her backpack at Rei so hard a mass of papers came out.

"Uwah! Verde, what're you-"

"God, right, with all this excitement I never got to show you *this*," Verde shouted, grabbing one of the papers and slamming it on the coffee table. Rei pushed the backpack off of her and looked at it.

Drawn on the paper with a felt tipped mark was a large circle, intricate geometric shapes layered atop it. In the center was two stylized gusts of wind, long straight lines curling up into a spiral.

"I was planning on showing this off later, but now's as good a time as any! Watch and be amazed... and sorry if this gets a little messy, Ma'am!"

Before anyone could react, Verde put her hands on the paper and spoke, her voice seeming to echo as she did.

"*Luft!*"

A small, emerald-green tornado burst out from the paper, scattering the rest of the papers even more and blowing the coffee table clean. It was strong enough that Rei had to bury her face in an arm to resist the wind. And as quickly as it came, it ended, utensils and plates falling to the rug unceremoniously as the rest of Verde's papers drifted lazily in the air when once they'd been spiraling.

"Holy *shit* Verde! You... you just did magic! I mean, I think that was magic!" Rei shouted. She could barely contain herself. For a moment, everything was forgotten in the mixture of awe and excitement.

Verde was laughing, clearly loving Rei's response. Everyone else; Gamma, Ella, even her own mother, didn't seem remotely surprised.

"I... you *hid this* from me! How could you hide something this cool from me!"

Ella ducked behind Verde, shivering. Gamma just picked what remained of his breakfast off the floor and ate it.

"For what it's worth, little bell, I only learned it this morning," Aria said. She gave Verde a dead-eye stare. "She could have warned me she was this powerful, though. You realize I need to clean this right?"

The both of them ignored Aria's complaint. "Okay, spill it! How'd you figure this out?"

Verde put an arm around Ella, shoving her forward. The latter squealed at that.

"Ella did it. She found a book in the library, searched it high and low. We've been uh, studying it. For about two days," Verde said, the cockiest grin on her face Rei had ever seen.

"Gamma's a pretty useless instructor, but thankfully I'm a natural."

They all laughed, even Gamma in his own way. But Rei laughed the hardest. *I wish I got to learn about this before... well, everything,* Rei thought to herself. It was hard not to; they were trying to go on like everything was the same, and a part of her knew it was to cheer her up. *And the thing is... it's working.*

Despite all that had happened, all that *would* happen, Rei felt a warmth in her heart. They'd rest, prepare, and tomorrow, they'd go and take down Kestrel. For now, it felt okay to indulge in this, to have some degree of fun. For now, they could be normal.

Then the news report started.

######

Chapter 20

"We interrupt the current morning report for an emergency announcement. Tragedy has once again struck our fair Laketown. What law enforcement are reporting as a lone assailant entered the Golden General Hospital at seven thirty this morning, harming dozens and fatally injuring two before taking Miss Chloe Nichols hostage. You may recall this is the same young woman who was hospitalized last Monday for second and third degree burns along her arm and face. Law enforcement has not commented on the connection between the two incidents."

The room had gone dead silent. Rei could feel her eye twitching, could feel flames begin to boil her blood. A strangled sound came from Verde as she pulled out her cell phone and dialed her mother's phone.

Rei could barely hear her friend's words. Everything had gone dull, but for the sound of the television.

It continued. "They have, however, made a statement regarding the kidnapping, tying it to another story still ongoing. At two AM this morning, road safety workers were assaulted by two individuals and rushed to hospital, where two remain in critical condition. One has unfortunately passed away. While law enforcement had initially considered this a tragic, self-contained incident, the chief of police has just announced that they will be turning over investigation into both the deadly attack on the hospital and the violent assault to the ONY Security Force. An official Security Force bulletin urges citizens to stay indoors, as the three individuals are known to them as dangerous threats and, as Golden General shows, are willing to take hostages. It is currently unknown at this time if the severed arm found last night is connected to these events."

The news report went on to a discussion of what measures the Security Force take with these sorts of events, talking about it like some abstract *thing* and not something happening now.

It wasn't until Aria turned off the television that Rei found she could breathe again.

"Verde, is... everything alright?" Rei asked. She tried to swallow the inferno building in her throat. Verde's mother worked at the hospital, and the report didn't say who was killed.

Verde looked up from her phone. She was crying, but only faintly. "Sh... my mom is fine. Kestrel, he... he only h-hurt the people who got in his way. Mom was with a patient, so she didn't... but he... he could have..."

Verde went to throw her phone against the wall, only stopped by Ella grabbing her shoulder. She was crying too.

That was answer enough. Rei rose to her feet. "I'm sorry Mom. We... we have to do this. Now."

Her mother stared right back at her. Rei expected an admonishment, a warning not to go.

"I understand. Be safe, little bell. And give him hell."

Rei took Verde's phone, and dialed Kestrel's number.

It rang once.

Twice.

A third time.

Rei held her breath. Finally, he answered. She switched it to speaker phone.

"Who is it?"

His voice hadn't changed a bit. Soft spoken and calm, like everything was fine.

"You know who it is, bastard. Where are you?"

There was a pause before he answered again. "You're right, Rei. I do. You want your best friend back, don't you? You know what we want in return, right?"

It was clear from his tone it wasn't a question.

"Yes, I... I do, Kestrel. You want me."

Another pause. "Correct. And no matter what happens, we *will* root you out. Chloe is just a... bargaining chip. An incentive."

Rei's grip tightened on the phone. "You... let her go. She has nothing to do with this!"

"And if you come to me, alone, I will. As simple as that. I'll even recall my... companions, who are currently hunting for you. To make it easier. We want as little bloodshed as possible, Rei."

"I understand. Tell me where you are... and I'll come. Alone."

"Good decision. I'll send you the address. And... you know what happens if you're lying, don't you?"

Rei hesitated. Before she could answer, another voice came through the phones.

Chloe's.

"R-Rei... is... is that really... you?"

"I-It's me. It's me, Chloe. I'm... I'm going to save you."

There was a pained gasp from the other line. Chloe was hurt. "D-... don't. Please don't. He... he killed people. He... he'll kill *you.* I don't want to, to see you get hurt. Rei, I lov-"

The line went dead. Moments later the little ding of a text message popped up. The full street address of where he was.

It was just a few blocks down the street from Gamma's home. Likely where he said he was living with his family. A house, hidden away at the end of a street, where no one would ever think to look.

Rei closed the phone, and a swarm of thoughts assaulted her. None distinct enough to latch on to. The edges of her vision were blurring with fought back tears. She tried to focus, and heard the crackling rumble of flames in her ears. Burning blood pulsing through her veins.

She took a deep breath and could of swore her breath made the air waver with heat.

Verde snarled. "It's a trap. *Obviously.* I... look, I get it, but we can't let you go al-"

"I'm not going alone. You're right, Verde, it's a trap. But... I realized something."

Rei handed back the phone and took another breath. Anything to keep herself from bursting into flames.

"When I fought him, I managed to catch him off guard. Once, but I did. He didn't see it coming, and I... managed to hit him. And as far as he knows, Gamma is the only person who even *can* help me. There's no reason to tell me to come alone."

Gamma chuckled to himself. "I see. He means to make you afraid. I should be dead as far as he's concerned. He's underestimating you again."

"Yeah. Yeah, he is," Rei balled her hands into fists. "And now that we know where he is... I've got an actual plan. Verde, you and Gamma sneak around to where he is and wait, and I'll go to meet him. Once he shows up... I'll get him talking. Do anything I can to get Chloe to be let go. Then, when he lest expects it... I'll give a signal. Attack him, and once he's off guard... I'll kill him."

Gamma got up from the couch with a groan, wounds clearly still hurting. "No, *I* will. He owes me a death."

"That's only if I don't wring his stupid neck first. He..." Verde said. She inhaled, sharply. "He owes me death too, man."

"It seems like a good plan, but... wh-what about me?"

It was Ella. She had been silent for the entire news report, cowering behind Verde. But still she had stood with them, umbrella clutched tightly between her hands. Her pale knuckles were snow white with tension.

"I... I d-don't think... I *can*. But... I, I'll fight, too. So, so what should I do, Rei?"

It was Aria that answered first. "Well, I can't really fight anymore. As much as I'd love to, I just can't work up the rage. Ella, you can stay here, and help make sure Rei has something to come home to. Does that sound alright, little bell?"

Rei nodded, and it almost looked like Ella was about to faint from relief. It was clear she wanted to help but... for Rei, just knowing her friend would be safe was support enough. One less thing to worry herself about.

"T... thank you. I promise I won't let you down."

Rei gave her a wave. "You won't. Verde... pack us some medical stuff just in case. And guys, prepare yourselves. This is it."

#

Rei thought over the plan in her head as she marched down the street. Small little burn marks melted the soft snow in a long trail behind her. Heat, growing in intensity as she worked it out over and over again.

There was a chance everything could go wrong. The thought festered at the core of it all like an errant wound. Kestrel could outsmart her, or avoid the attacks, and then what? Her friends could get hurt. She could die. And Chloe...

Rei shook her head, pushing grim concern away for the time being. Random factors, things she couldn't predict, all of that was going to happen one way or another. She'd come up with the best strategy she could. It wasn't great, but she had hope. All that was left was to push into the end game.

It felt stupid, in a way. Comparing this all to a game. It was so, so much more than that. But every time she thought about it, it came back to that. She had fought people like Kestrel before. Not in real life, not with any stakes that mattered now, but she had. Arrogant assholes who thought, maybe even *knew,* how much better they were.

It was always one little slip up that sent them falling. One little detail they missed, and her aggressive fighting style would pay off. All she had to do was trust that it would work this time, too.

Truthfully, there was no use worrying about it. She had reached the border between the commercial district and Gold Row. Verde and Gamma had already split off from her, snaking towards their destination through a path they'd traced out on Verde's phone.

Rei let out a breath, and focused.

The winter chill didn't even touch her.

#

Verde scurried her way through back alleys, light snow crunching underneath her shoes. Even with her sweater she was freezing, but she pushed on. A hunger was driving her, a familiar hunger mixed with something more.

She'd prove her ability. She'd prove that she could do whatever she sank her fangs into. But more than that, she'd finally pay Rei back for everything. Every little way Rei helped her, she'd pay it back ten times over and make them both shine brighter and hotter than ever.

That idiot didn't know what kind of storm he'd unleashed. She could feel excitement burning in her blood, and the slight weight of the stacks of paper she'd squirreled away in the massive pockets of her sweater. She had come prepared.

"He-hey uh, excuse me, miss?" a voice called to Verde. It shook her from her thoughts.

A woman in a long dress; a padded vest to keep the cold out. Her skin was brown and her hair long and black.

"Yeah? You know, you shouldn't be out like this. Things are uh... a little dangerous around here," Verde said.

"Oh, I know. But I'm looking for my son," she approached her, concern heavy in her voice. "I... he went out, to a friend's house, and I don't know where he's gone."

"Look, I'm sorry, I... I can't help you," Verde answered.

"Please... I know it's dangerous, but he's just a little boy, around your age. He'd gone to his girlfriend's house when the alert came in, but I haven't heard from him."

Verde grumbled. She didn't have time for this.

"Don't worry. He's probably safe. Get back inside and call him, he'll pick up. Kids do some dumb things when they panic or get scared, believe me on that one."

She wanted to help, but... with what was going on, helping would do more harm than good. Besides, Kestrel said he called back his goons. She doubted he *did*, but if he was dumb enough to actually give Rei his real phone number it seemed likely. It was safe to be out now.

But the woman didn't know that. She didn't know it wasn't dangerous anymore. And yet she'd left the safety of her home to find him. Why not just call if she knew where he was? Why hadn't he called her?

Why was she over in the commercial district if she looking for her son?

Oh, she's one of the bad guys, the thought came to her in an instant.

Just as a flash of steel sparked across the corner of her vision.

Gamma let the cold play across his chest, partially covered by the jacket Rei had gotten him. His body still felt numb from his injuries, and truthfully if a protracted fight broke out, he'd probably risk ripping his body in half.

The thought flitted by his mind for a second before being entirely discarded.

Not just because of revenge. Revenge was simple fuel, that they all shared. No, this was something else. An empty spot in his chest filled.

The doctors and their puppets had beaten every last good thing out of him. Rei had found at least one small part of him and put it back.

He looked down on the city from the small building he was sitting on. Soldiers in black combat gear, armed to the teeth, searching for Rei. Well, they'd found him instead. He just hoped Rei didn't mind he was a little late.

He descended into the alleyway the two soldiers were heading down, landing behind them as shadows swirled around his feet to cushion his fall. Not quiet enough, the one closest to him had heard. Had turned to aim her automatic rifle directly at Gamma. She shouted a warning.

With the flick of Gamma's wrist, a hooked tendril shot out from the darkness of her own shadow and through her neck, jabbing through her collar like an unfortunate fish. She was dead before the shadow reeled back into the ground, slamming her corpse into the ground with a sickening crunch. Her fellow Security Force member fired.

Swirling arms of darkness rose up around Gamma, forming a shield like a blackened egg shell. Bullets slammed into it with the sound of rocks falling into a lake, and did as much damage.

Gamma walked towards him, shadowy shield moving with him at a lumbering, discordant pace, inky darkness slowly dripping as the bullets, bereft of momentum, fell to the snowy ground. His target ran behind a corner, and started radioing for backup.

Good. He awaited them, ready to show what their weapon could do.

Ella paced around the house, a nervous wreck. So much violence and bloodshed had happened and it hadn't even been a full week since she'd gotten here. The fact that Rei, that Verde, that even Aria herself had all seemed to take it as well as anyone could was astounding. It was unbelievable. Aria was doing the dishes from breakfast. The *dishes*. This was no time for dishes.

Of course, here *she* was, umbrella in hand, ready to strike at whatever nasty creature or enemy appeared. She'd never hit anything before in her life, at least not consciously. She was even averse to play hitting.

And yet, after getting to know Rei for even this short amount of time, Ella felt ready to fight for her. It wasn't that big a surprise really; when she'd read Rei's blood in her first fortune telling session, she had seen it. A spark of flame, just a tiny one, caused by Rei's burning arousal that day. Then she'd done the second one, to get a closer look. Rei was clearly wondering if Ella's fortune telling was legitimate- a hard question to answer that she had tried and failed to explain multiple times- and Ella's own curiosity had been piqued by the pyromancer's enthusiasm.

The second time had filled her head full of all the horrible, chaotic things that could happen if she was reckless. If Rei lost control. This was no spark; it was a soul roaring like an inferno.

Ella thought about how to warn her, how to phrase it to her new friends who seemed to grow so attached so quickly. She had hoped to edge them into the shallow end of the pool, maybe show them a cute magic trick or something. Something simple and controllable.

Then they'd met Gamma, and any opportunity for that had flown out the window.

Worse, Ella had learned the fire in Rei's eyes were just *dreams*. She'd nearly *fainted* at the thought of it. If all that budding potential was Rei's base state of mind, what could she do if push came to shove?

So, there Ella was. Umbrella in her hands, jittering in her own skin, trying to find out how to protect Rei's mom from any number of unknown threats that she had a feeling Miss Scios could break in half anyway.

Aria had brought up two things the instant Rei and the others had left. First was that, due to Rei's call on Verde's phone, there was a high chance that Kestrel would track it and the house would be attacked. The only reason Ella hadn't collapsed on the spot was because she was so *jovial* about the whole thing. She asked if Ella was comfortable defending herself, and her answer was a half mumbled 'I will do my best' that seemed to satisfy her.

Then she'd asked for a fortune telling. Unprompted. Oh, she *said* she'd heard it from Rei and Verde, but Ella could tell. People who *knew* could tell, especially people like her. The only fear in Aria's voice last night was for her daughter's safety. Everything else, the violence and blood and magic, had been *normal to her*. So, she'd read her blood.

It was like gazing across a vast sea of cooling magma.

Fate. She knew it wasn't real. But if it was, it had thrown her an interesting card the day Verde was picked to show her around school. Reading the chaos in their blood had made Ella surer than ever of one single thing; she should have taken up tarot card reading. No chance of seeing something terrible in *that*, that was for sure.

There was a knock at the door, and Ella almost fainted.

######

Chapter 21

The ever-present scent of cigarette smoke that permeated Gold Row filled the air as Rei arrived. In retrospect, it was an obvious place to hide. Few lived here, and fewer still dared linger long enough to notice the former. Kestrel could have an army with him and Rei doubted anyone in Laketown would have noticed.

The old house was tucked into the dead end of a back alley; were it not for the footprints in the pink tinged snow it would have been ignored by any passerby. Rei got it in her head that, in its past, the home probably looked nice. It was slightly raised, a small staircase leading up to a front porch that connected to the building proper. With the snow starting to build on its overhanging roof, it looks almost friendly.

Rei approached with cautious steps and called out to him.

"Okay Kestrel. I'm here."

The front door opened, and the two of them stepped out. Chloe first, a dull iron saber against her neck. Kestrel behind her, holding the blade in his right hand while his left, wrapped in bandages, held her by the elbow of her unburned arm.

The two slowly inched out, Kestrel's eyes locked on Rei's.

"Hands up, Rei. If you want her to live, do as I say."

Cold, calm, precise. The voice she remembered falling for. Rei felt like an idiot, adding to the burning in her chest. She held her hands up.

"R-Rei... wh... what is ha-happening?" Chloe asked. She was shaking, and the bandages on her right arm were dripping red.

"Don't worry Chloe, I'll save you. Alright Kestrel... my hands are up. What next?"

"On your knees."

Slowly, he started to let go of Chloe. His sword stayed at her neck until Rei had finishing kneeling.

"Don't even think of moving. You're still a hostage," he said to Chloe.

Chloe shivered, trying not to move. Despite the obvious pain on her face, she wasn't crying. Something in her eye sparkled in a way Rei recognized. Chloe, as ever, was defiant.

"Wh-why... why are you doing this?" Chloe asked.

He ignored her and stepped forward. One foot, then another. Methodical, precise, slowly pointing his saber forward towards Rei.

"Why *are* you doing this, Kestrel? I know who you work for, at least I think so. And I've got my theories for what's going on. But please... tell me, at least. I don't want to die, or get captured or whatever, without knowing *why*."

It was a question she'd been mulling over in her head for a while. And she did need to stall for time until the others arrived, so why not at least try to sate her curiosity.

He grinned, yet no emotion hit his face. "No. Why should I tell you?"

Anger boiled, but she had to keep it down. Save it for the right moment. Her right hand twitched, begging for the release of flame.

Kestrel stopped and swung his saber backward. Chloe screamed, cut short by the blade stopping right against her neck. She could barely risk breathing.

"Careful, Rei. No fire, or she'll die."

Rei grit her teeth, trying to contain it. Every second she looked at him was a reminder of the pain. She could hear a rumbling in her ears like a roaring fire, could feel the edges of her vision crackle with heat.

"I... tell me, and I'll go. Tell me and let Chloe go, and you can have me. Kill me, take me away, whatever. Just... just don't hurt her."

"N-no! Rei, he'll ki-" Chloe shouted.

Kestrel twisted his saber. The tip of it dug into the underside of Chloe's chin, a string of blood dripping down the blade. Rei felt her teeth start to grind even harder.

"Quiet. Now, tell me Rei... how can I trust you, when you've already lied to me. My allies have already intercepted the friends you brought along. They're going to die."

Not smart enough. Not fast enough. Not *aware* enough. The thoughts that always plagued Verde echoed in her mind at that instant. It almost drowned out the pain. She'd never felt pain before, not like this. She'd hurt herself trying to do something stupid, broke her hand once trying to punch out someone who'd insulted her height, she'd even just recently sliced open her palm while trying to use magic for the first time.

But as she stepped back, narrowly avoiding the blow aimed for her neck, as the combat knife sliced across her cheek and left a bleeding wet slice upon her from chin to cheek that would almost certainly scar, Verde realized she had truly never felt *pain* before.

She kinda liked the rush it gave her. Verde pulled a piece of paper from her pocket and held it out towards the woman who'd just tried to slice her face open.

"*Klingenluft!*"

The magic circle on the paper shone green, and Verde felt the stamina *draw* out of her, into the spell. A torrent of wind burst forth from the paper and Verde's attacker, pushing her back fifteen feet.

And then it rounded on Verde, slicing the paper to ribbons and cutting into her hand, reopening the previous day's injury.

Damnit, I drew that one wrong! Verde inwardly cursed, winching at the pain. She cleaned her palm off on her sweater, leaving a red smear, then grabbed for the next sheet of paper from her pocket.

"Oh please, little girl. Won't you help me find my son?" the woman, if she even was one, asked. She advanced forward, blood stained steel in hand. She moved so human, her face full of concern and pity.

But her eyes were blank.

Verde dodged the second stab, felt the force of it pass by her face. She had to focus on the spell. A third swipe came, this one catching her in the shoulder.

The sweater took most of it, but Verde could feel the wet spot where it had nicked her. Her fingers threatened to drop the paper in her hand.

The woman reared back and went in for another strike. Verde grit her teeth and dodged toward her. The knife blow missed by miles.

Benefits of being short. Verde shoved the paper against her foe's stomach and said the spell again.

"*Klingenluft!*"

A blast of wind erupted forth, blades of wind scattering snow and sending the woman flying. She slammed into a building wall, cratering it. There was a snap like bones breaking. Clothes, hair and flesh were shredded, the discarded pieces dissolving red mist.

For a moment, it looked strangely, horrifyingly human. A woman missing chunks of her body, head twisted at an angle, jaw broken. But as the dust settled Verde could see the crystalline skeleton underneath, the ruby-red bones of the puppet Rei and Gamma had told her about.

"Huh... guess it's one of those puppet things. Well... that's good then. I can be traumatized about killing someone later."

Verde threw off her backpack, rummaging through it for a fresh bandage for her hand.

A creaking sound echoed through the snowy air, pulling her attention back to the puppet.

Shit, it's still alive!

The puppet pulled itself from the wall, enough of the flesh shell it wore hanging on to it to make it look all too human. That only made it worse as its legs twisted backward, inverting to the crystalline creation's default state. It hunched over, tilting its head to the side.

What remained of the woman's face dropped till it was upside down, a misshapen mask barely concealing the blank, vaguely skull shaped head of the puppet.

She smiled and spoke; its voice, once full of life and vigor, scratched out like a broken disc.

"H-help me fi-find my son-n-n."

"Oh *hell* what the-" Verde said. The puppet lunged forward, an unearthly shout reverberating from its humanoid covering.

Verde shot to her feet to try and avoid its strike, stumbling over herself in her panicked dash. The puppet's knife missed by inches, slicing through the front of her sweater. Green fluff accompanied the flurry of snow that was kicked up from Verde falling flat on her back.

The puppet loomed over her, sun glinting off what Verde could see of its true body. It lifted the knife up, poised to strike down at her.

Adrenaline coursing through her like wildfire. Verde flipped over, tried to scramble away.

The puppet stabbed downward, and the knife tasted blood.

Aria answering the door had been nerve wracking. The stranger's appearance was more so.

The man at the door was tall and thin, with dark skin and darker hair. He wore a simple shirt under a hooded button-up jacket. He looked almost exactly like an older Kestrel.

"H-hello, sorry. I... I'm looking for my son, Kestrel. I think he may have known your daughter?" he asked.

"Oh? Well please, come on in," Aria said in response.

Ella's grip on her umbrella tightened, so hard she could almost feel her knuckles pierce through her fair skin. Aria letting the enemy- an obvious enemy- into her home was the worst possible thing she could do.

"Thank you, really. I've been worried sick about him."

He came on in, a genuine look of concern upon his face. But if he really *was* Kestrel's father, Ella doubted he had anything but ill intent. She should strike him across the face right now.

For all that would do. She hadn't trained to fight like Rei, didn't know a thing about offensive magic like Verde. All she had was the athletic training of a decent ballet dancer, an umbrella, and her blood reading. A party trick at best.

I could also... her mind briefly considered trying something drastic, and the smarter parts of Ella's brain shut that down immediately. She couldn't risk it.

"Please, this way. You must be cold. I still have some pancakes left over, and breakfast always warms me up," Aria said, gesturing towards the kitchen. He seemed to hesitate, before nodding and heading in.

Aria gave Ella a quick, near imperceptible wink and followed after him.

Well, she had that at least. Miss Scios had a plan.

"Ella, be a dear and get the man some coffee. I imagine he could use a drink, given the cold."

He sat down at the kitchen table, looking around the room. Something in his eyes made it feel like he was searching for something, only barely registering everything else. Aria sat across from him.

Ella, umbrella stuffed under her arm, started preparing coffee. She kept one eye on their guest at all times. She had to find out who he was, *what* he was, then let Aria know. That at least she could do; proper blood reading involved prolonged contact, but a quick scan just a slight touch.

"So, your son... Kestrel, is it? I believe my Rei mentioned they were dating. Where do you think he's gone off to?"

He paused a moment before answering. "Oh, I really have no idea. Do you think he would be with your daughter?"

Aria shrugged. "Possibly. She did seem pretty sweet on him. Never told me much, though. What's your boy like?"

"Er, h-here you are, sir," Ella said, placing the coffee done in front of him. She barely had time to back off before he took the cup, took a sip of it, and placed it down. In that briefest of moments, Ella's fingertips brushed the back of his hand.

"Well... he's a good boy. He tries his best. Always talks about your daughter. I think he is... how did you say, 'sweet', on her as well."

Ella barely registered the conversation. She had frozen stiff from fright the instant she touched his hand. She had expected something terrible; a metallic demon or some kind of powerful mancer, but what she'd got was... nothing. Not even a single drop of blood.

Oh... oh NO. He's a puppet, but he looks so human! That cou-could mean anything is hidden on him! Knives, guns, magic... I can't see what it is. I should... I should...

Aria coughed, and it shook Ella out of it. She flashed a quick smile her way, which she just as quickly redirected towards the thing before them. Ella took a step back, as if to avoid the subtly venomous glare on Aria's face, directed straight towards the puppet.

"Yes, I imagine he is. My best guess is that right now, they're together. Any second now they'll phone us, tell us everything is alright."

He laughed. "Yes, quite. I have my phone on vibrate, I should... check, actually."

He reached his hand down into his pocket, but from where Ella was now standing, she could see it. It took all her effort not to scream.

The man had drawn a pistol from his pants pocket, looking down at it like a phone. He held it under the table, aimed straight for Aria.

"Nope, nothing. Sorry, Miss Aria. So... *do* you know where they are?"

Five.

That was all Kestrel had with him. Five Security Force members; the two posing as his parents and three that had survived Gamma's escape from their facility. In most cases that'd be *more* than enough, and they had it on good authority that 'Project Gamma' had died so all that remained was collecting the Scios girl.

In a way, Gamma felt insulted. And sadly, that was all the information the corpse he was currently sitting on had given before bleeding to death.

Well, that and his boots. Gamma's toes were getting cold.

Gamma held the soldier's radio in his hand, the beep of its emergency beacon barely perceptible. And in the distance, Gamma could hear the crunch of snow under combat boots. They were close now.

Two down, three to go. Gamma took quick stock of his surroundings.

A back alley, one that looked the same as any other in Laketown. Ten feet wide and with two entrances, not counting the one behind him. The maps he'd seen in Verde's books and on her phone made him wonder what madman designed it all.

That at least was an advantage. Neither he nor the guards knew the place all that well.

The first of the Security Force turned the corner into the alley and with no hesitation opened fire. Gamma leaned back, inky black shields enveloping him once more. He swished a hand forward and the shadows underneath the soldier blossomed into a dozen razor tipped tendrils that hacked his lower body to ribbons.

He fell to the ground, and the advance stopped. They were going to try and wait him out.

Gamma shifted his stance, flicking his wrist. A ribbon of shadow lashed out into the air, sharpening into a hook as it struck the topmost edge of a nearby building's square-topped roof.

He ran along the shadow to the roof, solid shadow dispersing behind him into black mist so nothing could follow. He reached the roof just as the two Security Force members remaining felt confident enough to turn the corner. One took a shot and the last of Gamma's bridge twisted into a shield to guard his legs as he pitched himself forward onto the safety of the roof.

He couldn't waste a second. They were sure to start doubling back the way they came, and he would be there to meet them. Gamma dashed forward, leaping back down to the alley, and thrust his arms forward just as they turned the corner once more.

A torrent of claws burst forth from the shadows, the alley growing dark with writhing arms. Gunfire flashed from their rifles as they retreated. Blood showered down as the slower of his two remaining foes was rent limb from limb in the storm of violence. The last managed to escape with his life, ducking back around the corner, into the clearing.

One left. A crooked smirk grew on his face. Five was far too small a number for him. He advanced, taking a deep breath.

His side felt wet. Over exertion no doubt, his wounds opening from the rush. He could feel exhaustion seeping in. Gamma touched at his bandages, to see how he was holding up.

He felt bullet holes.

######

Chapter 22

"W-what... no, you can't-no!" Rei stood up, every last fiber of her being trying desperately not to let her flames out. Her hands were aching. Tears were sizzling in her eyes.

She knew he was lying. He had to be. But the simple, calm tone of Kestrel's voice had changed. Confidence, subtle but there.

A part of Rei expected this honestly. It made sense to leave his men searching the town, to stop anyone trying to help her. Kestrel could easily take Rei himself, he didn't *need* back up. But to hear it still tore into her heart; her friends were caught out. Worse still, Kestrel had said 'friends'. He knew about them both.

Rei trusted them. Verde's magic could take them off guard, and Gamma even being alive was surprise enough. But the sudden surge of fear ate away at her. They could be hurt, or worse.

Kestrel's face read satisfaction. Something bad had happened, she knew it. He gave her an emotionless grin.

"Back on your knees, Rei. Or she dies next."

Rei, slowly, fell to one knee. Kestrel lowered his saber away from Chloe's throat. It seemed like only then did she next breath.

"Good enough. Now then. Why lie? What did you think would happen from lying to me?"

He took another step forward, now at the bottom of the steps. Chloe was far enough away she might be able to avoid a retaliatory sword swing. Rei could try to incinerate him right here and now. But the risk... the flames might not reach in time. It'd give him time to react, time to attack Chloe. And Rei wasn't going to risk her life on a 'might'.

She could try setting his hand on fire, but between the winter chill and the lack of any heat source to spark it up she doubted it'd light in time. And even then, Gamma had torn his arm off at the elbow and he was still standing. He'd even managed to replace it. Rei could still see the image of him leaping heedlessly through her fire to strike at her. Setting him directly ablaze wouldn't stop him either.

She'd have to play his game, just a little longer, hope that his confidence was just an act. Rei looked to Chloe, her face a mask of fear of determination, hoping for an answer.

And she saw it.

Rei had an idea. A stupid, terrible, risky idea that gambled with both of their lives.

But it was an idea.

"I... I didn't lie. My friends, th-... they forced me to let them come. They thought I couldn't beat you alone. That you'd kill me without their help."

He didn't laugh. What Kestrel did was hardly what you would call a laugh. It was more of a shockingly self-righteous 'hah'. Like Rei had said something ridiculous.

"An amusing thought. I'm... *loathe* to admit it, but between you and your friends you might have been able to take me out. But alone... you're all nothing. You never should have relied on them."

"We're not weak! We... *we* can still beat you..."

Kestrel took a step forward, putting Chloe out of range of his saber completely. His docile piece of bait forgotten; but not by Rei. She stared right past him to Chloe and let the faintest hint of a smile cross her face, more of a twitch of her cheek. A signal.

When Kestrel had stepped down from the stairs, Chloe had carefully, cautiously, reached into her pocket and drew out a scalpel, stainless-steel blade thin and sparkling in the morning light. Now she stood, poised to strike at the top of the stairs.

Chloe wouldn't falter. She never faltered. Rei *trusted* her.

Just... a little longer...

"Look at you. I can see you trembling, Rei. Full of rage and fire. But because of one girl, because of your friends, your *family*, you're afraid to fight back."

"Y... you're right, Kestrel. I'm weak. I can't beat you alone. I–I want to get stronger. I want to... to be able to control this power. Can you show me how?"

Rei swallowed the pain. Truth mixed with lies. Bearing her soul to someone who filled her with such righteous anger was tearing her apart. She was close, oh so close to erupting into flame.

He started to lower his sword, and Rei could have sworn he smiled. "No, I can't. But my master can. I imagine that's part of why he even wanted you alive in the first place. You *can* come willingly, Rei. Just step forward."

Rei stood, legs shaking from rage. Her arms pulsed, stiff from holding them in the air and sore from the crackling fire threatening to unleash at any second. Step by step she approached, until she was just out of range of his sword.

"Smart choice, Rei. Throw away the chaff. Lord Orochi will see to it you become what you were *meant* to be. You won't be alone, among these... weak *things* any longer."

Rei took a deep breath, one last attempt at calming herself. At *focusing* herself, for what was to come next.

"I... just have one question, Kestrel. Honestly, I have a lot, but for now I have... one question."

Rei turned her gaze to Kestrel, looking into his dead eyes. She wondered if he understood what she was feeling right now. That ungodly mixture of emotions; fury at what he was, regret at what she thought he could have been. Despair that her friends could be hurt or worse and she'd have no way of knowing. Hope that they'd be able to endure, and meet her on the other end.

Pride in knowing she'd found the one little thing he'd missed that would swing things in her favor, and love for the person that would do just that.

"What makes you think I'm alone?"

Ella's mind reeled. She could feel sweat budding at the back of her neck. There had to be a way to warn Aria. Had to be a way to destroy this puppet. Preferably without having to watch Rei's mother die in front of her. The thought of it zipped across her mind's eye and set her hands to shaking.

There was a ding, the coffee pot settling in to sleep with the pot now finished. It snapped Ella back to reality... and gave her an idea.

"Oh, Miss Scios! Your cellphone! I'll fetch it, and then you can contact Rei!"

Aria gave her a smile. "Good thinking. Give her just a moment."

Ella hurried to the living room; hearing Aria appease the puppet in the other room with small talk that didn't quite take him off the subject he was seemingly so obsessed with.

Such obsession was unsurprising; Ella had read about puppets before, in one of her family's books. Dutiful to their orders without question. Based on the way it spoke, this one was told to search for Rei. With what they'd heard on the news, and Rei's story about the 'crystalline skeleton' Gamma saved her from, it was clear what the order was if they interfered with that search.

They were dancing around a subject that, with one wrong step, could mean their death.

Their death. Ella was sure of it. She was going to die here along with Aria if she idled for longer than needed. Ella grabbed Aria's phone and hurriedly typed a quick warning on it.

[Puppet. Has gun, under table. Aimed at stomach. I have plan]

Carefully, she handed it over before scurrying back over to the sink near the coffee maker, umbrella held tight to her chest.

"T-there you are, Miss Scios. Your phone."

Aria looked at it, her expression unchanging. Then she smiled.

"Thank you, Ella. Well, sir, I've good news."

The puppet leaned in, her words finally getting its attention.

"It appears Rei, and your son of course, will be here shortly."

It smiled. "Wonderful. Apologies if I've... frightened, the other girl there. My wife always says I can be... intense. I've always been hard on the boy, as well. I just find life can be so dangerous at times. I am... overprotective."

"I see," Aria nodded. "Life can be like that, for children. But it's important to strike a balance. Truth be told... my own girl, I may have protected her too much myself. I should have trusted her. Ella, you know what I'm talking about, yes?"

Ella hesitated, but agreed. "I... I do believe I do, yes. Rei is... a very wonderful person, and stronger than you know. I-I wish I had that strength."

"You do," Aria said. "You're stronger than you think as well, little one."

As the two talked, Ella turned away from them both. She felt so ashamed; she wasn't strong, not in the slightest. Here she was, idly wasting time as Aria did all she could to stop a slowly burning fuse. And Aria gave her a *compliment* for all this? It was absurd.

Of course, *Rei* was absurd too. Running head long into what might be certain death, after barely surviving her first encounter with it. To save someone who, near as Ella was aware, had been nothing but a bully to her? There was a nobility to that, that Ella couldn't help but be inspired by. A burning, undeniable strength.

And here I am. Trying to share that strength, she thought to herself, looking down into the sink. Bloody bandages and dishcloths still lingered in one half of the sink, the other filled with lukewarm soap and dishes. The literal evidence of how far Rei would strive forward.

Ella reached a hand down to touch one of the dishcloths. It left faint red streaks on her fingertips. She could feel it, damp remnants of life. There was enough.

Slowly, she grabbed the bloody cloth. She had told Aria with her phone she had a plan.

Plan was, to be frank, a strong word.

What Ella *had* was a secret. Something she'd done her best to keep hidden; only someone like Aria, who already *knew*, would have been able to pick up on it.

Ella was a sanguimancer. She could control blood.

Beyond her blood reading she could do next to nothing with it. A lack of will to improve such a gruesome ability, a desire to just be a normal human girl; Call it what you will, Ella could do nothing with it... except the one thing she *could*.

Her grip tightened on the dishcloth, blood trickling out down her fingers in thin streams.

I have to do it. It's okay Ella, just... just keep yourself calm. It's okay... it's just a little blood. Just a little. It won't... hurt.

An easy thing to think, but harder to put in practice. But she knew she was running out of time; the puppet was getting more persistent with each passing second. She *had* to do it.

Ella took a breath, and bit down on the dishcloth.

The effect was immediate. Her hands shook as the taste- like cold ash and rusted copper coins- filled her mouth. Her senses doubled in strength and she was assaulted by the scent of the nearby coffee, by the subtle shuffling sounds of Aria adjusting herself in her seat to try and turn a potential, lethal gunshot into something survivable. Ella's body strained, muscles briefly finding themselves far stronger and begging for use.

It took everything she had to avoid going berserk with bloodthirst.

This is too much I can't take it I'm going to break I need more I have to stop it I should have gone with Rei I need to- she let out a sharp inhale of breath, held it for five seconds, then let it out.

She dropped the cloth, wiped any blood from her face onto her frilly sleeves, and turned to face them, her fingers wearing grooves into the handle of her umbrella.

As if on cue- *of course it's on cue Aria knows who I am what I am I--* Aria cleared her throat and gave the both of them a bright, warm smile.

"Well, sir, it was a pleasure to have you over. But given our children are together- and I put the utmost trust in my Rei and her friends- I believe it's time you left. I can call you once they've arrived safe and sound."

"Thank you, Miss Aria. I'll be sure to keep an ear out."

Its eyes went blank in an instant. Had Ella been in a calmer mental state, she'd have remembered what that meant. As she was now, it only said to her it was time to act.

Ella swung her umbrella down at the closet thing in range- the dinner table. It split in half, each end flipping upward with the intensity of her blood-fueled blow. The puppet bolted to its feet to avoid being hit by debris, Aria a half second afterward. It took aim at Ella with the pistol, the clearer more threatening target.

It pulled the trigger.

Or tried to, anyway. In the instant she had before it fired, Ella swung her umbrella once more, its pointed tip striking the puppet's gun.

With her enhanced strength what would be an inconvenience became a brutal wound. The gun was shorn from its hand, and the hand shorn from its wrist. What had once been an all too human arm was rendered into a jagged broken bone of ruby-red crystal.

Ella went to swing again and felt the edges of her vision grow hazy. She forced herself to hesitate, to stop herself for a brief moment, afraid to lose control.

The puppet retaliated, reaching for her face with its remaining hand. Too close to respond She had to move, to defend herself, to do *something.*

This time, she didn't have to do anything. Aria had shot forward the instant Ella had taken off the puppet's hand. She had grabbed onto its remaining one by the elbow, that bright smile not dropping for a minute.

"Good job, Ella. My turn."

Aria twisted the puppet's arm in such an unnatural way Ella winced. The thing's arm hung limp and useless. Before it could react further, Aria grabbed it by the throat with her free hand, the impact *crushing* its false flesh so hard, shards of its crystalline true form broke off and scattered to the floor. She lifted it up, feet dangling in the air.

"Hrm..." Aria's face scrunched up into a frown. "That red puppet again. I thought I'd killed the last of you five years ago."

She knocked on its head, giving it an annoyed look.

"Wh... what? What do you mean... again? And what're you looking for?" Ella asked. Already she was starting to feel a drain on her body. There had not been nearly as much blood as she expected, and she could barely stand.

"These things tend to have some sort of listening device. These red ones are... weirder, than regular puppets so I'm just-ah, there it is," she said. She had found something on its head, a spot just above the right eye of its humanoid shell.

"Hey, whoever's listening to this thing. I've got a message for you."

Aria tapped the puppet's face at the spot she'd found, as if trying to catch someone's attention. The puppet struggled in her grasp, but Aria just clenched tighter.

"Leave my family the hell alone."

At her words the entire puppet burst into flames. White and shimmering, an oppressive heat that caused Ella to fall backwards onto her butt. When the flames had finally died, the puppet's shell was nothing but ash, its crystalline structure burnt beyond recognition. Aria let go and it fell to pieces, crumbling into soot and mist.

Miss Scios clapped her hands together. "Well, that was fun Ella. Fetch me the broom."

Ella sat there, exhausted, and could only stare at wreckage around them.

An interesting card had been dealt to her indeed.

Gunfire rang out, sparks of light accompanying it. Gamma ran, swinging his hand behind him. A wave of shadows rose to block the bullets, only to be splattered and severed like melting butter.

It had been enough though. Gamma turned the corner, bullets slamming into the space where he had been just been not half a minute ago. The initial burst of gunfire had left him were bleeding profusely from new and old wound alike, and he could *feel* the pain overtaking him. Worse, his right arm was rendered all but useless. A second burst had riddled it with bullets. He wouldn't be moving it for the rest of the day.

If he didn't find a way to retaliate, he wouldn't be moving the rest of him either.

"Don't bother hiding, Project Gamma. I know where you are," said the soldier. His voice was thin and calm, despite the carnage. Gamma didn't blame him; anyone would be outfitted the way he was.

In retrospect it was obvious. Bullets infused with light magic to put down the shadowmancer, just in case. The other soldiers had simply been killed before they could load them.

"If you come quietly, you'll get to live. We might even let you keep the jacket."

Gamma cringed. He knew where he was, was just toying with him. It was now or never. He saw the man's foot stretch out past the corner and lunged.

And got the rifle's stock slammed into his face, knocking him down to the snow-covered alley. Blood sprayed from his busted lip and before he could do more but start to sit up, he saw the dull black muzzle of a rifle press against his forehead.

"Come on now. Settle down. I don't *want* to kill you."

"I don't care *what* you want."

The Security Force member laughed. "Oh, he can talk. The reports didn't say anything about that. That makes things easier. Project Gamma... why did you leave the facility?"

He started rummaging through his combat jacket for something as he waited for Gamma's answer.

Gamma couldn't help but smirk. This close to the edge of death, after everything, there was nothing left to do but smile. "You were there. You know what they did."

"I sure do. Same they put the other Projects through– more or less. Same with the Aves Class. You don't see them complaining."

"No, you don't," Gamma said, a defiant edge sharpening his words. "Kestrel didn't even scream when I tore his arm off. Disappointing."

"Heh, violent little bastard," the soldier pushed his rifle into Gamma's forehead a little harder. "You're going to be punished for that, by the way. Lord Orochi is forgiving but they put a *lot* of work into training that young boy. You almost killed him."

"*Almost?* With an injury like that... he'll die before today is done."

"From who? His other objective? She's a high school student."

Despite the pain, Gamma smiled. *Everyone is underestimating her. Just like she thought they would.* It wasn't his preference; he wanted to kill Kestrel himself, and there was something undeniably innocent about Rei that made him not *want* her to bloody her hands. But she deserved it more. Gamma would settle for this nameless soldier. All he had to do was survive.

A simple proposition. All he'd ever done is survive.

He spat blood and words at him. "Absolutely. Orochi's precious bird lost a wing, and soon he'll lose his life."

The soldier took out a pair of handcuffs from his jacket, keeping the rifle square between his eyes. "I bet you think you're funny, Project Gamma. Didn't figure a weapon would develop a personality, but there you go. The doctors in Center City are going to have fun finishing this interrogation."

"No," Gamma's grin grew. Black mist started to rise from his left hand faintly.

"I think you're all going to die."

Shadows flooded around them, cloying and viscous like a malicious bog. Gamma started to sink into it, drawing himself into pitch black darkness. He wasn't a hundred percent sure he could *survive* doing this, enveloping himself in shadows so completely he could feel his body growing numb. Could feel it pressing against him like a wall of writhing tendrils. The soldier shouted and fired wildly into the pool; both sounds dull to Gamma's ears as sheer nothingness enveloped him. Nothing but the unending void of true shadows.

Then there was light, a pinprick in his vision, and the shadows peeled from his skin like oil. He was behind the soldier now, inky darkness grabbing at his rifle and boots, threatening to pull him under.

Gamma allowed himself a brief moment of respite. He earned it; moving himself through the shadows was near impossible. He'd done it once out of sheer desperation; it was how he'd gotten into the dance club in the first place. And now he'd done it again.

"Sh-shit, I... you... you won't..." it was the soldier, calm and collected voice giving way to abject terror as the black mass of shadows slowly started dragging him down.

Gamma smiled a crooked grin, raw darkness oozing from his mouth as he spoke.

"Goodbye, soldier. Tell your friends Orochi will join you soon enough."

The man's screams were muffled as the shadow consumed him. Gamma could survive being so fully consumed by the dark, but this man... his screams faded away, and when the shadows dispersed nothing was left but a crimson red pulp that had once been a living being.

Gamma took one step forward before vomiting, body convulsing in pain. He wouldn't be doing this again any time soon. His wounds felt frozen, and he could barely stand anymore. His head was burning, a hazy fog coming over it.

Rei would have to get on without him.

On the one hand, the knife was stuck. That was a positive.

On the other hand, Verde could barely concentrate on anything but the raw, unending pain of the combat knife stabbing through her lower calve. It had missed the bone- she'd heard enough doctor stuff from her mother to know that- but it felt like a small comfort all things considered.

Verde swung back and hit the puppet as hard as her tiny fists could. It was enough to knock the puppet's hand away. Its other hand, meat long since fallen off to reveal the triple razor claw it hid underneath, was more than free to swing forward to eviscerate her.

It missed her skin, rending the front of her sweater to rags. And scattering the pages Verde had in her pocket.

"Shit shit shit *shit*!" Verde shouted. She tried to get up, the intense pain sending her falling flat to the ground again. Her glasses fell off, lens cracking. The puppet loomed large over her and swung again.

Verde turned, a crumpled paper in her hand. The circle was damaged, but she'd managed to grab at least one. One was all she needed. Or at least, all she hoped she needed. She rose to one knee, holding the paper out.

"*Klingenluft!*"

The crumpled, torn paper exploded into a hurricane of wind that sent the puppet flying, landing on its back with a thud. Verde was about as lucky- the explosion of wind slammed her down to the ground again, a sharp pain through her entire body.

At least her leg didn't hurt as much anymore. Verde stumbled to her feet as much as she could, her right leg dragging like the dead weight it was. She grabbed for any nearby papers. Blood and snow and claw had ruined many of them, but she had to make do. It wouldn't stay down for long.

There was a sickening creak as the puppet picked itself up off the ground. The last spell had shorn the rest of its flesh shell from its body, leaving nothing but the skeletal frame. Its pristine, smooth face was covered in scratches and gouges.

Wordlessly, it strode forward. Three steps were all it took for it to be on Verde again. Not even enough time to check the paper in her hand. It swung, and Verde tried to step back, to avoid its strike.

Another positive of a knife in your leg; it'll make you fall way faster than you intended. The puppet's claws hit nothing but air, Verde collapsing to her back before it. She tried not to think about how, had that not happened, its claws would be ripping into her rib cage.

Verde held out the paper and focused. Amidst the pain and blood, she saw it was pristine. She bared her teeth and snarled out the spell.

"Klu-... *KLINGENLUFT*!"

Pain shot through her as the spell blasted the puppet backward, wind buffeting its skeletal body. Shards broke off, superficial damage but damage none the less.

No time to celebrate. SHIT I messed up the wo- was the only thought she managed to get out before the spell rebounded, knocking her back twenty feet and completely shredding the last remnants of her sweater. Green fluff gently drifted down with the snow, covering the blood-stained alley. Verde skidded across the ground, and she could feel the wet streaks of blood from the scrapes and tears on her back.

"Oh... oh wow that, that *sucked.* That... grrck," Verde grumbled, managing to rise to her feet. The puppet started to stir, and Verde let out a curse. She hobbled away, grabbing at what papers she could as the blood trailed behind her in the snow.

Verde turned the corner and collapsed, back to the wall, and tried to catch her breath. With her sweater in ruins she was freezing solid, not helped by the blood loss. Casting was exhausting, having to dodge around while doing so only made it worse. Her heart pounded in her chest, as if she was running a marathon. The only thing even keeping her going at this point was pure, raw adrenaline and she knew it.

It was just what she was *hoping* for. The thrill, the *challenge*. Despite the shitty situation she was in, her spells scattered and useless, her leg and face leaking life, she smiled. She knew the puppet was approaching. Now she just had to think of a way out. Her spells were strong, but unrefined. Against something like this, it'd take something stronger. Something sharper.

She looked at the papers she'd managed to recover. Crumpled, bloodstain, torn. Not a one was left.

Verde knew what she had to do. She grabbed the knife handle, took a breath, and pulled.

The pain of pulling out the combat knife somehow hurt worse than it did going in. It left a hollow, vacant feeling in her leg. She had to work fast; cold air or not, two open stab wounds on either side of her lower leg would spell death in minutes.

Hands shaking, Verde sliced her right pant-leg from the knee down, and turned the resulting strip of cloth into a makeshift tourniquet. Anything to stem the flow of blood. This wouldn't be enough in the long run; already the beige material was turning almost black with blood. But it'd be enough.

Now, the hard part, Verde thought to herself with some degree of irony. *As if any of this has been* easy.

Verde knew three spells enough to draw them by memory. *Luft*, a basic showcase of wind, just to show that magic is real. *Klingenluft*, the chiming-air; called such because of how the blades of wind pinged off of armour as it sliced apart its target. Ella had gagged at the thought. It was otherwise just a basic offensive spell, perfectly reasonable. The third spell was too dangerous to use without being absolutely sure she made the circle perfectly.

Which was why that was the exact spell she was going to finish this with. Verde had cleaned the knife's leather handle as much as she could, and was carefully, methodically, drawing the magic circle in her own blood.

Desperate times, and all that.

The puppet turned the corner without a sound, jittering gait sluggish. Verde took the smallest of comfort in knowing she'd at least paid it back in kind. Then it splayed its claws and swung for her face. Verde thrust the knife out to meet it, eyes sparking with arcane might.

"*RASIERMESSER!*"

An experienced magic user, the book had told Verde, can tell when a spell goes wrong. They can feel the spell fail, can even point out what the errors where. Assuming they survive the backlash of course; as Verde had experienced far more than she cared to admit today, when a spell went wrong it hit her as much as it did the puppet.

So, when Verde cast the spell and felt an intense *stab* into the back of her brain that felt like a thousand migraines, she was absolutely certain things had gone completely wrong. The spell was supposed to send out a wave of razor-sharp blades of wind, eviscerating everything in front of her. Getting it wrong meant losing a hand, or worse.

But it didn't do that. Instead the knife shot from her grip- tearing the skin on her palms- and through the air.

And straight through the puppet's skull. It was embedded to the hilt, the magic circle on the handle so bright it felt like it was burning.

When it finally faded, Verde could see that it had; the magic circle she'd drawn on it had been permanently burnt into the leather grip. She had no idea what it meant, and no real energy to figure it out.

The crystalline skeleton fell to the ground, body shattering along the slice marks her earlier spells had made. Verde fell a half second after, coughing in pain.

She couldn't move a muscle, beyond the ones needed to smile.

"Verde, Gamma, NOW!" Rei shouted. Both her arms burst into flames so hard it *hurt*. Kestrel jumped backwards, to the foot of the steps. How could he not? Confident the others had been dealt with, could he risk not being sure? His eyes darted left and right, seeking the ambush.

It came from behind. With a furious anger in her eye, Chloe lunged forward and jammed her scalpel into Kestrel's right shoulder. Painful, but not enough to make him drop his saber. He spun on his heels, swinging his sword.

A fireball exploded against his back and side, sending the saber flying and the assassin face down into the porch steps. Chloe looked to Rei and despite the obvious pain she was in, she smiled.

Rei smiled back. "Chloe, run! Get away from the house!"

She nodded and ran past the smoldering assassin.

"I... I'll see you later, Rei. Live, please."

And with that she was gone.

Rei turned back to Kestrel, concentrating on her rage. She could feel her vision narrow as she lost sight of everything but her opponent before her.

Kestrel wordlessly stood and pulled off the burning hoodie, a white tank-top underneath. He was bleeding and burnt, neither the scalpel nor the fireball enough to stop him. The bandages on his left arm were coming loose.

Attached to the stump Gamma had left him with was a mass of dull grey metal, embedded into his flesh. Rei could make out screws and bits of pipe that had been molded by his ferromancy into a workable- if twisted- replacement. Each finger was like a talon, sharp and thin.

He readied himself, iron arm outstretched in defense.

Rei took up her boxer's stance; legs wide, left arm forward, the right close to her chin.

Their eyes met.

Someone screamed. Rei couldn't tell who. The fight began.

######

Chapter 23

With a roar, Rei threw out her right hand. A torrent of flames burst forth like a stream, exploding into the patio steps Kestrel had been standing on. *Had* been; he'd managed to avoid the flames by leaping up onto the railing and kicking off it, propelling himself over the raging fire.

It was clear from the outset what this fight would be. If Kestrel touched her, it was as good as over. But the thought of him turning the iron inside her into jagged, twisting spikes did nothing to cool her burning blood. She had the range advantage.

Or at least, she thought she did. Rei stepped back to put further space between them and threw a fireball at where he was about to land. Kestrel swiped through it with his iron claw, dispersing the flames. As he did so, a dull grey glow lifted from his iron arm and she could see it start to shift. Not from the heat, but from his ferromancy. Three thin spikes propelled themselves from his arm, launching towards her at a high speed.

It was all Rei could do to avoid them, weaving her body to the sides. Two missed, but she could feel the third slice across her torso, just above the hip. Wet blood spilled, and she staggered for just a moment.

That was all the moment Kestrel needed. He advanced and raked forward with his iron claw. She leapt backwards, almost falling from the pain in her side, and thrust her hands towards him.

Flames erupted forth and he was forced to back off, shielding his face with his iron arm. It shined faintly grey again, as though he had to focus his ferromantic powers on it just to make it move.

But ten feet was all that was between them now. If she overextended, he could land the one real hit he needed. Rei had no real idea how hard she'd have to work to put him down, so she had to play defensive.

That was her weakest play. Every fiber of her wanted to attack, to try and overwhelm him with fire. Against digital opponents it would work, but here... before she could think further, he dashed forward again.

Kestrel reeled back with his iron claw, intending to stab its talons at her. Rei dodged to her left, but it was a feint; his right hand swinging to catch her left shoulder. Rei increased the heat, flames flickering along her arm with her intensity and swung. A wave of flame billowed from her, cherry-red and hot enough to force even Kestrel to back off.

But as he did, something slowed his steps. Rei could see his left upper arm quiver. He wasn't used to fighting with such a weight, not when his ferromancy was aimed elsewhere.

Finally, an opening! Rei shouted internally. She charged forward; a right hook aimed for Kestrel's face.

It hit, flaming knuckles colliding against his cheek bone. His expression distorted as he fell backward.

Then he twisted mid fall, and a boot flashed across Rei's vision, slamming against the side of her head. He'd used the momentum of her punch to swing his foot up and kick her in the face, and the resounding strike rattled Rei's brain and sent stars flying across her vision. Blood dripped down the side of her face.

Kestrel recovered first, by seconds. He returned her punch with a jab to the gut that Rei only barely managed to sidestep, only for the iron arm to swing toward her like a club. She held up her arms in a defensive boxer's stance, still stunned from the previous blow to the head. The iron arm rattled her bones and pushed her backward half a step, jagged iron tearing her sleeves and leaving her arm bloody. She had enough room to safely swish her left hand upward, a pillar of flame rising with it to force Kestrel back as well.

The both of them took a breath, quick and sharp. That's all they allowed each other.

Kestrel grabbed one of the twisted edges of his iron arm and with a shimmering grey light, pulled out a thing rapier. He stepped forward and thrust it out, aiming for her center mass

Rei dodged, too slow. The rapier sliced across her torso; a bloody mark torn in her side. Another shallow blow. Before she could recover, he lashed out with a rapid series of thrusts aimed for her head and shoulders.

She ducked and weaved, feeling the blade swish past her face. Every thrust took him a step forward, took her a step back. He was getting closer each time, his most recent stab drawing a red line across her cheek.

Rei had enough experience reading opponents to know what was happening. He was wearing her down, bit by bit. Kestrel controlled the pace from the moment that spike had hit her, the wet spot spreading with every second. It was a slow dance towards her death, and she knew it.

No more. She grit her teeth, anticipating the next stab. It was aimed for her left shoulder.

Rei took a half-step forward, dodging to the right, and caught the rapier by its narrow blade. Flames surged. The rapier melted, molten iron torching Kestrel's hand as she took him by surprise. Rei smirked and threw a sudden right hook at his face once more. This time, she felt his nose *crunch*.

He stumbled, and before he could recover Rei went on the offensive. A left jab to the gut, the impact increased by the flames rocketing her fist forward. A right-handed straight to the jaw to send him spinning. She followed it up with a second left hook across his face, flames leaving a charred mark. He was staggering, blood flying with each punch. This was it, one more hit and-

A cold touch amidst the flames. As she was pulling back her left hand, he had grabbed her elbow. Rei felt a chill run up her spine, a tingling energy that made her feel numb. The flames continued to burn, but a pain built in her veins. She tried to retaliate, to land one devastating blow that could end it, but he slinked backward.

Kestrel was smiling. It was over.

Rei felt her knees begin to shake.

"You... put up a good fight, Rei. I won't kill you," he panted. She could see the exhaustion and pain on his face, the grey light lifting from his hand as he worked his ferromancy through her.

"In a few short seconds you'll pass out. It'll hurt, but you'll live. Then...

then we take you to Lord Orochi."

Rei coughed. She could feel it happening, feel the iron in her blood twist and harden. All that rage, all that fury, and what? A few blasts of flame, some fire wreathed punches? That was all she could muster? She was going to just... lose, like that?

She began to fall.

"No."

Rei was surprised by the power in her voice, despite the pain. The edges of it crackled like a roaring flame. She'd had managed to brace herself. Managed to keep standing. She could feel the heat rising, as Kestrel's emotionless smile burned into her mind. She let out a scream. She would not let him beat her.

Every inch of her body cried out in agony as fire burst out from within, the explosion of flames cracking the asphalt. Her hair lifted faintly, rising with raw power. She took a step forward, molten ground sticking to her shoes.

Rei felt the iron in her blood melt. It bubbled through her system, excruciatingly painful.

But entirely useless to Kestrel.

Rei gave him a wild snarl and dashed forward, flames trailing after her. Kestrel leapt backward, giving up a few inches of his iron arm to launch three more twisted metal spikes.

With a wave of her hand the spikes were turned into white-hot slag that fell to the ground unceremoniously. Her advance didn't stop. She reeled back her right fist and swung.

Kestrel caught her punch in the grasp of his metal arm. Talons dug into her knuckles, blood spurting out sizzling and hot; it was all she could do to uncurl her fist, to push back against his metallic grip. Kestrel swung at her with his spare hand, and Rei grabbed it. His skin started to bubble with the heat.

The two struggled, hand in hand, glaring at each other. Rei had unleashed every last ounce of anger in her, and it was burning away at her. The edges of her vision were going dim; she could barely breath through the heat and flames. The pain was overtaking her, she couldn't keep this up and she knew it.

But Kestrel was the same. He was straining, that cold, dead eye stare full of anger. His face a patchwork of burns and blood. It was just a matter of wearing him down first. Rei squeezed her left hand, the fire intensifying. His right hand wouldn't survive this, no matter who won.

And neither would her left. A spike, half a foot long, burst out from his iron hand and pierced through Rei's palm to the other side. It shone grey, as though he was pouring every bit of ferromancy he had into it.

Time seemed to stand still in that moment. The chillingly cold pain coursed through her in an instant, like a sudden lightning-flash. In one instant is was searing, indescribable, and the next... somehow dull. Whether it was from the strange clarity this blank of pain caused, or a stratagem Rei had thought up the moment he'd pierced her hand, she could not say.

She let go of his right hand.

Kestrel seized the opportunity and knocked her right hand aside. He reached out, to grab her face, a grey light came to his molten, cracked right hand. Every fiber of his ferromantic power focused in those fingertips.

Leaving his iron arm dead, dull, and unmoving. Rei focused on her right hand, and the cherry-red flames grew hotter, more intense. And then she pulled.

For the first time, Kestrel screamed. With his focus on his right hand, his left was just a clump of iron jammed into his arm stump by hooks. Hooks that, with Rei's heat, started to melt. She tore his artificial arm off in a single, raw *rip* that took chunks of his arm off and sent Rei falling to the ground.

Kestrel grabbed at his stump, his attack on Rei forgotten in the reflex of true, genuine pain.

It was the opening she needed. Rei started to rise. Despite the numbing pain in her right hand, fingers curled into a fist. Flames, cherry-red dyed with crimson, rocketed her upwards. She heard the impact instead of feeling it; a cracking, crunching sound as she uppercut Kestrel in the jaw so hard it must have broken some teeth.

For a moment, there was clarity. Rei was floating through the sky, propelled into the air by the force of her uppercut. Twenty feet by her guess, hanging in the air like a blazing star. It felt like she was flying. Then gravity reasserted itself and she fell, landing unsteadily on her feet. If she had fallen, she doubted she could get up again.

A half second later, Kestrel landed too; in a heap seven feet from where he started.

Breath ragged, Rei dragged herself over to him, flames leeching down her body to her hand. Slowly it built up like a raging inferno, burning bright- almost too bright to look at. She couldn't feel her hand anymore, but the fire licking at her puncture wound caused her fingers to twitch softly. She held her hand out towards Kestrel's prone form, palm forward.

Kestrel struggled to his knees. He was a bloody, burnt mess. Blood was running down his face in streams, and his right hand looked like hot charcoal, crimson life leaking out every crack. He stared up at her, and barely made a sound beyond his own belabored breathing.

Rei took a deep breath, body shaking.

"Tell me. Tell me everything. Why did you do this? WHY?!"

Her voice was strangled, worn thin by rage and fire.

Kestrel shook, trying to stand. "I... Lord Orochi wants you. Your fire."

He sounded as death, voice slurred with blood and pain.

Rei kicked him in the stomach, hard. Tears were forming in her eyes, sizzling into steam.

"No! I don't... I don't *care*! Why did *you* do this. Why, why did you try to kill me?"

It took a moment for Kestrel to respond. He coughed up his answer, blood splattering on the ground.

"It was a job. Capture... or kill. Nothing more."

Rei's working hand curled into a fist, sparks crackling along the knuckle. The flames on her right hand grew larger, hotter. Blood burned and set a black tinge to the fire's light.

"What do you mean it was just a *job*?! Yo-you, you tried to kill me! You tried to kill *me*! We... I thought we... we were friends."

"What made you think I was... your friend?"

The empty void of his answer seemed to draw her in. Rei's teeth started to grind, the flames growing so hot she could barely contain it.

She had known this, of course. Known it since yesterday when he'd attacked her. But in her chest a spark had held out hope that maybe... maybe it was something else. Maybe he'd been forced to do it, maybe he didn't *want* to hurt her.

"N... no, you're lying! Wh-what... what about all those things you said. I thought... I thought we co-could be..."

"We could be what? You..." he coughed, hard. "You were my target. I needed a way to get close. If not... for that, I wouldn't have even seen you."

Something snapped. Like shattering glass, or crackling embers. Rei's eyes went wide, and she thrust out her palm, a candescent swirl of primal flames rising from her hand. Just one single thought and it'd be over. He'd burn to ash, never to hurt her or her friends again.

No fire came. Rei fell to her knees and sobbed.

"I-I... I can't... I can't do it," she said, each word tumbling from her weak and lifeless. She looked down at her burning hand. It was alight with every last ounce of her rage. And yet, no fire came.

"I... I can't kill him. Why... *WHY*! Why can't I *KILL HIM!!*" Rei screamed. But she knew the answer.

Images of Chloe being engulfed in flames haunted her. The screams still echoed in her ears. She hated Kestrel, hated him with every fiber of her being. But seeing the destructive power of her fire... she couldn't bring herself to do it. Had she not seen firsthand how horrid it could get, not seen how painful it could be, she might have been able to do it. But now, she couldn't.

Rei couldn't take a life. Not even his.

She punched at the ground, leaving a molten impact with each sullen blow. Vision blurred with tears and flame.

"I-I don't, I don't want to hurt... I don't want to kill anyone. But I... I *have* to-"

Kestrel was up. He'd used the last of his strength to pounce forward. His right hand, blackened and dead, burst open as a blood-red spike erupted from the charred mess of flesh and bone, formed from his own blood. He thrust his hand towards her neck. Rei could feel the faint tingle of its sharpened end bite into her collar.

Rei thrust her right hand forward.

A brilliant flash of light exploded out. A torrent of white-hot fire erupted into a total maelstrom of flames. She saw Kestrel then, framed in the light. No pain, no fear. His dead eyes flickered slightly with surprise. And then he was gone, engulfed by the inferno. A dark spot in her vision, erased in an instant.

The flames died with the same immediacy at which they came. Before her was nothing but scorch marks, the asphalt glowing faintly with heat. It was melted down a few inches, with only the faintest discrepancy showing that something had been within the blast. Off to one side was the smoldering remains of Kestrel's right arm, from the elbow up. He'd gotten that close to her, that close to killing her. Blood welled up on her collar, a minor prick.

Nothing else remained.

Rei shakily rose to her feet. Her right hand was pierced straight through and releasing all the pent-up fire within her had scorched her hand raw. She couldn't feel a thing. All her wounds had stopped bleeding, and her clothes were burnt where blood had stained them.

She coughed, and smoke billowed out from her mouth, momentarily blinding her.

And then she fell forward, unconscious.

######

Chapter 24

For the first time in Rei's life, her dreams were quiet. No roaring flames, no crackling embers. Just sweet, soft darkness. It was so comforting and inviting, and in the back of her mind she wanted to stay like that forever.

Then her eyes shot awake. A faint beeping sound and the scent of unknowable medicine told her she was in a hospital. Pain and exhaustion laid heavy on her body, so much so she could barely move. A bandage had been wrapped around her forehead, likely from when Kestrel busted it open with a kick. She could feel further bandages all over. All of it stung, a sharp stabbing pain over the wear and tear the rest of her body felt. She made a promise to herself that when she got out of here, she'd *definitely* get back to boxing, if only so that the next time something like this happened, she'd be more used to moving so hard so quickly.

She took a deep breath and shakily let it out. Memories of her fight flashed before her eyes, and it was all she could do to keep from breaking down crying. It was over.

She had killed him.

"O-oh, Rei... you're awake," said a voice. Rei turned toward it.

It was Chloe, sitting by her bedside. Her own bandages had been replaced, and she was still dressed in the borrowed clothing she was in... yesterday? Today? Rei had no idea anymore.

Rei smiled. "Hey, Chloe. I... how are you?"

Chloe hugged her hard, and Rei cringed. "A-ahh, careful, careful. I still-aggh, that... not so tight."

"O-oh my god Rei you're okay. You're okay! I... I've been here all night. I couldn't leave. I wouldn't let them *make* me leave. Oh Rei, you're okay!"

"I... I guess I am, huh," Rei said. She hugged Chloe back, softly.

Only then did she realize she still couldn't feel her right hand.

It was bandaged completely, a splint around it to ensure it didn't move awkwardly. Not that it mattered, Rei could barely make it twitch.

"I uh... what, happened, Chloe? I mean, how long was I out?"

Chloe put a hand on her shoulder. "It's been almost a day. It's Thursday. I... I heard explosions and went back to find you. To see if you were okay. And you were all alone, unconscious an- and hurt. I called an ambulance, rode it back with you. I've been with you ever since. Mostly."

She blushed slightly, and Rei couldn't help but blush as well.

"Thanks, Chloe. Is everyone..."

"They're okay. I spoke with your mother. She... told me everything. More or less, anyway. She and Ella are okay, but Verde and your uh, other friend had gotten into a fight with the... puppets, I guess. Verde will be limping for a few days and has some frostbite, but she'll be fine. And Gamma will be, too. Verde's mother saw to that."

Rei laughed dryly, felt the pain shake through her. "Hah, wow. How'd she convince him to come in? He's kind of intimidating."

"Hahaha, intimidating? The instant Verde's mom saw what was happening she grabbed him by the ears and pulled him into intensive care. The poor guy looked horrified. She was livid that she wasn't told anything."

Chloe's laughter was like wind chimes and for a second Rei lost her train of thought. She shook her head, putting her mind back on track.

"Huh. I'd pay to see that. So... what about you? Are you hurt?"

She smiled, tears rolling down her cheek. From the stain on her face it was clear she had been crying for a while and was just trying to cheer Rei up. "I'm fine. We needed to clean my burns and rewrap them, but I'm not hurt. I'm just... just so glad you're alright."

Rei took a deep breath and leaned back on her pillows. The bed was tilted so she could sit up.

She wasn't alright, not in the slightest. The pain might heal, and she might regain feeling in her hand, but these scars would linger. It didn't matter that he deserved it... she'd still killed him. It was in self-defense and it had been by sheer instinct, but she'd still done it. She'd take that feeling to her death one day, she was sure of it.

Rei shook her head again, ridding herself of those darker thoughts for the time being. She couldn't let it linger. She focused on the positives. Chloe's right hand had made its way into hers, and though she could not feel it she could tell how soft her touch was.

"I'm... glad I'm alright too, Chloe. And I'm really happy to see you. Honest," she looked her in the eye, and Chloe stared back. "Wow, it's been awhile since I've said that, huh."

"It really has. We need to stop meeting like this. Hospitals have such a dreary atmosphere," Chloe said.

It hurt to laugh, but Rei did anyway. As hard as she could. She smirked.

"You know...you tried to tell me something, over the phone. When Kes-when *he*... you know, put you on the line. What were you trying to say?"

Chloe's face, what Rei could see of it anyway, went white. "I-I... I said I..." she stammered, tripping over her words. Then, she smirked as well, and her haughty tone returned.

"I'll only tell you if you beat me in a rematch, Rei."

The embers in her heart had cooled, but they began to spark again. "Heh, you're on, *Miss* Chloe."

"Please, I'll grind you into dust. And it's Chloe. *Just* Chloe," she said.

They laughed, Chloe jokingly punching her in the shoulder, Rei cringing in exaggerated pain. It felt good, to allow that moment of levity.

"I guess in that case, I should put up my own bet," Rei said. "If-*IF* I lose... I'll hang out with you. Just you. For a week. How's that sound?"

Chloe smiled wide, the edges of it fading into the bandages on her face.

"Sounds like a date. You're on, Rei."

Rei was awake. That was good, at least. It helped take Verde's mind off her own injuries. They weren't nearly as severe- though her mother's stern face and tone made it clear not everyone felt that way. Verde didn't blame her; no one ever wanted to operate on their own kid.

Truthfully, both her and Gamma were lucky to have escaped with their lives. Verde's leg would heal, but she'd be hobbling for a few weeks at best. Gamma's right arm was in a sling while it recovered from being shot, and the number of bandages needed for the rest of his wounds made him look like he *actually* wore a shirt.

They both needed their rest if they expected to get better any time soon.

Which was why he and Verde were sparring on the roof of the hospital. Oh, Verde's mother had told them to stay in bed of course. But she was, understandably, busy trying to keep *her* hospital running. Bothering her in this state would be tantamount to signing a death warrant.

So, no one had said no when Verde Guérisseuse, daughter of Chief Physician Estelle Guérisseuse, had asked to be given keys to the roof. Verde doubted anyone *could.*

Snow gently drifted down as they clashed, shadows swinging at Verde's legs and head in an attempt to trip her. Verde- hobbled though she was- did her best to avoid them, blasting off small training spells she'd printed onto some hand-held cue cards.

Ella watched them, partaking of a tray of hospital food as they fought.

"Not too hard now, Miss Verde. You might rip open your wounds. O-or his!" Ella called to them.

"We'll be fine, just make sure to stay out of the waaAAHY!" Verde shouted back. The momentary lapse in focus let Gamma knock her off her feet, her glasses scattering to the ground.

Gamma grumbled at her. "Focus, Verde. Letting even the faintest distraction in will be your death."

"Yeah, yeah, I got it. Asshole. Let's take a breath for a second, I wanna show you guys something."

Gamma sat down, snatching an apple from Ella's tray and gnawing on it. "Alright. You clearly need the break. What is it?"

Verde rolled her eyes, retrieved her glasses, then took out a small holster. With one solid motion she drew out the knife, a small gust of wind swirling briefly around the blade.

In the reflection she saw herself. Something in it had changed. She wasn't just hunting for something anymore, and she could see it in her eyes. The scar that went up from the bottom of her face to the cheek bone was a mark of it. She smiled.

Ella nearly upset the tray with her response. "A knife! Yo-you brought a *knife*! To the *hospital*!"

"Is that weird? Hospitals are full of knives," Gamma said. He gave her a smirk... not crooked. He was working on it. Mostly.

"Yeah. I think I might have done something to it in the fight. Think it might be like... enchanted, or something. You got any idea, tall dark and brooding?"

Gamma sighed and inspected it. After a moment, he gave her a one-armed shrug.

"No clue. Ella, you found the book, you look at it."

Ella shook her head. "N-no. No way. That's a knife! A *magic* knife! I'm not going anywhere *near* that thing."

Verde laughed. "Come on Ella, look at. For like, a second. Do some of that... that divination stuff on it. See if you can figure out what it is."

Ella crossed her arms, but something had clearly hooked her interest. "Er... I... alright, alright. I'll look at it. That's not how my blood reading works but I'll at least give it a look. And *no* bringing it to the hospital after this!"

Verde laughed again and looked out over the city as Ella studied the magic circle on the knife's handle. Despite the warmth in her heart, something was bugging her.

"They'll be back, won't they? For you, and Rei. We're gonna have to keep fighting, aren't we?"

It was a rhetorical question.

Gamma nodded. "We will. And next time we may not be so lucky. So, we prepare ourselves."

"Yeah. Next time we'll be ready," Verde smiled, despite it all. She'd sunk in her fangs and wouldn't let go. This was just the challenge she was waiting for.

###

A young man wearing a hoodie looked down from the old house. The burn mark in the street stretched back nearly thirty feet, and had cooled. He was more than confident that his decision had been a good one.

That stupid fool Kestrel had ruined *his* hunt for Project Gamma and acted all high and mighty about it. So, he'd let Kestrel have all the glory. Hunt Project Gamma *and* go after Scios. Take on all the responsibility... and all the pressure of it.

Then Rei Scios had killed him. Worse, it had turned out Project Gamma was alive and feral. Useless as a weapon. It honestly disgusted him, that one of the Aves Class could be killed by a little girl. But then, Kestrel was- *had* been the simplest of them. His conditioning had prepared him for assassination, kidnapping, but had broken him of anything else but that. A deadly killer who could finish a fight at a single touch if only he was prepared.

A skill that made him a consummate perfectionist. Both were wanted alive over dead, and Kestrel's nature demanded for the former. Capture them both, no witnesses, no trail. No wonder he was caught so unaware; juggling his two opponents spread him too thin.

Of course, Kite knew part of it was his own fault. If he'd have backed him up, maybe Kestrel would still live. Or maybe the assassin would have messed it up for them again and they'd *both* have died. The worst-case scenario for himself- and their master.

No matter. Where Kestrel's conditioning had failed him, Kite excelled. *He* knew how to play the long game, knew when to roll with a few losses.

Kite jumped down from the old house. It didn't take long to find it; a streak of cooling blood. The cold air had kept it fresh, and her pyromancy had likely kept it clear of any germs or bacteria. A nice, clean sample. Lord Orochi had wanted her body, dead or alive, but this would be enough. And as a bonus, Kestrel's remains.

As for Project Gamma... he'd observed the faulty weapon's fight with the Security Force. The recording would do nicely; sufficient combat data and visual proof of the Project's success was really all he'd wanted. They had it now.

Kite had beaten Kestrel one last time.

He smiled behind his scarf and walked off.

Aria sat in her favorite chair and let out a sigh. Unleashing so much power in such a short burst of time had been exhausting. She was forty-two now, not the young hothead she used to be. But little Ella had been so brave, how could she *not* show off, just a little.

In a way, it was good she had done so. It reminded her how soft she'd gotten over the years. Her days of glory had long since faded, and all she truly wanted now was to take care of her daughter.

A daughter who'd just had to fight someone to the death. Aria sighed, and wished Samson was here. He'd know what to say, how to help her come to terms with taking a life. He always understood it more than she did. Now all she had was his black book of names and phone numbers, contacts that might be able to help where he could not.

As she searched, the President of ONY gave a speech over the news. His white business suit prim and proper, with gold cuffs and a blood red tie. He held a cane, though purely for the fashion of it and his graying hair was slicked back into a mullet, the only wild part about his appearance. He was said to be only a figurehead, the prime minister being the real power, but he exuded strength from every fiber of his being.

His voice was silky smooth, cool and collected and without a trace of malice to it. And yet as he spoke, the world seemed to tremble.

"Thank you, thank you, for coming to the ONY Manufacturing Trade Show and Tech Exposition. Let us not waste any time. I present to you, fresh from ONY's factories, the latest in-home defense."

On screen, he gestured to a veiled curtain. And from behind it stepped an iron puppet. Aria stopped her search for only a moment to scowl at the screen. To all the world, it would look like just a simple machine. Few would realize the arcane energies animating it. Fewer still would realize what it meant to welcome it to your home.

He continued. "The Model X-Six Home Security Device. This humanoid computer will attend to all safety concerns the modern household may have, from stopping would-be robbers to house sitting to childcare. It runs on a clean energy engine, so you'll hardly hear a sound. Each comes with a variety of features, customizable for any home and any situation. In fact, the ONY Security Force, made up of loyal, hardworking volunteers such as yourselves, will be incorporating them into their ranks. Those who put their lives on the line for your safety, now have a shield themselves."

Aria glared deeper at the screen, could feel the small heat of the television's power source. A part of her wanted to set the thing on fire. But she knew better.

She sighed and turned off the television, unable to listen to that bastard's words. It made her sick to her stomach. Besides, she had found the name she was hunting for. An old contact of her husband's, from back in their youth. She dialed in the number and waited.

It was three long rings before the other line picked up. Her voice was gruff, but kind. Groggy with what Aria hoped was sleep.

"Eh... Hello? Luna Crescent speaking."

"Hello, Miss Crescent. It's Aria. Aria Scios. You knew my husband?"

"Knew your hus... oh, right. Samson. I'm... sorry for your loss, Miss Scios."

Aria took a deep breath. "Thank you, Miss Crescent. I... have a job for you. One that requires your... particular, skills."

The other line was silent for a dreadfully long moment. "What is it?"

"He's found us. Orochi Yamata has found us."

######

About the Author

Aya McHugh is a Canadian woman who has been writing all her life. She was born in and of the North, and intends to stay there despite the cold, surrounded by her friends and books. The latter often being thrown at the former (metaphorically, of course). She has a lot of dumb hobbies and mostly just kind of screws around.

She really hopes you liked her book, and hopes you have a good day.

You can connect with me on:

🐦 https://twitter.com/The_Zodi_Lady

Made in the USA
Coppell, TX
19 April 2022

76811130R00152